What's His
Is Mine

Books by Daaimah S. Poole

What's His Is Mine

Somebody Else's Man

A Rich Man's Baby

Diamond Playgirls

All I Want Is Everything

Ex-Girl to the Next Girl

What's Real

Got a Man

Yo-Yo Love

WHAT'S HIS
IS MINE

DAAIMAH S. POOLE

Dafina
Books

KENSINGTON PUBLISHING CORP.
www.kensingtonbooks.com

DAFINA BOOKS are published by

Kensington Publishing Corp.
119 West 40th Street
New York, NY 10018

All Kensington titles, imprints, and distributed lines are available at special quantity discounts for bulk purchases for sales promotion, premiums, fund-raising, educational, or institutional use.

Special book excerpts or customized printings can also be created to fit specific needs. For details, write or phone the office of the Kensington Special Sales Manager: Kensington Publishing Corp., 119 West 40th Street, New York, NY 10018. Attn. Special Sales Department. Phone: 1-800-221-2647.

Dafina and the Dafina logo Reg. U.S. Pat. & TM Off.

ISBN-13: 978-0-7582-4621-9
ISBN-10: 0-7582-4621-8

First Kensington Trade Paperback Printing: October 2010

10 9 8 7 6 5 4 3 2 1

Printed in the United States of America

Thank you to Allah for making this and all things possible.

My boys Hamid and Ahsan, I love you. Thank you to my mother, Robin Sampson; father, Auzzie Poole; stepmother, Pulcheria Ricks-Poole; and sisters Daaiyah, Najah, and Nadirah Goldstein. Also, lots of love to all my extended family. It's a lot of y'all.

Thank you to Ieshea Dandridge, Tamika Wilson, Maryam Abdus-Shahid, Miana White, Carla Lewis, Darryl Fitzgerald, Gina Del Lior, Sharon Long, Elaine Petitt, Fred Holman, Nyla Goldstein, Lacretia Saunders, Linda Saunders, Devon Walls of Starshooterz, Camille Miller, Candice Dow, and Allison Hobbs.

Special thanks to Black and Nobel bookstore, Khalil at City Hall (Philly Book Man), DC Book Diva, and African World Book Distributors.

To my readers, I thank you a million times for your constant support and for spreading the word. Thank you for e-mailing, Facebooking, and always showing love. I so appreciate it. E-mail Daaimah@14aol.com, DSPbooks.com, Facebook.com/DSPbooks, and Twitter.com/DSPbooks.

Thank you so very much to Audrey LaFehr and Martin Biro of Kensington Books. You will never know how much I appreciate you both. Also thanks to the entire staff at Kensington Books.

Thank you, Karen E. Quinones Miller. I owe you the world—you are the greatest agent, friend, and mentor.

Thanks,

Daaimah

Prologue

Tanisha Butler

"Hello. Hello. *Hel-lo!*" my daughter Alexis yelled.

I didn't say anything, because I couldn't. I just listened intently from the other end of the call. I wanted to tell my oldest child to stop yelling, but I was getting comfort from just hearing her voice.

"Ugh, I wish they'd stop playing on our phone," she said as she hung up.

I wish I were playing. What my daughter thought was a prank call was actually me, checking in. If she only knew how desperately I wanted to say, *Hello, it's Mommy. I'm in Detroit. I miss you. Don't be mad at me—I'm sorry I killed that woman and I want to come home.*

I wish I could say that to her, because I missed her. I missed my children, my boyfriend, and my entire life that I left behind. When life gets hard, people say, *I wish I could just get up and walk away.* I used to have those types of thoughts, but it is not that easy or fun.

Last year, I accidentally killed a woman, and instead of turning myself in, I ran. And since then I have experienced the hardest twelve months of my life. When life goes wrong, all you can ask yourself is, How did I get here? If someone were to ask me, I wouldn't know what to say. My life hadn't been great, but it hadn't been like this, either.

I had my daughter Alexis at sixteen and my son, Jamil, was born a year later when I was seventeen. Then by the time I was nineteen, I was married to my ex-husband Tyrone, a truck driver thirteen years older than me. We had a daughter, Kierra, and our marriage lasted about fifteen years. I wanted out of the marriage because I was tired of being tied down. So I divorced my husband and decided I wanted to make up for lost time.

I began hanging out with my coworker's ex, Adrienne. It was all so exciting at first. We went and did everything. Adrienne took me to some really nice parties filled with young, handsome, and rich professional athletes. My life changed instantly—I went from sitting on the sofa watching movies to partying all night in Vegas. My life had become so exciting, and then to top it off I met the man of my dreams. I met my Kevin at a basketball game and we hit it off.

Kevin was the most compassionate, romantic, humble, and attractive man I had ever met. We fell in love quickly and had a beautiful, long-distance relationship. I visited him in Rome, Italy, where he played for the Italian basketball team, Lottomatica Roma. My life was like a fairy tale. Then the fairy tale began unraveling when Kevin came back to the States to play basketball for the Philadelphia 76ers. That's when I learned I was pregnant and I had to come clean about all the lies I had told Kevin. I deceived Kevin about so many things in the beginning of our relationship because I didn't think we were going to become serious.

I lied to him about my age. I said I was twenty-nine when I was actually thirty-three. I told him I was a nurse, but my real job was in the hospital's billing department. I also told him I had only one daughter, who was five, but I failed to mention my two other teenage children. When I came to

Kevin with the truth, he was upset with me, but he forgave me and things went back to normal.

Everything was fine until I started receiving threatening notes. The notes said *Go kill yourself bitch! Six million ways to die . . . choose one,* and *Watch your back, bitch.* I didn't know what to make of the notes, so I just threw them in the trash. I figured they were from a crazy groupie. Not keeping the notes was the worst mistake I could have made. If I would have just told Kevin, I would have been prepared when Kevin's ex-girlfriend—not "crazy groupie"—tried to kill me.

She came to the hospital while I was visiting my newborn and put a gun to my head and carjacked me. Then she made me drive to a park and basically let me know she was going to kill me. I didn't want to die, so I fought back and we tussled for the gun and it went off. When I stood up she was on the ground, bleeding and lifeless. At that very moment I should have called the police and explained, but instead I got scared and called Adrienne.

Adrienne helped me dump the gun and suggested that I go on the run. At the time, running made sense. I had just committed a murder, I didn't want to go to jail, and I didn't have any proof that she was stalking me. I didn't mean to kill her—it was self-defense. But who would believe me? What proof did I have? The only thing I could think of was being sent to prison for life. I couldn't go to jail, so I ran. I wanted to get far away from Philadelphia, so I ran all the way to The D—Detroit.

The D is cold. Literally and figuratively. A lot of the auto plants and a bunch of other companies have closed, and people just don't have jobs here. There is so much crime and drugs, and the unemployment rate is horrible.

Adrienne dropped me off at the train station and I just jumped on the first train and somehow I ended up here. The train ride was crazy. I just remembered asking myself, *Where the hell am I going? What am I doing?* But I couldn't turn back. I knew the police were looking for me and had a warrant for my arrest. I knew my DNA was all over that park and on that crazy lady's clothes.

In my mind I envisioned my face plastered all over the news and on posters with "WANTED" in big, bold, capital letters. But I figured the longer I stayed away, the easier it would become to disappear. Big news stories only last for a few days . . . weeks at best. I knew eventually I would be able to simply blend into society.

On the train ride I found the driver's license of a woman from Milwaukee. Surprisingly, the photo sort of resembled me. To make myself look more like the identification photo, I cut and dyed my hair blond and started wearing glasses. I don't really worry about anyone recognizing me, because I don't recognize myself. I've been living under the name Brenda Douglas and have everything in her name.

I worked in a Detroit restaurant owned by a Chinese man named Mr. Kim. There was a bar in the back of the restaurant. I was employed as a waitress during the day and also worked as a barmaid a few evenings a week. I found the job looking through the classified section of the *Detroit Free Press* newspaper.

Mr. Kim trusted me enough to let me run his Laundromat on the nights when I was not working the bar. At the Laundromat, I basically made sure the machines didn't overflow, gave out change, and sold laundry detergent. I didn't make a lot of money, but on the side I washed and folded clothes.

I think my coworkers at the restaurant assume I'm a battered woman on the run. I heard two other waitresses talking about me. They asked me a lot of questions that I never answered. I just acted busy and ignored them. I always looked mean and unapproachable. I kept my guard up. I basically lived like a hermit over the last year, because I didn't need anyone in my business.

I rented a studio apartment—one big room. I didn't have any friends and I didn't socialize. I read a lot of novels and tabloid magazines. I watched television, but I stayed away from the *Law & Order* type of shows. Every time I tried to watch the news my body shut down and I got really scared and extremely nervous.

I lay in bed every night and I thought about my family. I wondered what they were doing and how they were. I wished I could kiss them and hold them. Sometimes being without them was so hard, I felt like I was going to go crazy. So to keep my mind off of things, I prayed. I prayed a lot. I thought of going to church, but it was too crowded. So I just developed my own personal relationship with God. I prayed that I would be forgiven for taking that woman's life. I prayed to be united with my family. I prayed to get my old life back. I prayed for the strength to do the right thing. I thought I was ready to do the right thing, which was go back home and turn myself in. I didn't know what was going to happen to me when I did, but being alone was miserable. It was hell. I had my freedom, but I didn't have peace. I wanted to go home. I wanted to see my children. I was ready to go back to face my fate. If I got five months or even if I got a life sentence, I knew I would be able to pull through. If nothing else, at least I would be able to see my children again.

From working all my jobs, I was able to save six thousand dollars and I was thinking about getting a good attorney to prove my innocence. Six thousand should be at least a good down payment on an attorney.

After a little more thought I decided it was the right time. I was ready and my decision was made. I was going home. I didn't have any choice. I wrote down everything I wanted to do once I got back and mentally prepared myself to leave. I even wrote Adrienne a letter and mailed it. I thanked her for her help and let her know I would be home soon.

Chapter 1

Adrienne Sheppard

What's wrong with wanting half? Some women dream of becoming doctors, athletes, and lawyers. Others dream of marrying them.
—Adrienne Sheppard

It was 7 a.m. and it was already forming into a hot August day. I was off from my job as a nurse at the Mantua Nursing Home. I couldn't wait to get home and get in my bed. I was so exhausted. I did three double shifts in the last week and was so happy I had the next two days off. I planned to get some rest and get refreshed.

Right now the only thing standing in my way of getting home was the slow-moving traffic on 76 West in Philly. I tried not to fall asleep at the wheel of my Nissan Maxima. I turned on the radio and rolled down the window. I was so sleepy and really needed rest. Sleep right now was a privilege. It was the equivalent of money, an exotic vacation, or some real good sex. I wished I had all those things right now. I was so deprived. I was one hour away from sleep. I had it all planned out, how I was going to get to my bed faster. I was going to go straight to my mom's house and pick up my daughter, Malaysia. Then I was going to drop her off at day care and after that I was going to keep my appointment with my bed. I could not wait.

After fighting traffic for forty minutes I arrived at my mother's home. I walked in my mother's eccentrically decorated home. Since my grandfather had passed, my mom tried to fix up the old row home. She got an E for effort. You're not supposed to put new furniture in a house with old carpet and wallpaper. There were touches of zebra and leopard prints here and there, with mixtures of chiffon and a lot of bright-ass colored Ikea furniture. In two words: hot mess. But that was my mother, Debbie, for you—over the top, crazy Deb. My mom is white and my father is black, which makes me black. I was raised by my white mom and white grandparents, but I still always felt like I was a 100 percent black, even though I didn't necessarily look it. My complexion was cocoa butter yellow, and I had long curly hair that without a flatiron would be big and curly. I have had Spanish people try to speak Spanish to me and I always say "No español" back to them. My mother raised me without my father's assistance. Neither he nor his family ever accepted his mixed race child, and I never cared.

My mother was feeding oatmeal to my daughter, Asia, in high chair. As soon as Asia saw me she smiled and raised her hands so I could pick her up. I took her out of her high chair.

"Hey, Asia, girl. Hey, Mommie's baby," I said as I kissed her all over her dimpled cheeks. She was only sixteen months, but so smart and adorable. Asia has her father's chocolate skin and my naturally curly hair. The combination of complexions made a beautiful, cinnamon baby doll.

My mom handed me the bowl of oatmeal and said, "You can finish this. I have to get ready for work. I hope you brought her some clean clothes, because she doesn't have any."

"There's nothing clean in her bag? Mom, you couldn't do me a favor and wash her clothes? You know I have to take her to school."

"No, I couldn't have, Adrienne. I'm tired. She is your

daughter. Sometimes I think you forget that and take advantage. You are going to have to find yourself a teenager or someone else to babysit. I love her, but I can't watch her all the time."

"You don't watch her all the time." I sighed.

"Yes, I do, and I can't watch her this Saturday because me and Joe are going to Foxwoods out in Connecticut. We're seeing a show and going to dinner."

"Huh? This weekend? I have to work," I said, annoyed.

"Adrienne, I told you two weeks ago to try to find someone else to watch her, because I have something planned."

"Great, Mom, now I'm going to have to call out," I said as I packed my baby up and headed toward the door.

Whatever, I thought as I put Asia in her car seat and I got back in my car. My mom really irked me. She was always complaining about watching her own grandchild. I didn't get it. Since she'd been with her boyfriend, Joe, and lost her weight from gastric bypass surgery, she thought she was young now and it was so damn irritating. She was always talking about going out and how she was not a built-in babysitter. She stayed talking trash about watching Asia, except for the days it was time for me to pay her. Then she was all smiles.

Forget her! I was tired and ready to fall asleep at every light. I was mad I had to go all the way home to get Asia dressed. I honestly thought about letting her do a repeat at day care. Who would notice? But I couldn't send my baby girl to school looking unwanted and unloved. The other option, if I didn't take her to day care, was to let her stay home. That wouldn't work. I would never get any rest with her there. She would be up all morning bothering me. It would have worked when she was a little younger. I used to be able to feed her, give her a bottle, and sit her in her playpen in front of the television. Now I can't do that, because she has learned how to get out of there. So I had to find the strength to take her to school so I could get rest.

I took Asia to school and came back home, took off my scrubs, showered, and fell onto my bed. As soon as I dozed off the phone rang. I picked up the phone groggily, only to hear my daughter's father, DeCarious Simmons, shouting, "When can I see my daughter?"

"I don't know. In a few weeks," I said as I yawned. I turned over on my stomach to look at my alarm clock. I couldn't believe I had only been asleep for about fifteen minutes. I was sleep deprived and not in the mood to have a conversation with him.

"I'm tired. I'll call you back," I said.

"No, don't hang up. Why do I have to wait a few weeks?"

"DeCarious, because that's what I said. That's the only time I'll be able to take off again. I wouldn't have to work like a slave if you gave me more money to take care of your daughter."

"Since when is four thousand a month not enough to take care of a one-year-old? I pay my child support," he yelled in my ear.

"Who are you yelling at?" I asked, sitting up in the bed. I wasn't about to let this moron get me upset. "No, four thousand is not enough, DeCarious. You spend that on drinks and dirty whores in the club."

"I don't . . . Whatever, man. Can I just come up there and get my daughter?"

"No, you can't take *my* daughter anywhere without me. As a matter of fact, I just got off work and I'm tired. Goodbye," I said as I powered my phone off. If I didn't turn the phone off, it was guaranteed he would call back.

I hated my daughter's father, DeCarious Simmons. He is a certified asshole. In the beginning of our relationship he would do anything for me. The first day I met him in Vegas, he took me shopping and had a car take me to the airport. Back then you couldn't have told me that I didn't hit the jackpot. He was a rookie in the NFL and played for the Seattle Seahawks, making great money, and wanted to be with me. When I got pregnant he was so happy. But then his hating-ass cousin Rock told him he wasn't my first athlete and a bunch of other shit. Some of it was true, some of it wasn't. Okay, so what if I hung out with other guys in the league before . . . And? I didn't think it was a deal breaker, but DeCarious thought it was.

Once he heard about my other indiscretions, he confronted me and I did what I was supposed to do, which was deny, deny, deny, and deny some more. I wasn't there, it wasn't me, wrong girl, and I don't know what you're talking about. But it didn't work or matter, because his whole attitude changed toward me.

He changed from "Baby, whatever you want" to "I'm going to do whatever I want and you can take it or leave it." I decided to leave it, and as soon as I did, I felt like I took a flight from the glamorous life back to the below average life. Let me tell you, it was not a fun transition at all. I had to go back to work and pay my own bills and do everything for my daughter on my own. And it's been so hard.

And to make matters worse, he was not in Seattle anymore. He got traded to his home team, Atlanta, and was doing good. So he thought he was somebody for real now, and he was not. He was just a dumb jock who was making a lot of money. You would think that since he was in the NFL and made two million dollars a year, I would have had it made. Wrong! I only got four thousand a month in child support. How the judge did that math, I will never know. You might think four thousand a month was a lot, but it wasn't, because I had real bills.

My mortgage was twenty-seven hundred dollars a month. Then let's not forget day care, student loans, my car note, car and home owner's insurance, gas, electric, cable, cell phone, clothes, and all the money I paid my mom for keeping Asia overnight. And then I had so much debt. When I was with my daughter's father, I paid my credit cards down, but over the last year, I'd run them all back up. I didn't know how, but I guess because I found a reason to shop all the time. I just liked shopping. Me and Asia always needed things. It's like after the third time I wore something, it lost its newness and I didn't want to wear it anymore. I just couldn't walk past a store without buying something. When I was at the mall, I always saw cute shoes or sneakers for Asia and I had to buy them.

So, long story short, living off of my child support was not an option. I was about to try to see if I could get my child support modified. I needed seven thousand a month to take care of myself and daughter properly, at the very least. That's not asking a lot. And don't try to judge me and say I needed to be happy with what I had. Please. My daughter needed to be living the same lifestyle as her father.

Okay, let's get something clear right now. Everybody wants money and likes money. Everyone wants to be comfortable and not have to work hard every day. That's why people play the lottery—to get ahead, to get that extra. I was trying to get my extra by having my daughter by someone rich. I thought I was securing my future for the next eighteen years and making an investment, but I wasn't and I didn't. All I did was buy myself a lot of headaches. My first headache would be DeCarious's ass. My second headache was my missing friend, Tanisha, who I haven't seen in a year.

Tanisha was not really missing. She just ran away. She thought she'd killed her boyfriend's crazy ex-girlfriend, who was trying to kill her. The ex-girlfriend carjacked Tanisha and then tried to shoot her. Somehow Tanisha got ahold of the gun and ended up shooting the ex-girl. She came to my house all upset, bloody, and crying, saying she killed a girl in the park. I tried to calm her down and reassure her that everything was going to be okay. I consoled her, gave her new clothes, and drove her back to the park so we could see if the woman was really dead. At the park there were red and blue flashing lights and yellow crime scene tape in every direction. Just looking at the chaotic scene, we knew she must have killed the woman.

Tanisha was hysterical and I had to help her. The first thing I did was to dump the gun. I thought if there was no gun and no one saw them together, how could they link her to the shooting? But then Tanisha's daughter called and said the cops had already been to her house and wanted to speak with her about something really important.

At that point I was so scared for her that I drove her to the train station. I just couldn't see her going to jail. The only thing I could think to tell her was to run and never come back. I shouldn't have told her to run, but at the time it seemed like the best idea.

When I told her to run, never would I have thought that the woman she thought she'd murdered really wasn't dead. And secondly, I wouldn't have dreamed that Tanisha wouldn't get in contact with me or her family for an entire year. After watching the news, I found out that Tanisha hadn't killed anyone, I ran back to the train station to get her, but she was gone. I was hoping she would call, even though I instructed her not to.

When all of this first happened, I was going crazy. I used to try to go and check on her children, but I couldn't look in their faces. They were devastated. They weren't sure what exactly happened to their mother, and I knew but couldn't say anything.

A few days after the shooting, the cops found her car down the street from my house. They questioned me twice and asked me if she had contacted me. I told them I spoke to her the night of the shooting, but our conversation was normal and she didn't mention anything unusual.

So, for a year I have been going through it. I wanted to tell the authorities what I knew. I wasn't sure if she was dead or alive. I had no idea what happened to her, until she wrote me a letter a few weeks ago saying she was okay, living in Detroit, and coming back soon. I was so happy because I felt so guilty and it had been weighing me down.

Initially, I thought about going to Detroit and finding her myself, but I decided against it. I was glad she was coming back, but I didn't know what kind of charges she was going to face. She didn't murder anyone, but she did shoot that girl.

Knowing that she was okay was a relief, but now I just hoped that I didn't go to jail, too. They could charge me with . . . I think it's called aiding and abetting. I should have dropped her off at the police station and kept it moving.

So I was already so over this. I lived with the guilt of her leaving. I'd already gained weight over worrying about the situation. I'd come to the conclusion that it was not my fault. I didn't know that the woman wasn't dead. I didn't know the lady who tried to kill Tanisha shot Kevin, too! I told Tanisha to run, but she didn't have to listen to me.

Chapter 2

Zakiya Lee

"Aunt Kiya! Aunt Kiya! They fighting again."

I was startled out of my sleep by my six-year-old nephew Kyle's voice. I jumped up and threw some clothes on.

"Stay here," I ordered him as I ran downstairs to the kitchen. My sister, Lisa, was throwing canned food and anything else she could find at her boyfriend, Mikey.

"You want to stay out, so just stay out. Don't do me any favors coming in at three in the damn morning. Just stay out all night," she screamed at him. Mikey just stood against the stone-colored countertop, trying to explain himself and duck the objects Lisa threw at him. This was a common scene in our household. Fight. Love. Fight. Love. *I hate you! Get out! No, never mind . . . come back home.* My sister and her boyfriend had been together for as long as I could remember. You see one, you see the other.

Growing up it was always Lisa and Mikey. They were the cute couple that dressed alike and had the perfect prom picture. Back then, you would have thought they were going to grow up and have the big wedding and live happily ever after. I don't know what happened to the happily ever after. I guess they both grew up, had the twins, and reality set in. Everyone was so over the Lisa and Mikey drama. Especially me, because I was always in the middle, breaking it up. I hated Mikey, and Mikey's parents hated Lisa, and I wished they would just break up for good. But anytime you suggested breaking up with Mikey, Lisa would use the excuse that she had the boys, she was stuck, and she had already put too many years in with him to leave.

I coughed and stood in the doorway, letting my presence be known, in case Mikey got the dumb idea to throw something back at her, and then we would have to jump him. They both looked over at me. Instead of ending the argument, Lisa continued to cuss Mikey's ass out.

"Listen, go back out into the streets. I don't care. I know you were out there cheating on me, probably at the bar with some bitch."

"I wasn't cheating on you. I don't want to go back out there. I just want to go to sleep, Lisa. I'm tired," he said, sighing and rubbing his forehead.

"You are a damn liar," Lisa said as she threw the toaster directly at his knee. He bent down to grab his knee.

Miles ran over to his father to make sure he was okay and said, "Mommy, please don't hurt Daddy."

Before Lisa could pick up anything else, Mikey looked over at Lisa and shook his head. He picked up his son and walked past Lisa. She stood in place—he knew she couldn't throw anything else. After he walked out of the kitchen, Lisa looked at me like *why was I up?* I began picking everything up off the floor.

"I don't think it is good for Miles to hear or see y'all fight," I said.

Lisa flagged me and said, "It is not good for his father to come home in the middle of the night. I am so tired of this shit, I wish he would leave."

My sister knew she really didn't want Mikey to leave. Because the moment Mikey left for a few days she was going crazy. She would go out and track him down. She would beg him to come home, he would apologize, and then they would be blissfully in love for about a week.

Lisa was very pretty—she could get another man easily. She was twenty-six, and people always asked if we were twins, but I'm seven years younger. We had the same build, but I was slightly taller, same brown skin, high cheekbones, slanted eyes, past-our-shoulders long permed hair, and big spearlike noses. I hated our noses. My nose was a little larger than hers. I thought it took up the majority of my face, but people said it fit me and I was cute. One day when I got money I was going to get a nose job. Not like Michael Jackson's or anything crazy. I just would like to make it a little smaller.

Lisa worked as an administrative assistant and Mikey did what he could. Which was not much. He was smart, but only wanted things the easy way. The easy way had landed him in jail a few times. No long stretches, but he had a record. Which made it harder each time for him to come home and get a real job. Somewhere along the line, Mikey decided if he couldn't be a baller, then he wasn't going to be anything. I don't know.

I was tired, and knew I had to be up in a few hours to take my nephews to school. They went to a charter school that had classes year round, and I had to get up on time to take them.

As soon as the alarm went off, I got up and got Kyle and Miles up for school. They're twins. Miles was my baby and always wanted to hug me, hold me, paint for me, and talk to me. Kyle was the opposite. He liked wrestling, skate boarding, and being a daredevil.

When I told them that it was time to get up for school, Kyle always pulled the covers over his head or hid under the bed, and Miles ran into the bathroom.

I wasn't in the mood to fool with them today. "Kyle, get up. I'm not playing with you. If you don't get up, then when you come home, you can't play the game."

That was all he needed to hear. Kyle jumped up and started getting ready.

While they showered, I ironed and put their clothes on the bed. After they were dressed, I fed them and we walked three blocks to their school. We made it just as all the other students were rushing into the building. I told my nephews to have a good day and I kneeled down and tied Miles's sneaker. He thanked me and gave me a fast hug and told me bye. He looked around to see if anyone was watching.

"Are you going to give me a hug, too?" I asked Kyle. He looked around and shook his head no, and said, "After school. Not here, when I get home."

"Okay," I said as I watched him run after his brother into the building. I walked back home and cleaned up their mess. There was cereal and spilled milk all over the table, but I didn't mind. I always clean. I like to live in a neat house. That's one of the things I do remember about my mom. She used to always keep our house spotless. I got up every morning and cleaned. I don't have OCD or anything, but it just made me happy to be in a clean space. Sometimes it made Lisa upset, because she couldn't find things in her own house. Well, that's what she said. But I don't think it's that. I think that being really clean and organized reminded her of our mother. And neither of us liked to think about our mother because she committed suicide.

My mother wasn't a real weak woman, but she just couldn't handle the stress of taking care of two kids on her own anymore. My mother killed herself eight years ago, when I was eleven and my sister was seventeen. I came home from school one day and my mom wasn't home. It wasn't until my aunt arrived from Maryland that I found out my mother was dead.

My mother's sisters, Vicky, Tina, and Darla handled everything. Since Lisa was almost eighteen, they let us stay at our small south Philly row house and just helped us with the bills. If we needed anything they were there for us, but mostly me and Lisa had to do for ourselves.

I worked at Pathmark on Grays Ferry Avenue as a cashier. I had been working there for two years. I liked it, but everyone from my neighborhood tried to come into the market asking me to hook them up. I was not getting fired for them. I started off working part-time, and then when I graduated from Overbrook I started working full-time. I was going to go to college, but I didn't get any scholarships. Hopefully, by the fall I'll sign up for community college. Outside of work, I didn't have much of a life. I talked to guys, but it seemed like all they did was make you sad, get you pregnant, then make your life miserable. It happened to this girl Mina at the job. Her boyfriend begged her for months to be his girlfriend, then as soon as she got pregnant he said the baby wasn't his. Now she had the baby and no babysitter, so she couldn't work. Then my sister and Mikey loved each other, but he was always cheating on her. I don't know, I would always meet guys, but I would never call them. I just didn't like guys who aren't about anything. I didn't want the kind of guy who would bring me down. I'd rather not talk to anyone, plus as soon as I told guys I was still a virgin at nineteen, they usually ran when they found out they were not going to be my first. So right now, I was just taking care of my nephews. They were my world. I took them everywhere and bought them whatever I could.

*   *   *

Today I had to work from nine until three in the afternoon. The market was wild; filled with crazy people, and there was always something going on. I walked in the break room and put on my blue polo-style shirt. Lenora, my shift manager, said, "I need you on register ten."

The market was busy for a Tuesday morning. I took my till to register ten and turned on my light and began ringing up customers. Some lady in my line had all these coupons. I understand trying to save money, but she had stacks of clipped coupons and was trying to save on things she didn't even buy. I looked over all her purchases and had to break the news to her that she couldn't use all her coupons.

"Ma'am, this Tide detergent isn't on sale and you can't use that coupon."

"Yes, it is," she insisted.

"No, miss, it is one hundred ounces on sale, not this one."

"The sign back there said this is the one on sale," she said as she pointed at the detergent. "I can go and get the sign— matter of fact, can I see a manager?" the woman asked angrily.

All I could think of was *all this for a dollar off*. Could she see a manager—that's what I didn't want to hear. *Ugh!* I thought. People behind her were getting mad. One lady called out, "Come on now, I have to go to work." There was nothing I could do but get her a manager. I called for Lenora to come to my register. She tried to explain to the woman that we couldn't use a coupon for something she didn't have. The lady wasn't hearing it. The one-hundred-ounce container was on sale, not the sixty-four-ounce container that she had, but Lenora just gave it to her anyway to keep the line moving.

*   *   *

When I got off work, I was supposed to be taking the boys to GameStop and to Burger King. I wanted to take a nap, but as soon as I came through the door, the twins came running.

"Aunt Key, you taking us to the GameStop to get a new game today, right?"

"Yeah, Kyle. Let me take a shower, then we are going to go. Where is your mom?"

"My mommy sleep. Her head hurt."

I walked into Lisa's cluttered room. There were shoes and clothes piled knee high in heaps all around the room. An empty Pepsi bottle and an open bag of potato chips were in the bed with her. She was sprawled across the bed with the blanket covering her head.

"Lisa, you okay?" I asked.

"No, my head is hurting. This migraine is killing me."

"Did you take anything?"

"Yeah, a few Excedrins. If I don't feel better by tomorrow, I'm going to go to the doctor."

"Do you want me to get you something?"

"No, just close my door. I'm going to take a nap. Can you make sure the boys eat dinner?"

"I was going to take them out with me anyway."

Lisa muttered, "Okay." I tiptoed out of her room and went downstairs and told the boys to be quiet so their mom could rest. I felt sorry for my sister—she always got bad headaches. I think they come from stressing over Mikey. So until she left him her headaches were going to stay.

Me and the boys caught the bus to the plaza where the GameStop was. I was planning to spend only fifty dollars on them. As soon as we walked into the store, I steered them into the Used section of the store. I could not afford to buy them a single game for sixty dollars each. They didn't know any better, and picked out games in my price range and were happy with them.

From GameStop we went to Burger King, and then came home to play their new games. That would keep them busy the rest of the night. Once we were home I checked my messages. No one had called and that was sad. I needed to get a life besides my nephews. I walked out of my bedroom and into the living room and took a seat on the sofa.

"You going to play us in Smack Down vs. Raw?" Kyle asked. I told him I would and held my hand out to take the controller. It only took me a few moments to beat Kyle on the game.

"Aunt Kiya, you cheating," Kyle said as my player pinned his down.

"How come every time I win, I cheated. You are a sore loser, Kyle."

"I'm not a sore loser. I don't want to play anymore!" he shouted and threw the controller down and then he ran to the steps and began crying. Miles was teasing him and calling him a cry baby. I tried to comfort him, telling him that he couldn't cry every time he lost, but he was still huffing and puffing and refused to play. I'd had enough of the game and went and checked on Lisa.

I peeked in on her. She was sleep, but Mikey was in bed with her. I told him I was sorry for opening the door and not knocking. I was tired myself and couldn't wait for the weekend to come.

Chapter 3

Cherise Long

I was waiting to hear the countdown in my ear before I went live. My producer gave me a two-minute warning.

"Okay," I said as I checked myself out in my mini compact. My photographer turned the bright light on and it was showtime.

"Good evening. I'm here in College Park, and there is an explanation tonight as to why when the people in this neighborhood order pizza, they get more than they'd bargained for. In the past two weeks, residents in this neighborhood have been plagued with missing televisions. With us now is one of the victims.

"Ma'am, can you tell us what happened?" I asked as I looked over at the woman I was interviewing. Right before the camera lights came on she was very poised, but now I could tell she was becoming nervous. Her eyes became very big and she started stuttering.

"All I know is a few days ago, I came home and my television was gone."

"At the time, did you have a clue as to who had taken your television?" I asked.

"None whatsoever. I just knew someone had climbed in

my window and stole my TV. They didn't take anything else. Just the TV. And then I was talking to the lady down the street, and her television was gone, too. That ain't right. We are working people. We all had one thing in common though: Jerome! He's the man who delivers all of our pizzas."

I nodded a few times, and then I turned my attention off of her and looked straight into the camera.

"Tonight our sources are telling us that pizza delivery man Jerome Reid of Riverdale is in police custody this evening and is being charged with a string of burglaries. This is Cherise Long, reporting for Action 7 News."

I waited to get the signal that I was clear, and turned my mic off. I thanked the woman for the interview and then took my earpiece out.

I jumped back into our Action 7 News van with my photographer, Gary, and headed back to the station. I was a general assignment reporter at Action 7 News. I had been on the job for four months, but in the news business almost five years.

After attending Northwestern University, I landed my first job in Corpus Christi, Texas, for two years. Then from Texas I moved over to Birmingham, Alabama, as a general assignment reporter for almost three years. Now I was here in Atlanta, and I loved it. Atlanta is the eighth biggest market in the country, and I was still adjusting to the fast pace. In Texas, I was always reporting on cow tipping and a bunch of other farm stories, and Alabama was a little busier, but not like here.

My sister Toni and her husband lived right outside of Atlanta, so it made the transition easier. Toni was five years older than me, but she acted like the younger sister at times. She and her husband had been living here for the last ten years. They didn't have any children together, but her husband had a smart-mouthed preteen daughter, Tatiyana, from his first marriage and she was always over.

Toni was a teacher and her husband, Dave, owned a real estate company. Their marriage was currently on the rocks, though. Dave's company hadn't been doing so well and my sister just lost fifty pounds. She dropped the weight, but gained the *I look better than anyone* complex. She began losing the weight last year when she found out Dave was cheating. He apologized and was remorseful, but she blamed it on her weight. So her husband now had to deal with a wife who was skinny, made more money than him, and was still mad that he cheated.

Toni was my best friend as well as my sister. Most sisters argue, but I always wanted to be like my sister. She was five years older than me, which meant she was always a step ahead. She helped me with my whole life. She had already made the mistakes and told me what to do once I reached certain points in my life.

She taught me how to ride a bike, jump rope, and braid hair. In high school, she told me that my body was a prize and not to reward just any-ole-one. I listened to her because she was always right. Anytime that I didn't listen to her, I paid for it.

I believe that our dysfunctional family back in Charlotte assisted with our closeness, too. My sister and I knew from the beginning that normal families didn't cuss each other out and fight, but those Longs did. They fought, cursed, stole, and got sent to jail. My sister and I were never like them. We grew up living without our mother and father. Our father had his own blues band and he traveled overseas most of the time. They would send us money from his shows. At first my mother stayed home with us, but by the time I was in kindergarten she was back on the road with him. My father, Stanley, said he wanted to play bass all over the world. My mother said, "Okay, baby, follow your dreams." It didn't matter to them that they had two children. Rita just went along with whatever Stanley said. They would come into town, check on us, give our grandfather money for us, and then be back on the road. But from the very beginning, Toni and I just knew since we were little that we didn't belong with our father's family. The Longs were, for lack of a better word, ghetto. It was nothing for my uncle to drink beer for breakfast, fix a car on the lawn, or get locked up every other weekend for robbing someone or fighting with his fat girlfriend. When I was in college on breaks, I would go stay with friends at their houses instead of going home. Even today, I never went home to visit. I always tried to stay away. The Longs suffered from too many secrets, lies, and madness. No one would believe that the beautiful, doe eyed, golden brown news reporter with a perfect physique and a winning smile had a family like mine.

My condo was a long way from my Charlotte family drama. My ninth-floor Peachtree Street condo in downtown Atlanta was serene and peaceful. My place was very diva-ish and gaudy, but I loved it. I had plum leather furniture, a huge fireplace, a big chandelier, and a balcony with a view of the city.

I was thankful for it being a slow news day. I had enough time to go home and relax for a little while and then head to the National Association of Black Journalists reception. Just as I was taking my clothes off, my phone rang.

"Do you have time for drinks?" Toni's squeaky voice asked.

"No, I have to go to a NABJ event this evening. You know I'm new to town—I have to network, but you're welcome to join me."

WHAT'S HIS IS MINE   27

"A roomful of journalists sounds boring." She laughed.

"Well, if you change your mind, let me know. I have to get ready. I'll try to squeeze you in this weekend."

"You better."

My sister was so crazy. I loved her, though. I loved my life, but there was something missing. Yes, that four-letter word, L-O-V-E. I know you have heard it before. So here it is again—I was a very successful African-American woman, but yet I was very single. I wanted to fall in love. It's just that I was too busy working and the right person hadn't come along yet. So I'd been celibate for two years. I should have been having sex all the time at twenty-seven, but I was not getting it at all. This celibacy thing didn't start off as some spiritual journey, I just hadn't met a worthy candidate.

People thought because I was on television that it was easier for me to meet men. But to be honest, it was much harder for me than the average woman. I hate to use the *I* word, but it's true—many men I met were intimidated. They thought, *Why would she be interested in me?* or *I know she is already taken.*

My last relationship was with my college sweetheart, Travis. He was perfect while we were in school, but after graduating we both knew it wouldn't work. I had to go where the jobs were, and he already had a job waiting for him in Louisville, KY. Of course he moved on, he had a live-in girlfriend, and he was happy. I was happy, too, but would be happier if I was in a relationship. So in the meantime, I distracted myself with my career and tried not to focus on my single status.

I looked at the clock and realized I had wasted a lot of time thinking. I only had a half hour to get ready for the NABJ event.

The event was being held at the W Hotel. I walked into the crowded room and ordered a chardonnay and looked around to see if I saw any of my colleagues from the station or anyone who looked familiar. I saw Gavin. We went out a few times. He was a columnist at the *Atlanta Journal-Constitution* and he just so happened to live in the building I was initially going to move into, but at the last minute the deal fell through. Nothing's really wrong with him. He just has a bad sense of humor. I'm not going to say the ridiculous line that he is too nice. But he wasn't my type. He was about five-foot-nine, and when I wore my heels I was taller than him. Aside from the height issue, I just didn't see Gavin in that manner.

I went up to him and tapped his shoulder. "Hey, Gavin."

He turned around and said, "You look great."

"Thank you."

"How's everything going?" he whispered as he put his hand around my waist.

"No complaints," I said casually. I wanted to come and meet new people, not be stuck with Gavin.

"When are we going to spend some time together?" he asked with a hopeful look on his face.

"I don't know. Soon," I said as I removed his hand from my waist. We talked a little and then I went to mingle about the party.

I saw Deborah Ellerbe, who was someone I wanted to meet. She had been at the station since the late seventies. She was the station's first African-American anchorwoman. I read her bio at the station, and I was so impressed and wanted to get to know her. However, I never wanted to go up to her like a nervous fan. She had a great career. The National Media Association honored her with a lifetime achievement award and she was in the Georgia Association of Broadcasters hall of fame, and she won a regional Emmy for editorial excellence nine times. She also served as a chair on several charities. I was getting so excited. Deborah Ellerbe was just the type of person or mentor I needed. I looked over and saw her stop Gavin. Gavin left, then he came back over to her with glass of wine. As he was walking back in my direction, I pulled him over to me and asked, "Gavin, do you know her?"

"She is my mom's sorority sister."

"Really? Can you introduce us? You never told me that."

"I did a couple of times. Shows how much you pay attention to me. After she finishes up her conversation, I'll introduce y'all," he said. The couple she was talking to was walking away and she was headed in our direction.

"Here she comes, Gavin," I said.

He turned around. "Auntie, I want to introduce you to a good friend of mine, Cherise Long. Cherise is a reporter at Action 7."

"Well, nice to meet you."

"It's a pleasure to meet you, Ms. Ellerbe. Congratulations on all of your success."

"Thank you."

"I'm new at the station," I said, managing to keep the nervousness out of my voice. "You have had an amazing career."

"Well, thank you. I've seen you around. You're pretty and I'm sure you will do well at Action 7," she said.

I felt so honored I wanted to break out in a big grin, but I maintained my professionalism. "Thank you, it is really an honor to have met you. I hope to have such an illustrious career as yours."

"Well, thank you. You are so sweet." She looked over at Gavin and said, "Honey, she is a keeper."

We both smiled.

"Gavin, have your mom call me. And, Cherise, you should come to my ladies only luncheon in a few weeks."

"I would love to."

"Okay, I'll send the information through Gavin to you."

"See, you might want to roll with me," Gavin said with a bragging tone. I laughed at him. I still didn't want him, but I was grateful for his connection.

Chapter 4

Zakiya

I was in the bed, totally drained. Yesterday was the first of the month and three people called out. The first of the month was when everyone got their stamps and Social Security checks. Every customer that I rung up was the wrong price or size or something. Then all the customers acted like they couldn't help me bag their food. I bagged so many bags yesterday my arms were sore. My check was going to look real good, though, with eight hours of overtime on it.

But this morning I was paying for my sixteen-hour workday. I hit the snooze button six times already. The first time I hit snooze the clock read 6:30. The second time 6:45, and the last time I looked at the clock it was 7:18. I hit the button and closed my eyes and thought, *I just need ten more minutes of rest.* That was an hour ago. I opened my eyes and looked at the clock. It read 8:15.

I immediately jumped up. The boys were going to be late for school. I threw my clothes on and ran in their room screaming, "Miles and Kyle, get up!" Their room was empty. I peeked in Lisa's room. She was folding clothes and singing along to the Mariah Carey song that was blasting.

I screamed over the loud music, "Lise, where are the twins?"

"At school."

"You took them to school?"

"Yeah, I did. I got up early. I feel much better. That migraine had me down yesterday."

"Did you make their lunch?"

"I bought them hoagies from the corner store. There is a little breakfast left on the table," she said, not looking up from folding clothes.

"Oh, okay. Well, I'm going to eat and then get ready for work," I said, closing her door. Something was going on with Lisa. She hadn't gotten the boys ready for school since last school year. I was confused, but I was just happy that the boys got to school on time. I walked into the kitchen and served myself eggs, bacon, grits, and toast. Lisa came downstairs dragging a bag of clothes.

"What are you doing with all that stuff?" I asked as I munched on my bacon.

"I just went through my closet. I have all these clothes I don't even wear. I'm going to give them to the Salvation Army. You can look in the bag and see if you like anything."

"Okay. I have to get ready for work," I said as I jammed a piece of toast into my mouth. "I'll look later."

I ran upstairs to get dressed. I took my uniform out of my neat closet and placed it on the bed. My shoes were perfectly aligned and all my hangers were going in the same direction. I started to take off my clothes to go get in the shower when Lisa knocked on the door and handed me her black shoe boots.

"Here, you can have these," she said.

"These are your favorites. Why are you giving them to me?"

"I don't like them anymore. I want some new boots. I want everything new."

"You sure?"

"Yeah, I'm sure. I'll drive you to work. I have to stop past Aunt Darla's house."

Lisa dropped me off and I only had five minutes to clock in. When Lenora saw me coming in she looked down at her watch and told me to hurry up because I was going to be handling returns. I didn't mind. I knew where everything was located, and walking around made the day go by faster. There were three shopping carts full of returned items. I would be busy at least until lunch.

After lunch, they put me on the express lane because it was becoming busy. I hadn't even had a break. By the time they tried to give me one, it was going to be time to go home. Lenora came over and tapped me on my shoulder at four and said, "I need you logged off your register. Come to the back. It's important."

"Okay," I said, startled. I turned my register light off and told the man who was next in line that he was my last customer.

My nerves were getting the best of me. I was a wreck, trying to figure out why they would take me off my register. What was going on? I hoped I hadn't forgotten to give someone the right amount of change again. As I scanned each item, I tried to remember any errors I may have made. Each beep of the register had me jumpy. Finally, I logged off and walked to the back of the store. "Your sister's fiancé called. He said it was an emergency and for you to call home because your sister is in the hospital." Her fiancé? I figured Lenora was talking about Lisa's boyfriend, Mikey. What could have happened to Lisa? I couldn't gather my thoughts or belongings fast enough.

"Did he say what was wrong?" I asked Lenora.

"No," Lenora responded.

I thanked her and clocked out. I pulled out my cell phone and called Mikey.

"Mikey, what's going on with Lisa?"

"She is at the hospital. Your aunt Darla is with her."

"What hospital? What the hell happened?"

"Man, I don't really know. Just meet me at UPenn." I told him okay as all kinds of thoughts ran through my head.

I caught a cab to the University of Pennsylvania hospital. I went to patient information. As soon as I exited the elevator, I saw my aunt Darla, her husband, and Lisa's best friend, Yvette.

"What's going on, Yvette?" I could tell by the expression on their faces that it was something bad. Real bad.

"She took some pills," Aunt Darla said.

"Some pills?" I said, shocked, as tears began to stream down my face. "How many? What for? Was it an accident? Her head has been bothering her lately and she's been getting migraine headaches."

Yvette butted in and said, "I don't think it was an accident. She left a letter and she took a bunch of stuff. I called her around three when school was out and Kyle said, 'My mommy sleep.' I said wake her up, and then he said he couldn't. So I called back again and then Miles said she looked like she was dead because she wasn't breathing. I thought the boys were exaggerating, but then I called back and I told them to smack her to get her up because it was really important. I heard the smack and Kyle told me she was still asleep. So I drove over there and they opened the door for me and I found her unconscious in the bed."

"So what are they saying? Is she going to die? Where is she?" I asked as my aunt Darla came up and started hugging me. I broke down, almost falling on the floor.

"Lisa is in a coma. They have her in intensive care. She is

down the hall and it doesn't look good. You can go in there, but you have to calm down," Yvette said, as my aunt Darla tried to hold me up. I tried to get myself together as I walked in Lisa's room.

Lisa was hooked up to all these monitors. I cried quietly as I touched her hand. It felt cold. I couldn't look at her. I couldn't see my sister hooked up to all those machines. I started crying hysterically.

"Calm down, Zakiya. Don't count Lisa out. She might still make it. We just have to wait and pray," my aunt Darla said as she held me up and walked me out of the room to a seat in the family waiting room. I tried to get my thoughts together.

Tears began to fill my eyes. "Where are my nephews?" I asked Yvette and my aunt Darla.

"Mikey's mom has the boys. I had them call her and then I told her what was going on," Yvette said as she attempted to console me, too. I saw Mikey coming down the hall and I became instantly mad. I tried to contain myself, but I just couldn't. I broke down and I couldn't stop the tears from flowing. My chest was heaving up and down and I felt like I couldn't breathe. This couldn't be happening. I couldn't take it. First my mother and now my sister. I kept asking myself why Lisa would do something like this. She knew how hard it was on us to grow up without a mother. Why would she do this to her children and to herself? It didn't make any sense. When our mom killed herself, everyone was always pointing and staring and feeling sorry for us. We never had a mother to give Mother's Day cards to or celebrate the holidays with or comfort us by simply telling us that it was going to be okay. We had different dads, and neither one of them was around for us. *So why would she think it was okay to do it to her boys?* I thought as I cried uncontrollably, sobbing on my aunt's shoulder.

She gave me some tissues and hugged me. She told me it

was going to be okay, and then asked me how Lisa had been acting the last few days. I tried to sit up and wipe away my tears, I collected my thoughts and said, "I thought she was happy. Like really happy. She had music blasting and she was cleaning up, folding clothes, and bagging up clothes for the Salvation Army."

"That's strange. If she was happy, why would she try to kill herself?" Aunt Darla asked.

"Actually, it is normal before a person attempts to commit suicide. They usually get really happy and give away their prized possessions. They get this euphoric feeling. I learned it in my psychology class," Yvette said.

"Really? I didn't know that; I could have stopped her," I said as a doctor came over to talk with us. He introduced himself as Dr. Mead. We all gathered around him in a huddle as he began explaining Lisa's condition.

"The next twenty-four to forty-eight hours will be touch and go. Anything can happen. However, does she have a will, or do you know what her final wishes were?"

Final wishes! I couldn't take any more. I walked away. This was way too much for me.

"Second generation is crazy," I heard my aunt Darla whisper as I walked away. I looked back at them. "Did she hear me?" she asked Yvette. If they were supposed to be supporting me, they were doing a bad job of it. Mikey stood up and walked down the hospital corridor, throwing his arms up at the ceiling and letting out a long, loud sigh.

I walked out of the hospital and saw Mikey. He was pacing and smoking a cigarette. I wanted to be mad at him, but it wasn't his fault. He didn't pull the trigger, but he did give Lisa the ammunition. He was the one who made her want to kill herself. He always made her sad. Damn. Why couldn't he just do right by her? That's all she ever wanted. As he approached me I had mixed feelings. I wanted to hit him, but I just gave him a hug and started breaking down again. He hugged me back and said, "It's going to be okay, Kiya. She is going to make it through this shit."

"I hope so. I don't know what I would do without her," I cried as we separated.

"I know everyone thinks it is my fault, and to an extent it may be. But listen, I got Lisa. I love her. I don't want anything to happen to her or my sons," he said, shaking his head.

"So why do you keep doing stuff, Mikey?"

"Your sister be tripping. I go get my hair cut and she accuses me of being with another woman. I put on cologne and she asks me who I'm trying to smell good for. Last week, she came down to the pool hall and busted my car headlights out because I was playing against my man and his girl, and she thought the girl was with me."

"Well, you have to do something to make her feel more secure. So she won't think anything."

"I've been trying, Zakiya. Come on, you know your sister be acting up for no reason." I knew he was telling the truth, but still, maybe if he hadn't cheated in the past, then she wouldn't always accuse him. It didn't matter now. What mattered was just praying that Lisa made it.

I wanted to see my nephews, but I knew they were going to ask questions and I didn't have any answers. I had to seriously think about the future. If Lisa died, there would be so many things that had to be addressed. Her funeral arrangements. Who would take over the house? Would Mikey fight me for the kids? God, I didn't know how I would handle all of this.

By the time I came back upstairs to the family waiting room, my mom's youngest sister, Tina, had arrived from Maryland. She used to come and get me and take me out when my mother was alive. I hadn't seen her in years. She had her hair cut short and it was dyed honey blond. She was wearing a

pink velour sweat suit. She always was the somewhat fash-
ionable sister. Her husband was older. He did something for
the government in D.C. I knew he made a lot of money and
she didn't work. As soon as she saw me she gave me a hug
and kiss on the cheek. The rest of the night we prayed and
hoped that Lisa would make it through.

Chapter 5

Zakiya

For the last two days, I had just been crying. I mean crying hard. You always take things for granted until something bad happens. I didn't know what I was going to do without Lisa around. It was already so difficult. I was just trying to deal with it. I was on my way back to the hospital when I saw Mikey's number come up on my cell phone. I was scared to answer. I couldn't bear to hear any bad news. I just couldn't. *Damn it, Lisa, why?* I thought. I pushed his call to voice mail and then he called back again. I looked down at the ringing cell phone, picked up, and said, "Mikey, don't tell me any bad news. I couldn't take it. I really couldn't."

"It's not bad news. Lisa is up."

"She is? Oh, thank you, Lord. Oh my God, I'm on my way down there now."

I rushed down to the hospital. I was so happy that Lisa was conscious. When I walked in her room, Lisa was sitting up looking normal. She didn't appear like anything was hurting her. She saw me and she smiled. I walked in and gave her a hug. I wanted to remain calm, quiet, and pleasant—but I couldn't. I couldn't act like what she just tried was okay.

"Why would you do this?" I asked angrily.

"I don't know. I felt hopeless. I felt like I wanted to give up. I don't have a job, I have all these bills, and Mikey wasn't acting right. I don't know; I just lost hope."

I wanted to scream at her, but I used a normal tone. "So killing yourself would make it all better? Who is going to take care of Kyle and Miles? Your children need you. That is so selfish. You had everyone so scared. If you don't care about yourself you should at least think of them."

"I know, Zakiya, I know. I'm not going to do it again. I'm glad I wasn't successful."

"I'm so mad at you," I cried. "You're so fucking dumb, Lisa. I told you to leave him alone. If Mikey's the problem just leave him." I knew I was supposed to be nice to her, and not cuss her out, but I couldn't hold it in. I was so upset at her. I walked out of her room and went down the hall, crying. Aunt Tina followed me. She came behind me and began consoling me.

"Calm down, Kiya. It's going to be okay. Let's go to the cafeteria. I want to talk to you anyway." We took the elevator down to the second floor. She asked me if I was hungry and I said no. She ordered herself soup and insisted that I have a sandwich. I wasn't hungry, but I hadn't eaten in days, so I let her order me a tuna sandwich and an ice tea. Once the sandwich was in front of me, I began to nibble on it.

"What are you doing with yourself?" Aunt Tina asked.

"I'm working at the market."

"And what else?" she asked.

"That's it," I said. I knew she was trying to change the subject. Take my mind off of Lisa, but right now was not the time.

"Listen, don't take this the wrong way, Zakiya, but you need to be doing more with yourself."

"Huh? I'm going to go back to school, probably in the fall."

"I think that is a good idea, because I told Lisa to go to school before she had them babies and she didn't listen. Now look at this mess. You need to get a better job and get in school. Do you understand me? If not, you will end up with a life of nothing, with a no-good man like Mikey. Lisa needs to break up with him. He is bringing her down."

"I know. I know, but she won't leave him or listen to anyone."

"Well, she needs to listen to somebody, 'cause he ain't shit. He is in and out of jail, doing whatever he wants to do with his money, while she's struggling," she said, upset.

"You're right. He don't help her at all."

"I know. See, that's a problem and I don't want you to get caught up like that. I'm going to tell you what's gon' happen. You're gon' sit around here and meet one of these little boys and you're gon' wind up pregnant. Then you're gon' be talking the same stuff Lisa's talking about. And it's gon' be too late. You'll be stuck with no way out. Is that the kind of life you want for yourself?"

"No," I said, shaking my head.

"I think you should get out of Philly. I think that you should go stay with Vicky."

"I'm not moving. Lisa needs me."

"No! You need you, and . . . um . . . You know she's in LA now."

"I thought they lived in Florida."

"No, they moved to California. She's doing real good out there and she got a real nice place. Her boyfriend is a white guy. I think he's like a producer of movies, and I'm going to buy you a plane ticket. And you are going to go! Because I'm going to tell you something—time don't wait for no one and you are nineteen. You are not in school. You need to be having fun, living your life, seeing the world. But all you're doing is working in that market and taking care of Lisa's kids. And Lisa's depression . . . that stuff is contagious. If your mom was living, she would be telling you the same thing."

"B-b-ut . . . " I stuttered.

"There is no 'but,' Zakiya. At least just try it out for a few weeks. Zakiya, you don't have any children or responsibilities. You're going to listen to me and you're going to go. I'm going to call Vicky now."

Before I could say no, she had dialed her on her phone and passed it to me.

"Zakiya, how are you, hon?"

"Hey, Aunt Vicky. Y'all living in California now?" I asked.

"Yeah, we are in Los Angeles. You need to come out here. You would love it. The weather is pleasant all year round. It is so busy and everyone is doing something with themselves. Tina told me about everything that's going on out there. Why don't you come out here for a while and get away? Jade and I would love to have you."

"I might. Thank you for the offer, Aunt Vicky. I have to think about it," I said as I gave the phone back. I heard Aunt Tina say, "I'm going to make her come, Vicky. I'll call you when I buy her ticket."

She couldn't make me do anything. If I didn't want to go to California, I didn't have to. I hadn't seen my Aunt Vicky and cousin Jade in years. They were always moving. They lived all over the country. Vicky was my mom's second to youngest sister. She was always on the go—city to city. She was a makeup artist, a dancer, a singer . . . and a bunch of other things.

I remember growing up, my mom was always so happy

when Vicky would come into town because she always had some fabulous story to tell my mom. Like where she had been and who she was working for. My aunt Vicky was blessed with the gift/ability to never work too hard and always had a rich boyfriend to take care of her.

Chapter 6

Adrienne

I was in the middle of my overnight shift. In front of me were stacks of charts and paperwork that I had to complete. I only had the next four hours, but I would need at least six days to complete it all. I was counting down to 7 a.m. when I could go home and go to sleep like a normal person. Some RNs preferred nursing homes, but I didn't. I hated working nights. It used to be easy—no visitors, everyone asleep—but lately it seemed like the overnight shifts were when all the residents decided to go crazy. It was a very depressing place. I hope to grow old someday, but I hope my daughter doesn't send me to a retirement home. It is the worst.

Just two days ago, I had two patients die on me in the middle of the night, and if the residents aren't passing away, then they are falling. What that equals for me is a lot of paperwork. Nursing homes are really the last stop, the end of the line, before, well . . . going home literally. I'm trying desperately to get back in a hospital, but haven't come across the right position. Some people don't come and visit their parents, others come and yell at them the entire visit or yell at the staff about what we are not doing right for their parent. My response for that is, *How about you take them home and take care of them yourself? Then you can make sure they have everything they need.*

Kalisha, a CNA, came to the station and handed me a menu. "Dina said do you want to order with us?"

"Where are y'all ordering from?" I asked as I opened the trifold menu. "Probably from the pizza place," she said as I stared down at the menu. Nothing looked appealing and I wasn't really hungry. Plus, I knew I shouldn't be eating at night, but I decided to order something anyway, just in case I got hungry later. Dina, another nurse I worked with, called down from upstairs. She was in her midthirties, but still fun. We helped each other out covering for each other when were late or needed a nap.

"I want a chicken cheesesteak and French fries," I said to Kalisha as I closed the menu and went back to my charts. "Tell her I'll be up with the money. I have to go to the ATM."

A few moments later when the phone began ringing I knew it was Dina asking for the money for the order.

"Adrienne, I need you to come upstairs."

"I'm about to bring the money up. Give me a moment, Dina."

"No, I need help with Mrs. Fein. She's hanging at the elevator doors, trying to leave again. And I can't calm her down. You know she likes you."

"Ugh. Why me?" I sighed out loud as I took the last sip of my room-temperature coffee and left the nurses station.

"I'll be right up. Keep her calm and stay with her."

Once I was on the third floor I saw eighty-nine-year-old Patricia Fein balled up crying on the floor. She was balding and what was left of her hair looked like white sticky cotton. Her pale blue nightgown was sagging off of her wrinkled neck.

"Mrs. Fein, we talked about you trying to leave. You cannot just walk out of the building." She didn't respond, she just looked at me with frozen, deerlike eyes. It was like I was talking to myself. Sometimes talking to the elderly when they were suffering from dementia or Alzheimer's was like speaking to a child. She was not responding and I was angry with Dina for calling me up for this. I looked over at her and whispered, "What do you want me to do?"

"Make her go to sleep. I'm tired," she whispered back.

"Mrs. Fein, I want you to stop crying, okay? Tell me why you are trying to leave." I walked over to her and tried to rub her back. She pulled away and kicked at me. I reacted fast enough to move away.

"Mrs. Fein, you can't kick at me. I'm here to help you. So, tell me what's wrong." She relaxed a little and then said, "My daughter said she was coming today, but she didn't come. She promised she would come and see me. She doesn't love me anymore. She is supposed to help me get out of here. I want to go home. I want to be back in my house. I want my daughter to love me."

"She does love you, Patty. She was just a little busy today. I just spoke with Maureen a few minutes ago, and she said she'll be here first thing in the morning to see you. So how about you get your rest and when you awake, Maureen will be on her way, okay?"

"Are you sure?" she asked as she looked at me with uncertainty.

"Of course," I said, reassuring Mrs. Fein. "When you awake she is going to be here, so go get in the bed and when you awake it will be time for your visit with Maureen." Mrs. Fein reluctantly let me walk her to her room and she got in the bed.

"Whew, I'm glad that is over," I said as Dina and I walked out of the room.

"The food is here," Kalisha announced as she handed everything to Dina to sort.

"How much do I owe?" I said as I dug into my scrub pants pocket for money.

"You don't owe me anything. I got it. You just did me a huge favor getting Fein to sleep," she said as she handed me my order.

I thanked her and I was on my way back downstairs when Dina ran up to me with the medicine log and asked me to sign.

"What's this for?" I asked as I handed her my bag as I signed.

"I have to go upstairs and give Henderson his medication. It's morphine—you know he only has a few more days."

"Yeah, I was up there yesterday." I signed the log and she handed me my food and I handed her the clipboard back.

After eating all my food, my scrubs felt extra tight and I felt like a nasty fat beast. It was four in the morning and I had a few more hours to go. All the residents were asleep and we were all just talking and watching videos. Dina was doing her favorite thing, which was shopping. I think Dina was the only person who shopped more than me. However, she didn't necessarily buy nice things. Like she wasted money on Pandora charm bracelets and expensive key chains. She bought everything online for her house and her husband. But right now she was looking at something I heart, and that was shoes.

I peered at the computer screen and said, "They are so cute."

"Girl, aren't they? I had to track these shoes down. They didn't have a size eight anywhere in the country. I'm going to New York to pick them up."

"You are—when?"

"Tomorrow."

"Really? Who's going with you?"

"No one. I'm just picking up my shoes from that boutique I was telling you about—Lena Charles. It's in midtown."

"I should ride with you. I wasn't doing anything tomorrow but sleeping," I said as I got excited thinking about shopping in New York.

"You should. And remember that bag of mine you liked? I got that from there, too!"

"That's where you got that bag from?" I thought about it momentarily. I didn't really have any money, but I did need new shoes and a new bag. Lately, I didn't really have enough money for bills. But I was going to make a way. I deserved it. I worked hard. I knew I shouldn't be shopping, but I was going to pull money from somewhere. It had been a while since I bought me and Asia something. I thought it had been at least three weeks. I didn't care if something didn't get paid—I was going.

The next day I was on my way to New York City with Dina. I hadn't been anywhere besides work in months. Just being a passenger driving down the road was relaxing. Dina and I talked the entire drive about our kids, the job, and celebrity fashion. I lied to my mom and told her I had to work so she would pick Asia up from school for me and I wouldn't have to rush home.

We went to Lena Charles's boutique in Manhattan. Looking through the window I could see a huge chandelier and pink walls and every shoe imaginable. There were rows and rows of shoes lined up against a white brick wall. I stood by the door. I was afraid to go in. I knew I wouldn't be able to control myself. It was like a shoe heaven, and before I could even think to say it, Dina said, "Just breathe. I won't let you do too much damage." I took her advice and took a deep breath. Dina held my hand and we walked in and went straight to the register. She gave the short, blond saleslady her name and said she was there to pick up the shoes she had on hold. The saleslady looked up the information and then brought out a big black box with gold writing on it. While Dina tried on her new shoes, I salivated over all the designer shoes I was seeing. I wished I could buy every pair. There were everything from embroidery flats to seven-inch dominatrix heels. Dina got up and modeled her new pair. I took one look at them and loved them. They were so worth the two-hour drive. They were so cute I wanted a pair myself.

"Dina, you are about to be mad. I'm about to get a pair."

"Get them. I don't care." As soon as Dina gave me the okay to copy, I asked the saleslady if she had a size eight.

"Yes, I think we do, but not in black. Only green," the saleslady said.

"Green? Let me see what they look like."

She went in the back and came out with my shoes and I fell in love. They looked even better than Dina's. I put them on and walked to the mirror.

"They are so cute. Buy them," Dina said.

"I am," I said. "How much are they?"

"Five forty-five."

Ow! I thought, but I had to have them, okay?

"How about I don't have anything green," I said, thinking about what I would wear with them.

"Well, you are going to have to buy something green."

"You're right—another excuse to buy something." I laughed.

We shopped all through New York City. Store after store. I forgot about my budget, but I could not resist so many one-of-a-kinds, last markdowns, and I-had-to-haves.

By the end of the day I'd bought three pairs of shoes, and I treated myself to YSL sunglasses and a Michael Kors dress that I found marked down sixty percent. I also bought Asia a bunch of clothes and shoes.

After shopping, we went to have lunch outside at a little café in busy Manhattan. I felt like I was in *Sex and the City,* shopping, drinking cocktails in the middle of the day. *Why couldn't life always be this good?* I thought.

"My husband is going to kill me. I'm going to be working overtime for the next three weeks to make up all the money I spent," Dina said.

"Well, at least you have a husband. I am going to be paying this credit card down for the next six months." I laughed even though it wasn't funny.

"You better go find you a husband. A cute girl like you. You could get a rich one, too."

"You think?" I laughed. She had no idea. I tried to get a rich man before and it didn't work out.

I picked up Asia from my mom's house and came home and made us dinner. After dinner I read her a book, played a little, and then ran her bathwater. She was in the tub smiling and splashing the water.

"Asia girl! Asia girl!" Every time I would say it she would slap water in my face. She was such a happy and playful child. I love my daughter.

After her bath I dried her off and tried her new clothes on her. The pink skirt and pink and white hoodie looked so cute. I took that off of her and then tried on the aqua drawstring one-piece. That looked adorable, too. She didn't care about the clothes; she was trying to get off the bed and run around.

"Asia, stay still so I can take your picture," I said as I reached for my bag to get my camera phone. She kept moving around, but I finally got her to sit still and smile and take a perfect picture. I instantly sent the picture to my mom. I couldn't wait for her to get older, so I could really dress her up and do her hair.

I put Asia to bed, and then began trying on everything I bought myself. I pulled my boots out of the bag. They were so damn cute. I was so happy I went to New York, but sad that I couldn't go shopping all the time. I wished I could buy whatever I wanted whenever I wanted it. I didn't like this being-on-a-budget stuff at all.

Dina was right—I needed a rich man. And in order to get a rich man, I needed to get back on the chase. And in order to get back on the chase, I had to get back on the scene. Damn, I had to find my friend Angelique's number. She would be my link to a new sponsor. *It is time for me to try to get back on my mission again*, I thought as I searched for my old cell phone so I could find her number. There is no need to work hard all day, when I can just find someone who will give me their money. I met Angelique at a game and she put me on to all these parties. We used to have so much fun together. She would have me in D.C. on Friday and New York on Saturday night. She knew everyone, and whenever there was an exclusive party she was there. Angelique's only flaw was that she had too much confidence. She thought that anyone who wasn't drooling over her and asking for her number was gay. I would have to deal with that, but I thought I could stand her long enough to make some connects. I found my old phone and powered it on and scrolled thought the A's. I found her number and dialed her on my new phone. After two rings she answered rudely, "Yeah."

"Angelique?" I asked.

"Who is this?"

"It's Adrienne, girl."

"Adrienne. What's up? Where you been at?"

"Nowhere, I just haven't been doing too much since I had my daughter. How about you? What have you been up to?"

"Me? I just been doing the same old thing, piling up my frequent flyer miles. I'm living in New York now. I sold my condo in Philly."

"Really?"

"Yeah, I wasn't down there as much anymore. Yup, oh, and you know Princess got married. I was in her wedding a few months ago in the Cayman Islands."

"To her boyfriend who plays for the Nets, right?"

"Yup."

"That's nice. Well, I called to see what you been up to and maybe go out one night."

"Girl, just come up here. I'm going to this industry party on Wednesday. I kinda deal with this promoter, so of course all the bottles will be on him." She laughed.

"Damn, I think I have to work."

"You working?" she asked, as if it was a crime to be a woman and have a job.

"Yeah. I have a baby now. I have to work."

"Wow. What happened with your daughter's father?" she asked like she felt sorry for me.

"Long story. We're not together, but he plays his part. I get a check every two weeks."

"Well, that's all that matters. So I'll see you Wednesday. Call me before you come up."

Chapter 7

Adrienne

For the next few days I thought about whether or not I should go to the party with Angelique. It wasn't really a hard decision. I had been working around the clock like a slave and I deserved a damn break. A night out and a chance to have fun and meet my someone special who was rich was overdue.

I called out from work so I could go out with Angelique. I lied to my mom again so she would watch Asia. I told her I was doing a double. I planned on not working a double, but drinking a few doubles. It was a little lie, but it was justified. I wore a black, deep V-neck dress that dipped low in the front and back. My shoes were six-inch stilettos, and they hurt like hell, but made my calves look like they were extra toned. I couldn't wait to get to the club.

Traffic was heavy in the Lincoln Tunnel, but I still made it to NYC in just under two hours. Angelique's building was a nice high-rise equipped with a doorman. She buzzed me up and I took the elevator up to the twenty-second floor. I knocked on her door and I heard her say the door was open. I walked inside her spacious apartment. It was furnished with a white suede love seat and sofa. She had white and black artwork on the walls and a chrome bar set and matching dining room set and end tables. Angelique instructed me to come on back to her bedroom. She was doing her makeup and her two friends were sitting on the bed. She stopped doing her makeup and gave me a fast hug and said, "What's up, girl?" She still looked the same. Angelique was model pretty and tall. Her skin was flawless brown. Her hair was in loose curls, but she had it all pushed to one side. Angelique's royal blue bandage dress and six-inch blue and black heels just looked like money. I came in and had a seat on her bed. She introduced me to her friends Shavone and Nytika. Nytika looked like a doll. She had golden brown skin, pear green eyes, and dark long hair down to her chest, with a part in the center. Not only was she beautiful, she had the nerve to have a perfect S shape, too. She was wearing a black dress that had slits on the side and left nothing to the imagination. Her other friend Shavone wore a jet black Cleopatra weave that made her light skin look a little pale, and her face was big like a pie. Her body was nice, but she wasn't that cute and was wearing way too much makeup. But her emerald-colored dress and red-bottom shoes were nice. Both of their bodies were almost perfect. I just needed to drop thirty pounds so I could be back at my fighting weight.

"So, what's been up?" Angelique asked.

"Nothing, I'm just happy to be out of Philly."

"Yeah, girl, I'm glad you came up. Tonight is going to be so much fun. You know how I do. Girl, you should have been with us this summer. We nicknamed it the million dollar summer. All we did was hang with millionaires," Angelique bragged as she added more blush to her cheeks.

"Really," I said jealously.

"Yes, they all had money," Shavone said as she slapped hands with Angelique.

"It was fun, but I'm trying to get married. Get one of these dudes to lock it down for the long haul. That's next. It's all good being the girlfriend having nice seats at the game, but I'm trying to lock it in. I need some paper work." I agreed that was the perfect phrase: lock it in.

"You right, Angelique; lock it in and get paper work," I said.

We took a taxi from Angelique's building to the club. As always, when we arrived at the club there was no waiting in line. Angelique's friend pulled us in through the side door and straight back to the VIP section. The party was crowded and the music was really loud. Angelique's friend pushed through the crowd and took us to a table with a reserved sign. Immediately he had a bartender bring us over two bottles of Ace of Spades and a bottle of Cîroc. Angelique introduced everyone to her friend. His name was Mario and he wasn't that cute, but just from the clear diamonds in his watch and ears, I could tell he had a lot of money.

We were there for less than five minutes before people were already looking like "who are they?" because of the extra special treatment we were receiving. So Angelique had to be extra, and opened the champagne and began pouring, letting it spill and bubble over each glass a little. She handed us all a glass and with one sip I felt like my old self. I was back, and anything was possible. I was in a club in the middle of New York City and in every direction I was getting winks and smiles from countless rich men. I turned to my left—million-dollar-contract football players. I turned to my right—actors, rappers, and some more athletes. Angelique knew where to go. It was like I couldn't stop smiling, because I knew all it would take is one dude. Just one to come over to me and make me his and I would have VIP status for life.

I took a look around the club for a come-up. A cute guy at the table across from us caught my attention. He looked familiar, real familiar. I wasn't sure who he was so I tapped Angelique. "Who is that guy?" I asked, looking at him, still smiling and keeping my eyeball tennis match going with the cute stranger.

"Who, him?" Angelique asked, turning her nose up and looking in the cute guy's direction. "Girl, don't talk to him. His ass is broke. He used to have money, but now he is just living off memories."

"Really," I said and immediately sucked my teeth and turned in another direction.

"Yeah. Focus your attention over here, boo," she said as she tilted my head ninety degrees in the other direction. "You see that group over there? That's the starting line-up of the Pacers. They played the Knicks tonight and look, Shavone's funny-looking ass is already over there." I didn't want to say anything.

"What's up with her, anyway?" I asked.

"I ask myself what people see in her, but she gets money and has plenty of connects."

"I can't see it," I said as I downed the rest of my drink and swayed to the blasting music just as Angelique suggested that we leave VIP and walk around the party.

As soon as we were leaving our table, someone grabbed my arm and said, "What's up, Adrienne?" I knew that voice, but I had to look up to see who it was. And I couldn't believe it was this guy I used to deal with named Mark Owen. He played for the Cleveland Cavaliers, and I hadn't seen him in over two years. I was with him—well, chasing him hard—before I met DeCarious. He was supposed to be my baby daddy. He wasn't ever a looker, but his charisma and personality and money made up for it.

"Mark? What are you doing here?" I asked, surprised.

"You know I be in New York all the time. Where you been at? You must have got married on me?" he said as he hugged me.

"Not yet. I had a baby, though."

"Yeah, you got a baby by who?" he asked, scrunching his face up.

"You don't know him," I lied.

"Damn, that's supposed to be my baby." He laughed, but I was seriously thinking the same thing. I wanted to have his baby so bad, but his sperm would not cooperate.

"What about you? You get married yet?" I asked.

"Hell no. Who you here with?" he asked, changing the subject. He looked around and grabbed my hand. I pointed to Angelique. She looked over, saw I was going to be a while, and told me she'd be back. Mark ordered a round of Patrón and began dancing with me. We caught up briefly, but I had to leave him to catch up with Angelique and them. I gave him my number and told him to call me later and began to walk away.

"Where you going?" he asked.

"To find my friends."

"No, stay with me a little longer," he said, biting his lip and pulling me in to dance with him some more. I looked around and didn't see Angelique anywhere, so I agreed and danced off a dozen more songs and took more shots with him.

By the end of the night Mark demanded that I leave with him. All I could say was okay, because my panties were already about to explode after all the dirty winding we were doing. Plus, I remembered how spectacular his dick was and he always took out a couple stacks at a time. I texted Angelique that I was good and I would pick my car up from her place in the morning.

Mark was staying at the Soho Grand hotel. We were both out of it, but all over each other. I couldn't wait to get him inside of me and he didn't waste any time undressing. My dress came off as soon as the door shut. Damn, it was the only thing I could think of as his pants hit the floor. His man was thick, juicy, and long like I remembered. I got on my knees and treated him like he was royalty. I began to taste and savor every inch of his dick. He loudly moaned and exhaled as I consumed him. He then stood up and bent me over the dresser, spreading my legs apart, and penetrated my body. Our bodies came together hard, like a fist hitting a palm, making a loud tapping noise. He had my breasts bouncing and my ass clapping together every time he pounded my insides. He demanded for me to take every inch. I kept pulling back, unable to accept all of him.

If I didn't know better, I would think he was on Viagra or something, because no matter what I did he would not release. We were both sweaty and panting and I gave it to him until I almost passed out. When we were finally done, he slapped my ass and said, "Damn, I missed your ass, Philly." He then picked up the room service menu and turned on the television. I went into the bathroom and took a shower. By the time I came out of the shower wearing the hotel's white robe, the food was there. He ordered us jumbo cocktail shrimps, fries, and cheeseburgers. The food was perfect to calm my drunken, unsteady stomach.

I had the best night. Mark was a babe. After one night with him, I remembered why I used to be so into him. But it was daylight and it was time for me to leave. I was trying to gather my things and he was no help. I kept trying to wake him to ask if he had seen my phone. He threw his phone at me so I could use it. I dialed my number and "Good Pussy Groupie" appeared on the screen and my phone began ringing. I was in shock that Mark had my name listed as a groupie on his phone. Wow, that was crazy. That's all he thought of me. Damn. I thought as I looked over at him. He wasn't shit. But I should have known that by now. I let him play me again.

Not only did I fuck him all night and not get anything out of it, I had a history with him and he thought I was just a groupie. I didn't ask to stay with him, he was the one who had handcuffed me all night. Whatever. I found my phone underneath the bed. I put my clothes on and walked out of the suite without saying good-bye, after erasing my number out of his phone. Fuck Mark Owen again. I got his groupie.

Chapter 8

Cherise

Sometimes, if I didn't have anything better to do, I would entertain Gavin's conversation. Gavin should be happy, because he is very handsome and has a great career. But something was missing with him. There are more than enough women to go around here, but he still doesn't have one. I think he turns even the most desperate women off with his negative persona. His whole life is humdrum and he just complains and gossips more than the average woman. I guess that's the journalist in him. In this phone conversation, he was trying to explain to me why he didn't like taking his dates out to dinner. It was funny to get him riled up and hear him complain.

"So why didn't you want to take her out to dinner, Gavin?" I asked as I flicked through the channels on my television.

"Because I don't feel like driving to a restaurant, paying for parking, and then waiting for a table. I don't feel like going through all that. I work all week, restaurants are overcrowded and overpriced, and I don't feel like waiting in long lines just to eat. I eat out so much I don't want to go out to another stupid restaurant, get fat, and be unhealthy. Can I get a nice home-cooked meal, how my grandma used to cook?"

He just kept going on. I was pushing the mute button and laughing at him. I laughed and said, "Ladies want to go out on dates when they first start dating you, Gavin."

"But don't women know there are things we can do other than eat and go to a restaurant and spend money? Let's do something different. Let's go rock climbing. Let's go to the gym and work out. Eating is not telling me anything about you."

"I don't know what to tell you, Gavin. You are not going to ever meet a woman who doesn't want to be wined and dined."

"There's some out there. When are you and I going out again?"

"I don't know," I said as my phone beeped in my ear. I took the phone away from my ear and I looked down at the screen. It was Toni. Gavin was still rambling on. I interrupted him and said, "That's my sister. I will call you back." I clicked over to answer Toni's call.

"Hey, sistah."

"Don't sistah me. What were you doing?" Toni asked.

"Talking on the phone. You just saved me from another dead-end conversation with Gavin."

"Gavin—oh, that reporter guy. You should date him."

"No, I shouldn't," I snapped.

"I'm telling you, date the one who likes you more. It beats a blank. So I see you are not doing anything—get dressed so you can go out with me. I'll be at your house in ten minutes." I told her okay, but as soon as I hung up I closed my eyes. About fifteen minutes later she was at my door. I let her in and sat back on the sofa and yawned.

"How did you fall asleep that fast?"

"I'm tired. It's called working hard," I said. She sat across from me wearing this cantaloupe-colored ruffled silk shirt, dark jeans, and black heels. Her honey blond hair was short in the back and flicked up in the front. Her gold hoop earrings completed the look. She looked like a fresh-faced teen instead of a thirty-one-year-old stepmother.

"You look cute," I said as I sat up.

"I know. That's why I need to go out," she said, striking a pose.

"Where is Dave—you know, that man you are married to?"

"Who?" She laughed.

"Your husband?"

"In the house where he should be. He begged me to stay in and wanted to watch a movie. I said nope, I have plans. He had fun for all these years—now it is my turn."

"But he is trying."

"Whatever, I don't care. He wants to be the best husband now that he has no money. I think not. No, keep going out and doing whatever you want. Forget about Dave. I need for you to get dressed and go out with me," she said as she pulled the covers off of me.

"I really can't, Toni."

"Let me ask you a question. Are you getting hyphenated this year, or what?"

"What?"

"You know, your Cherise Long-hyphen-Smith or Cherise Long-hyphen-Thompson."

"Toni, you are crazy. I need my hyphen, but you have yours and you don't want to go home to the man who gave it to you. Okay, makes sense. I'm going to sit right here and get my rest," I said, pulling the covers back over me.

" 'I'm going to sit right here and get my rest.' You sound

like an old lady," she said, mimicking me. "What you need is a life."

"I need a career more than I need a life. I have to get up early. I have a big meeting. Then I have to work the rest of the day. I do not want ugly eyes. The last thing I need are viewers writing in, saying I need more rest and 'buy her some eye cream.' "

"So I have to go out alone," she said as she stood up and headed for the door.

"Yes, ma'am. Maybe next time. Have fun, but not too much fun."

"I'm not listening. Good night—have fun at work."

I always got to work at least a half hour ahead of schedule. I walked into the busy newsroom. Something was always going on. Lights, cameras, and lots of live action. I loved it. I fed off of the news. When I was younger, I didn't even know what a newswoman's proper title was, but I knew I wanted to be one. I looked it up one day and learned the correct name was anchorwoman. I remember thinking, *What a dumb name.* I thought anchors had something to do with boats and sailing. I didn't like the name, but I decided at about eight I wanted to be one on television. Every time I would watch the news, there was this pretty woman on television named Lisa Thompson. She was just so smart and pretty, and I wanted to be just like her. I wanted to tell the news, talk to the people, and get to the bottom of the story. She represented everything that I wanted to be: beautiful, intelligent, successful—and she was brown like me. I knew if she could be on television, so could I.

I sat at my desk in my cubicle and checked my e-mails. I had to prepare for the morning meeting. In the meeting we usually discussed what stories we're going to cover and be assigned to. If it was a slow news day, you were supposed to be enterprising and come up with new story ideas. Because I was new to the city, I didn't have any strong ideas. Just as I logged off my computer, my news director, Thomas Oliver, came over to my desk and said, "I need to speak with you in my office."

"Yes," I said. He asked me to please close the door. As soon as I went to close the door the sports director, Paul De-Santis, entered with a cup of coffee and had a seat. I was seated and waited for them to tell me what was going on.

"We like the job you are doing. You have showed a lot of growth in the short amount of time you have been here." *Okay, I'm doing a great job, so what's going on?* I thought.

"As you know, we had to let Phillip Goodwin go because of that whole underage sex scandal investigation. Anyway— well, we wanted to speak with you about bringing some femininity to our sports team in the interim."

"But I've never covered sports before," I said, puzzled.

"We know, but you're pretty and have an infectious smile and people will like you, whether you know sports or not. And we can guide you. You will pick it up easily, and your photographer, Gary, can assist you with anything else you may not know."

Paul butted in and said, "And the other stations that have women on their sports team—their numbers are through the roof. So what do you say?" Thomas looked over at me, waiting for my response. I knew I didn't really have a choice in the matter. They were asking me to help them out for a little while.

"And my salary?" I asked.

"For right now, it will stay the same. However, as soon as we can get a strong replacement in, you will be first in line for the news desk. Michelle Hartley, who does weekend anchor, is taking maternity leave in the spring and you'll have her position."

I knew I had to say yes. If I did them this favor, I would definitely get rewarded and be on the fast track to becoming an anchor.

I walked into the conference room for the meeting and all eyes were on me. Richard Hall was an old, Uncle Tom, still-in-the-streets reporter. He wasn't that fond of me, he never had anything pleasant to say, and always grimaced at me. But it is not surprising. Tammy Chan on weather, Bruce Nichols, and Audrey Brooks were the night correspondents. I was still the "new reporter" and I was still encountering a little hate, and now, with this promotion, I didn't know what people would think. In this industry, everyone is out for themselves. Your job can be in jeopardy as soon as a prettier, wittier girl or guy comes to town. I knew I had to work hard to get what I wanted. I tried not to be jealous of anyone and didn't expect for anyone to hand me anything.

Paul started the meeting. "Good morning. By now you have all heard that Phillip Goodwin is no longer with the Action 7 team. We have decided to temporarily replace him with Cherise Long while we look for his replacement. This will take effect immediately."

I looked around the room. No one really had anything to say about his announcement. There were a few short claps and then the meeting returned to normal.

When the meeting was over, I got one snide remark from Richard Hall. "Four months on the job and a promotion already. Congrats. It must be nice."

I started to respond, but I didn't. He was just mad that he had been working at the station for five years and had never been promoted.

Chapter 9

Tanisha

I emptied out my studio apartment. When I first arrived, all I had were the clothes on my back and the first two weeks' rent. Over time, I was able to make a room into a home. I had a small beige velourish sofa with dark brown wooden arms, a twenty-seven-inch television, a futon bed, and a cheap DVD player. My place looked full, but it only took one big trash bag to empty it out. I gave all my belongings to the lady downstairs, Justine. She was very thankful and said she would give the clothes to her granddaughter who lives over on 7 Mile. Leaving Detroit was going to be bittersweet. It had been the loneliest twelve months of my life. I wasn't sure what was going to happen next, but I was ready to go home. I looked around the room one last time and flicked the lights off and began walking to the bus stop.

I took the bus downtown to the train station. As I exited the bus, my heart began to beat rapidly. I was beginning to feel like I couldn't breathe, and my chest was becoming tight. I was very nervous, but I still walked toward the ticket window in the train station.

"One way to Philadelphia," I said to the woman behind the glass window. She typed my destination into her computer.

"Okay, sweetie, that will be one hundred and twenty-four dollars." I pulled out the money and handed it to her. She counted the money and swiped a marker across the money to make sure it was real. Then the cashier handed me a napkin and said, "Honey, why did you run here? It's okay—the train doesn't leave for another half hour." I thanked her for the napkins. I walked to the restroom and saw beads of perspiration covering my entire face. I wet a few paper towels and wiped my face. I looked into the mirror and tried to stop all the crazy thoughts I was having. I knew I was about to do the right thing, but it didn't make it any easier. Just not knowing what was about to happen next frightened me. But on the other hand, I couldn't continue to live my life in fear and in limbo. I still wasn't sure exactly how I was going to pull everything off when I got back home, but I did know I was tired of running.

The train pulled into the station, and I boarded. I took a seat in the middle of the train by the window, and took several deep breaths. It was going to be a long ride home, but I couldn't wait to see my children and my baby. I wasn't sure if I was going to try to see my family first, or go straight to the police to turn myself in.

Seventeen hours later I arrived in Philly at the 30th Street Station. I was very tired and couldn't believe I was home. Everything was busy—people walking to and from trains, rushing home from work. During the course of the ride, I decided I wasn't going to call anyone—I was just going to turn myself in. I didn't want to change my mind or get scared again. I was home, and needed to get the unpleasant out of the way first. I walked outside the train station and jumped into a Yellow Cab. The cab took me to the Roundhouse, the central police station on 8th and Race Streets.

God, I am so sorry. I didn't mean it. Please have mercy on me, I prayed as I walked into the police station. There were a few people seated in the waiting area. I walked past them. I was shaking and full of anxiety as I approached the bullet-proof window. I saw a female officer in her early thirties with red hair, wearing brown reading glasses and snug navy blue uniform pants and a light blue, creased shirt. She was sitting at a desk, typing something. I knocked on the window and she got up from her desk and walked over to the window. I was still going over what I was going to say in my head. *My name is Tanisha, and I murdered a woman last year in FDR Park. I'm here to turn myself in.* Or maybe I'll say, *I'm wanted and I'm here to turn myself in.* I didn't know what to say, so when the woman came up to the window and said, "What can I do for you?" I said in almost a whisper, "I need to turn myself in."

She leaned her ear over to the window and said, "I'm sorry, I didn't hear you. What did you say?"

I didn't want to scream, but I needed her to hear me, so I spoke up a little louder and clearer. "I need to turn myself in."

She looked at me, alarmed, but then all she said was, "Okay, have a seat. Someone will be out to speak with you."

Someone will be out to speak with you, I thought. I just told her I was there to turn myself in and all she could say was have a seat. Wasn't she supposed to march out with the handcuffs and throw me in jail immediately? I stood dumbfounded for a few seconds. I didn't want to have a seat, because I'd had too many months and weeks of excitement and frustration and not knowing inside of me. I had to tell what happened. Maybe it was a sign. Maybe I wasn't supposed to turn myself in—maybe I was supposed to just keep on going. I reluctantly took a seat as my hands and legs began to shake nervously. Instantly, I thought about running again. I looked at the door, then back at the officer. I looked around the room. I looked back at the window. The officer had sat back down. Was she crazy? What was she doing, just sitting? I thought about going back up to the window again. If she didn't call me in five minutes, I was going to leave. It was 6:14. She had until 6:19. I took a deep breath and waited. One minute, two minutes, and then at 6:19, nothing. I looked up at the window again and the woman wasn't even at her desk. This overwhelming feeling took over my body and I couldn't wait anymore. I got up out of my seat and briskly walked out of the police station door. There were a few officers outside smoking cigarettes. They didn't pay me any attention as I hurried past them. I walked down the block and the first cab I saw, I flagged down. The cab stopped and the driver asked in a thick African accent, "Where you going to, miss?" I wasn't sure. I didn't know what to tell him. We got a few blocks away from the station and I began sweating again and tears streamed down my face. I started wheezing and my chest was becoming tight again.

"Do you need to go to the hospital, ma'am?"

"No," I said as I attempted to calm myself down.

"Are you sure?"

"Yes, please just drive. Go straight," I yelled.

"I can't just drive straight, I need to know where we are going," he said rudely. I guess I was going home, and from there I could figure something out.

I had the cab drop me off at the corner of my block. My tree-lined block of row houses appeared to be the same. I could see my house from the corner. It seemed so big. I remembered when it looked and felt so small, and I had felt trapped. Back then, I couldn't wait to get out. Now I would do anything to go back in.

Chapter 10

Zakiya

I was going to Los Angeles, and now I was so happy about it. I told my job that I was quitting. They were a little upset that I wasn't giving much notice, but Lenora understood. I'd never been on a plane. Aunt Tina said the flight was about five hours. I was packing my clothes. So far I had almost two suitcases filled. I was sitting on the edge of the bed, trying to decide what I could live without because I couldn't take everything. The weather is supposed to be very nice all year round, but I heard it gets cold at night. So I did want to pack some sweaters and long pants. As I packed Aunt Tina kept calling, making sure I was really going. She said she was calling around trying to get the best deal on my ticket since it was last minute. I thought Lisa would be upset that I was leaving, but she was like, *Go. If you don't go, I'm going to be so mad at you.* I felt a little relieved. I told my nephews I was going to Hollywood and they asked if I was going to be a star. They said they would miss me, but once they realized they could now have their own rooms they were over it.

My phone began ringing. I heard it but couldn't find it. I searched around for it on my bed. I found it. It was my Aunt Tina.

"I'm packing."

"Good. Um. Okay, I had a little issue with getting you a plane ticket. Since it is short notice, the tickets were just way too high. The cheapest I found was like twelve hundred, and that was with two layovers. So you're still going, but it's going to be on the bus."

"The bus?" I had never been to California, but I knew it would take forever to get there on the bus. "How many hours is that like—thirty hours?"

"No, two days."

"Two days." *Was she crazy? Did she really think I was going to ride the bus for two days?*

"You will make a few stops and you will probably be asleep, anyway, and you get to see the whole country." I didn't want to see the entire country, but she had already bought the ticket and I was leaving the next day.

Lisa and Aunt Darla dropped me off at the Greyhound station downtown. There were long lines of people and the buses' engines were buzzing. I saw my bus, 1651 to St. Louis, MO. From there I would transfer to my next bus. Lisa was tearing up a little and told me to be safe and call her when I got there. I thanked my Aunt Darla and gave Lisa a hug.

I handed the driver my ticket and he tore off a piece and handed it back and asked me how many bags I had. I told him three, and he helped me place them in the storage compartment under the bus. I walked to the back of the bus and sat in an empty seat in the middle. I was still tired, so I turned and placed my jacket over my head and nodded off.

When I awoke, the bus was bumping down the road. It was pitch-black outside the window. I couldn't see anything but car headlights and dark traces of trees. Someone near me had their headset blasting, because I faintly heard a Lil Wayne song. I checked the time—it was almost 1 a.m. I had only been asleep for four hours, but I had to go to the restroom. The woman sitting next to me was doing a crossword puzzle. I excused myself and walked to the bathroom. There was someone already in there and that gave my legs time to stretch.

The man who came out of the bathroom said, "You might not want to go in there." I knew what that meant, but I had to go, so I was going to have to take my chances.

As soon as I entered the tiny stall I smelled a strong mixture of urine and something that was dead, but I had to go really bad, so I covered my mouth and blocked out the smell. It was so disgusting I thought I would gag. I walked back to my seat and placed my jacket back over my head. I already couldn't wait for the bus ride to be over.

I was halfway to my destination. Lisa had texted me, to check on me. I texted her and said I was good so far. I was stuck. I was in the middle of nowhere. I couldn't turn around now, but it would have taken the same amount of time to get back home. I had only made it to Topeka, Kansas, and we were still a day away from Los Angeles. This bus was so slow. I had passed through every small town in the United States. I thought if I started walking I could probably get there faster. I was so tired of seeing trees and the highway. I swore we were just riding around the same town in circles, because every town had a Wal-Mart and a bunch of McDonald's. The other thing I was tired of seeing was crazy people. I had realized crazy people are not allowed on planes, so they catch the bus. A crazy man took down his pants and peed at the last stop. Then a woman was arguing with her children and smacking them up. The bus driver asked her to stop and she didn't, so he called the police and pulled the bus to the side of the road and they escorted her and her kids off.

*   *   *

I tried going to sleep, read, and just look out the window. None of it was working, because I was not tired. I was restless. I wanted off this stupid bus. It seemed like we'd been riding through Colorado and Utah forever. And that didn't mean anything, because the man sitting in front of me said as soon as we got to California we still had another six hours. Oh, my God! The only thing that was keeping me from going crazy was I kept telling myself when I woke up I was going to be in Hollywood. This bus had to have stopped at least eighty times and I transferred onto two buses. It was like riding a never ending local bus. I wanted to go home, but at this point I was closer to California than I was to home.

We were an hour away. I couldn't take it any longer. My legs were aching. I felt so tired, but I couldn't sleep. I felt claustrophobic and I wanted to scream, *Get me off this damn bus now!* We had reached Los Angeles but now we were stuck in traffic on the freeway.

We finally pulled into the station and my Aunt Tina was wrong—it did not take two days. It took two days and sixteen hours. I wanted to break a window to get off the bus. *Let me off,* I wanted to scream to the people who were taking a long time to get off. *Get the hell off the bus!* I thought. When I got off the sun was shining brightly in my eyes and I felt a warm breeze tap my skin. I wanted to scream, *I made it!* That was the longest journey of my life. I felt sick and was in need of a shower, and I felt like I smelled.

I called my aunt and told her I was here. She said to come around to the other side of the bus terminal. I dragged my bags and walked toward the exit. I stood by the door and was ready to call her again, but then I spotted her.

"Auntie Vicky," I shouted.

"Hey, little girl, you look just like your mother with all

that long hair. You're so pretty. I knew you were going to grow into your nose," she said as she gave me a hug.

"Thank you."

She turned to the older, portly white man standing behind her and said, "This is my boyfriend, Martin." We both said hello and he smiled and took my bags. He had thinning blond hair, very dark tanned skin, and dark shades. He was a nice-looking older man.

"How was your journey?" she said as we walked out of the terminal.

"I'm never catching the bus across the country again. It was awful."

"I can imagine, but you made it here and that's all that matters."

We walked over to a black Mercedes-Benz convertible. I don't know what model it was, but it was very nice. He placed my bags in the trunk, opened our doors, and we headed to their home in North Hollywood.

On the way to their condo all I saw were these palm trees. I inhaled the air. It was different, and everyone just looked joyful and lively. I looked around in amazement because everything was so pretty.

We pulled up to my aunt's apartment complex, which was like a mini resort. There was a large pool and a tennis court. The condo had a big living room, two bathrooms, two over-sized bedrooms, and one small room.

"This is your room." There was enough room for a single bed and tall dresser. There were yellow and white sheets and yellow curtains. It wasn't as fabulous as the rest of the house, but I was very thankful. I began unpacking and getting situated. Jade came in and squealed.

"Cousin, you made it!" She hugged me. "You are going to love LA. Hurry up and finish getting dressed so I can show you around the city."

"Okay, can you show me the Hollywood sign?"

"Yeah, I'm going to take you everywhere."

Jade was about five feet tall and very thin. She was cute and had her hair smoothed back in a ponytail with sunglasses on her head. She was wearing a green baby doll dress and cute multicolored sunflower flip-flops.

I saw the Hollywood sign and it was just like on television. It sat so beautifully on top of a hill in the distance. I took a bunch of pictures. We went to Rodeo Drive. There was every big-name designer store you could imagine. Some of the stores even had big security men at the door to protect the merchandise.

Then we walked around the corner to a restaurant named Mr. Chow. Jade said we might see someone famous.

There were all these stores. It was just amazing. I just peeked into the stores from the outside because I knew I couldn't afford anything inside, but it didn't cost anything to look. There were all these paparazzi lined up.

"Those men with the cameras—are they paparazzi?" I asked.

"Yeah."

"So, they are trying to catch celebrities shopping, like on television?"

"Yes."

"This is too funny. Wait until I call home and tell Lisa I saw real paparazzi."

From Rodeo Drive we drove to the Walk of Fame on Hollywood Boulevard. It was in front of this Chinese theatre. There were so many handprints and signatures. I saw Eddie Murphy's handprints. I placed my hands in them and had Jade take my picture. There were street performers dancing and people dressed up like superheroes. I took a picture with a man dressed as the Terminator. There was so much going on. My nephews would love this place. I knew I had to get a job and save my money and soon. As soon as I had enough saved, I was going to fly the boys out here. I wanted them to see all this.

We ended the day at Roscoe's House of Chicken and Waffles. Jade's boyfriend, Theo, met us there. As soon as she introduced us, I didn't like him. I didn't like the way he looked, talked, or acted. I never saw a man be so fake. His jeans were too skinny and they made me uncomfortable. She said his father was a writer on a few shows and his mother was an actress.

I ordered the specialty chicken and waffles. It was so good. I was hungry and wanted a second serving, but Jade was still working on her first wing and only taking sips of her Diet Coke and water. Her boyfriend left half of his burger and still had French fries left on his plate. So I just asked for another glass of water to fill up my stomach and so I wouldn't seem greedy.

I awoke startled. I sat up, scared. I looked around the room. It took me a moment to realize where I was. I think I was still having flashbacks of that damn bus. I stood up, stretched, and then looked at my cell phone. It was 7:10, which meant it was 10:10 back home. I was so excited, I had never even bothered to text or call Lisa and Aunt Tina and my cell phone had died. I plugged it up and turned it on and a bunch of text messages came through. I listened to my messages first. My nephews had left several messages and Lisa left two, just telling me to call her to let her know I was fine. I couldn't believe everything I had crammed in the last thirty-six hours. I was really in LA. I had really left Philly. I dialed Lisa. She sounded happy to hear from me.

"How is it? How was the trip?" she asked excitedly.

"Lisa, I'm never getting on another bus again in my life."

"It couldn't have been that bad."

"It was. But so far, California is so nice. I'm looking out the bedroom window—it is so beautiful and peaceful. I just see trees and sunshine. I think I'm going to like it here. Last night we drove to Hollywood, like where the stars' handprints are. Where are the boys?"

"At school. I'm at work. The temp agency called me."

"You are? That's good, Lisa. You sound good."

"I feel real good."

"That's what's up. Um, have the boys call me."

"I will." Lisa was doing well and that put my mind at ease. The apartment was so quiet. So I walked into the living room to see where everyone was. I saw Jade was out and Aunt Vicky's bedroom was empty. I walked into the kitchen and opened the refrigerator and there was nothing in there that wasn't healthy. Even their eggs were egg whites. All the food was fat free or was free of salt or sugar. I don't think Aunt Vicky is a vegetarian and Jade just doesn't really eat. I saw a strawberry and banana yogurt in the back of the fridge, so I ate that. I would have to find a market and go and pick me up some regular food.

They came in an hour later, dressed in black tights, running sneakers, and fitted baby T-shirts. They both looked like fitness instructors.

"Where were y'all?" I asked.

"At our yoga class. We started to wake you, but you were knocked out. Maybe tomorrow you can go out with us."

"Maybe," I said, but I knew there was no way in hell I was getting up before the sun to go and work out.

"So what's the plan for today?" Aunt Vicky asked.

"I have to work, Mom, and then I'm going to dinner with Theo."

"I should go to work with you and look for a job," I said, getting up from the table.

"Girl, you just got here. Relax. You'll have plenty of time to look for a job. Let me take a shower and then I'll make breakfast."

Breakfast with Aunt Vicky and Jade was interesting: egg whites, toast, and some kind of meatless sausage. They weren't vegetarians, but they ate very differently. Really, they didn't eat much of anything.

The rest of the day I sat by the pool and then went to Ralphs market and bought real food. I was not going to be drinking any more soymilk or eating any veggie burgers. It had only been a little over twenty-four hours, but so far I loved LA.

Chapter 11

Adrienne

I let a millionaire fuck me for free. As much as I liked Mark and we had history, that was not acceptable. Angelique asked me how I knew Mark, and she said she knew I had a nice shopping spree afterwards, because he was the biggest trick. How he gave money to everyone and was always trying to boo love somebody. I felt like a fool because I kept thinking about seeing "Good Pussy Groupie" in his phone and that shit hurt. It hurt and I felt so stupid. I promised myself years ago that I wasn't going to let anyone disrespect me, and I did. Since I'd been going out with Angelique and her little squad, everything made sense now. They all behaved as if the world owed them something—even the ugly one. That was a reminder to me that I needed a man who is going to bow down to a queen. I really needed a rich man to pay my bills, take me on trips, and buy my dream house. The next rich dude, I get no games. I was reeling his ass in, I was holding on to that line, and I was not letting go. I wanted a man with money. Lots of it. A man who didn't mind sharing.

What's wrong with wanting half? Some women dream of becoming doctors, athletes, and lawyers. Others dream of marrying them. The difference between the two groups of ladies is that the doctors, lawyers, and athletes are all single, because they were too busy following their dreams to land a good man. Instead of being in the books, I should have been at the games. By now I would be married and rich. The smartest thing you can do is grab an athlete in college, or even better, be their high school sweetheart. That way it doesn't look like it's all about the money, even though it is. Anybody who's NBA or NFL bound, chances are everyone knew they were going to the league since middle school. Their chicks are just premature gold diggers who just jumped on the bandwagon early. If you don't get them early, you are just another chick scrambling to prove that you don't want them just for their money. Why the hell did I do four years of college? And what had my degree got me? Not more than Angelique. She had way more than me. But it is never too late and now I was on my job, because I refused to be working all hard in that nursing home, when I could just have someone take care of me. I deserved to be arm candy at the ESPY Awards. I was supposed to have a Maybach and a mansion. I needed all of that. Clear-ass diamonds adorning my wrists, ears, and hands. The mission was officially on. I needed a ring and a piece of paper making me a Mrs. and making my only job in life to luxuriate.

And back at my job, I hadn't been working as much, and I could tell Dina had attitude with me. I think she thought that I thought I was better than her now. She kept asking me if she could come to New York with me. That would be no. She would not mesh really well with Angelique and her friends. She was cool for shopping, but not partying. If she came out with us, she would be so out of her league.

I was driving back to New York again. I was going out with Angelique later and I still had to find something to wear. I couldn't have anything average on, because money recognizes money. First I was meeting up with Wesley, an enter-

tainment lawyer. I met him at M2 last week, at an album release party. I talked to him on the phone a few times. I knew
he had lots of money, because he had quite a few high-profile
clients. I usually tried to stay away from professional men,
because they are too reserved with their currency. Hopefully
he was different. His only flaw was that he was engaged, but
that's not married yet. So until he walked down the aisle, he
was single as far as I was concerned. His fiancée was a dentist
in Harlem and was busy herself. But that was her fault because today I was going to be spending time with her man.

Wesley was always in meetings or on an important phone
call. I hinted around about him taking me shopping when I
arrived, but I just wanted to make sure we were clear before
I got there. I called his phone and he said, "Adrienne, beautiful. I need to place you on hold for a moment." He came
back to the line and I wasted no time asking him what he had
planned for us.

"Well, I have a meeting or two and I guess we will do dinner."

"While you are at your meetings, I can go shopping," I
suggested.

"Yeah, you can go shopping if you want." He wasn't getting it that I wanted him to foot my shopping bill. So I was a
little more direct.

"I mean, like you can give me money to go shopping. I
need a new dress."

"Oh, really."

"Yes. Really," I said.

"Sweetie, oh no, I just can't give you money to go shopping."

"Why not?" I asked.

"I don't have a problem buying you something here and
there, but I'm not just going to take you shopping."

"Well, okay. I guess you won't see me then, because I don't

date men that can't do anything for me." I said as I hung up on him. He had money and he was going to spend it or we weren't going to be friends. I needed a dress and a pair of shoes to wear out tonight. My cards were basically maxed and I wasn't going to be able to get anything I wanted with the three hundred dollars that was in my pocket. A few moments later he called back and said that he would take me shopping.

He wanted to have dinner at Ruth's Chris Steak House. Luckily Bergdorf Goodman was in the same neighborhood. I walked into the expensive department store and went straight to the dress section. I held his hand and picked up a few dresses, took them into the dressing room with me, and came out and modeled them for him. I looked in the mirror—this black dress was perfect. "I want this one," I said, smiling at him.

"This dress is like seven hundred dollars," he said, noticing the price tag attached.

"But it looks good on me. Don't it—right?" I said as I modeled it for him some more. I asked him to unzip the dress for me so he could get a feel and look at my naked back. Maybe that would hype his engaged ass up. *He better buy me this dress,* I thought. I pouted a little. If I didn't walk out of the store with the dress and shoes, then he could forget he met me. I looked at him. And then he caved in and bought the dress.

It felt good to get him to buy me the dress without lying on my back. I felt like I could manipulate and get money from any man I wanted. Call it materialistic or whatever you like, but the world revolves around money.

I met up with Angelique and the girls at the party. It was at the art gallery. I knew I was going to meet someone, because I looked good in my new dress. The art gallery was nice, but too crowded. There were sculptures and paintings, but no one was paying attention. Shavone and Nytika went about their business from the very beginning. They left the table holding hands. I hated that girlfriends-holding-hands crap, but I watched them mingle through the crowd and I studied their mannerisms. Shavone didn't have anything on Nytika, but she just oozed confidence in her walk.

She went up to this strange-looking guy and the next thing I knew he was pulling out money, giving it to her. I watched the man count out hundreds and then hand them over to Shavone. I calculated about two thousand. Shavone came back over, placing the folded money in her bag.

"Look at her. I don't know why she deals with that guy, he is so local—and look at him pulling out a knot, in the middle of the club. Who does that? That's how you can tell he doesn't have any money." Angelique sighed. "Shavone, how can you mess with him? He looks like a gargoyle with those 3-D eyeballs. I could never wake up next to that," she said in disgust, shaking her head.

"Shut up, Angelique. Fuck it, I don't care. He just gives me money and I never had to do anything for it," Shavone said.

"You ain't never fuck him?" Angelique asked, twisting her lips to the side.

"No, I didn't have to. I told him I'm saved and he believed me." We all started laughing at that lie. It was official: If just-okay girls were getting paid, it was time for me to get back on my job.

I spotted someone I was interested in. He played for the Knicks. I recognized him from his Adidas commercial. The only problem was there was a three-layer ring surrounding him. He was tall enough to see above most of the crowd of heads. But it would be hard to infiltrate without looking like a groupie. I needed him to come over to me and say something. The first outer ring were groupie girls obviously trying to get noticed. The middle ring were friends of his friends and were talking to the groupies. The inner ring were his real boys and security. There was no way I was going to walk over to him. I had to get him to notice me. I stared in his direction until I got his attention. When I saw him looking at me, I smiled. He smiled back and waved. I said, "Come here," and he did. He made a part through his entourage, and grabbed my arm gently.

"What's your name, sweetheart?"

"Adrienne," I said seductively.

"Okay, Adrienne. So what's going on after this?" he said, straight and to the point.

"I don't know—you tell me," I said, smiling and taking a sip from my glass. Right as he was about to tell me what was up after this, this tall Hispanic woman with long wavy hair came up to him and whispered something in his ear. He smiled and then held up his finger to say "one minute" to her. Then he turned his attention back to me and said, "I'm having an after party back at my place—maybe you can come through." I was thinking no, but I would go out with him another time. I was going to just give him my number, but before I could, the woman returned, more desperate to make her point this time. She grabbed his dick and kissed his neck and whispered something in his ear. He laughed and said he would be right back, but shortly after I looked over and he and his entourage were leaving the building. What a waste of a cute dress and night. I only met one young dude.

Chapter 12

Cherise

The buzz circulating in the newsroom was that I slept with Paul to get my new position. I wonder who started that rumor. It didn't matter because it wasn't true. However, it probably appears a little suspicious that I was new and inexperienced in sports and still got a new position. But anyone who was paying attention knew that it was a lateral move.

I wasn't the most knowledgeable person about sports, but I was going to prove them wrong. Tonight I was covering the Thrasher game at the Philips Arena. We were sitting in the press box. I hated hockey—it wasn't really that I hated it, I just really had no idea what was going on. It was very noisy and rowdy and the crowd was into it, but I didn't get skating on ice while swinging a stick. I was about to interview the team, which had just lost to the Ottawa Senators. I really was out of my league. Gary being an avid hockey fan was a plus, because he gave me pointers and tips. I didn't know anything about hockey. But I was going to cover the game with so much enthusiasm and act like I knew what I was talking about. "Okay, Gary, now what is it called again when the puck goes into a net?"

"A goal."

"And tonight he had three in one night, so that's called a what trick?"

"A hat trick."

"Right," I said as I pulled down my skirt and fixed the collar on my jacket and practiced in my mind what I was about to say.

"You'll do fine, Cherise."

"I sure hope so," I said. "Gary, how do you say that player's name again–Aper-chock-o-nov?" I said phonetically. Russian last names were so hard to pronounce, but I was determined to get it right.

"That's it." Gary laughed. It was time for me to get ready.

When the game was over I walked back to the locker room, trying to not pay attention to all the butts halfway covered with towels, wet muscles, and missing teeth. I kept telling myself that I was a professional and I had a job to do, and I couldn't stare or laugh at the absent teeth or naked bodies.

I was on my way to Ms. Ellerbe's luncheon. Her home was a big, beautiful mansion that sat by itself in Duluth. Every house in the neighborhood was easily over a million dollars. All the other women were out on the large deck—they were all in their mid to late fifties. They had this very classy elegance to them. I felt honored just to be in their company.

"Thank you for inviting me to your home," I said as we walked out back on her deck.

I continued to walk to the back where all the other women were seated. I was the youngest woman there. I didn't see anyone else I recognized.

They were speaking about things I wasn't interested in. I thought they were going to inspire me and I was going to make new alliances with professional women, hear about changing the world. Instead, I had to hear about menopause, how much they hated their husbands, and why their children didn't call. The conversation was boring me, so I excused myself and went to the ladies' room. It gave me more time to look around her stunning home. On her mantel were pictures of her with famous people and politicians. There were other photos of her standing in front of the Sydney Opera House in Australia and the Eiffel Tower in France. In all the pictures I saw her alone or with her friends. I didn't see any pictures of a husband or children. I knew she had to be married. Before I could make it back outside, Ms. Ellerbe was back inside asking if I was okay.

"Yes. Your home is very nice."

"Thank you."

"I was looking all around and I noticed you don't have any pictures of your family."

"No, I dedicated my life to my career. I guess I missed out on the family. A husband and children are not for everyone. I have godchildren. It's very hard to have it all. I chose a career over a family."

"I see," I said, trying to hide my disappointment.

"Yeah, if you want a long-lasting career, don't get caught up with that sports director Paul DeSantis. There is no way to sleep your way to the top. Paul is the kind who will use you up. Sell you a dream and then get in a meeting and turn on you."

"Really? I didn't get that impression. However, I have heard rumors about myself that aren't true."

"I wouldn't worry about it. The best advice I can give you is cover the news—don't become the news." I thanked her for her advice and followed her back to the deck. I stayed for a few hours and then I left. I was no longer inspired by Ms. Ellerbe. She seemed lonely. What was the purpose of being rich and successful, having a huge home and no one to share it with? I didn't understand it. I wanted a family and children. She had everything but nothing at the same time. I didn't want to end up like her. Just as I was leaving, Toni called.

"How was your big diva luncheon?" she asked.

"It was nice. I just left. Actually, it was kind of depressing."

"What was depressing about being invited to a successful woman's beautiful home?"

"Well, she had all these possessions, but no family, no children or husband. She had all these things and no one to share them with. I don't want to be in my seventies and be alone. It just gave me a reality check—I want to settle down very soon, get married, and have children."

"Now you are going to listen to me. I've been trying to tell you this all along that it was time for your name to be hyphenated."

"I still don't need a man, Toni, but I think I am ready to at least try to find someone."

"So what are you about to do now?" she asked.

"Go to the house and get ready for work."

"Well, how about this? Don't go home. Come and get me and let's go out and have a few drinks. I'm meeting up with Lou, the guy I met the other night in Atlantic Station. I'm going to ask him if he has a friend you can meet."

At first I was going to say no. Toni wasn't slick; she was using me as an alibi to meet her young guy. I wasn't going to be an accessory to cheating.

"Okay, I'll come and pick you up, but I can't stay out late."

* * *

I pulled up to Toni's single-family home. It was very nice, the kind of home I was going to buy when I settled down. Everything from the outside looked perfect. Inside was another story. Dave opened the door for me. He had a big brown round face with a trim mustache and beard. He was wearing sweat pants, a T-shirt, and old sneakers.

"Were you working out, Dave?" I joked.

"No, just cleaning out the basement. I don't have anything else to do—business is real slow. This economy is crazy," he said, sighing.

"Things will pick up."

"It has to. Everything that goes up must come down. Vice versa."

"Yeah, very true," I said as Toni came rushing down the steps. It was so obvious she was being sneaky.

"Babe, you know it is girls' night, so don't wait up," Toni said as she grabbed her jacket and we walked out the door.

TL Zone was a bowling alley that had billiard tables and an arcade. We were going to grab a table and wait for Toni's friend Lou to show. I wanted to see what he looked like. Before long, he came up from the side and gave her a kiss.

"I have a table over here, babe," he said. He was tall, with coal-dark skin and a beautiful body. I was mad for Dave's sake. If this young guy was his competition, he didn't have a chance.

"Cherise," I said as I extended my hand.

"Cherise, Toni told me you were looking for a man. I was trying to bring one of my boys, but they were all tied up." I gave Toni a look like *what?* She smiled and Lou asked if we wanted anything to drink. Toni answered for us both and said two Cosmos. Lou took our drink order and walked over to the bar. Lou was cute, but he also seemed like he was very young.

As soon as he stepped away, I grabbed her arm. "How old is he, Toni?"

"Twenty-four."

"Twenty-four? Are you crazy? *I* wouldn't date a twenty-four-year-old."

"You wouldn't and I would, and remember—I'm married, so I'm not dating him, I'm just hanging out being a friend to a younger guy." She laughed.

Lou came back and placed our martinis in front of us and gave Toni another squeeze and kiss on the cheek. He was overly affectionate, which made me very uncomfortable for Toni and myself. I just kept thinking, *What if Dave walked though the door?* He would beat me, him, and her.

"Why is it so crowded here tonight?" Toni asked, looking around.

"The Falcons are having a charity event," Lou said, not taking his eyes off of Toni.

"Oh, that's nice," I said as I looked around, noticing the extra crowd.

"See, this is a good event for you to be at. You should know about this event, Miss Sports News Reporter Lady," Toni said.

"You're right, but when I'm not at work, I'm not at work," I said as I winked at her and drank the last of my martini.

"But, Cherise, there are a lot of nice men in here. I want you to pass your business card out. You better start self-promoting, or I will."

"Please don't," I said as I got up from the table to go to the bar to get another drink.

The bar was crowded, and the bartender looked like he

was either new or wasn't used to dealing with a large crowd. It took him fifteen minutes to take my drink order.

I handed him my credit card and began sipping the drink he placed in front of me.

"That's my drink," a deep male voice said.

I looked down at the drink and said, "I am so sorry."

"It's okay," the man said, laughing. "I didn't drink out of it, but you didn't have to steal my drink. I would have bought you one."

I laughed. Ms. Nosy came up beside me whispering, "Who is that?" I told her I accidentally picked up his drink.

"He's cute—talk to him," she said, trying to nudge me to him.

Toni took matters into her own hands and said, "Hi, your name is?"

"Tim Hughes."

"Nice to meet you, Mr. Hughes. What are you doing here tonight, and why do you look so familiar?" Toni asked.

"This is my event. Did you give a donation or bid on anything at the silent auction?"

"No, we didn't know about it. So do you play for the Falcons?"

"Yeah, I do. And you ladies need to take a look at some of the items we have. All the proceeds benefit my organization, Brothers Helping Themselves."

"Well, you need to talk to my sister. I know she looks familiar, too. You don't recognize her from the news? She is the new sports reporter for Action 7 News—Cherise Long." I was uncomfortable with Toni's big sister pushiness and bragging. But the man's demeanor did change when she told him who I was. Immediately he went from being slightly defensive to asking me for my business card.

"Really. Oh, can I have your card? I would like to let more

people know about my organization, which I've been running for about a year."

A dark man came up. "Bruh, what's taking so long?"

"Man, this bartender. And I'm talking to these nice ladies about doing a story on the house." The man turned to us and spoke. Tim was handsome, but the guy he introduced us to was even better looking. He was muscular, and you could tell he was an athlete. His body was amazing and smile perfect. His jewelry was a little flashy.

After Tim got his drinks, he was back, talking more about his organization.

"I want to give back to the community that helped me. Brothers Helping Themselves—my organization—is everything. It's job training for ex-offenders, help preparing résumés. Eventually we want to include women, but right now, you know, we need to get corporate sponsors. DeCarious has a studio and employs some of the youth, and I've poured a lot of my own money into it. But I would like to get more sponsors and mentors on board. People always ask me if I'm scared of getting robbed. Hell no, I'm from Zone One, Bankhead. But it is hard trying to save the hood alone. Do you think you can do a story?"

"Yes, it sounds very doable and interesting. Yeah, let me talk with my boss and we will see what we can do."

Toni couldn't wait until we walked away before she was asking me, "Did you give the dark-skinned cute one your card, too?"

"Yes. Why?"

"Good, because he was looking at you."

"That's nice, but I don't date athletes. Especially now that I am covering sports."

"Does it say somewhere that you can't?"

"No, but hello—conflict of interest. You can't be objective if you are a part of the story."

"If you say so." Toni sighed.

We enjoyed the rest of the night bowling, laughing, and having a good time with Toni's boy toy, Lou. I didn't know how I felt about my sister being a baby cougar. I wanted her to just make up with Dave and live a happy life.

Chapter 13

Tanisha

I knocked on the door and heard my six-year-old daughter, Kierra, yelling, "Daddy, someone's at the door." I didn't know what kind of reaction I was going to receive from my daughter and my ex-husband. Were they going to be happy or mad? Cuss me or hug me? I just wanted the door to open so I could see my baby girl.

I could hear Tyrone's slippers approaching the door. I took a step back as the door opened. I was so scared. Tyrone opened the door and his mouth dropped before he could say anything. Kierra ran past him and screamed, "Mommy, oh my God, Mommy!" She jumped in my arms and hugged me. I hugged her back.

Tyrone stood still, his thick body frozen in place. His hair had more white in it and his middle was rounder. My ex-husband appeared as though he had aged several years.

Kierra was holding on to me, crying and saying, "Mommy, Mommy, Mommy, where were you? I missed you. Why did you leave me? I thought I wasn't going to see you again." I just held her and swayed her back and forth, while patting her back.

Tyrone finally snapped out of his daze. "What the hell happened, Tanisha? Where have you been for all this time?

What's going on?" he said, looking around to see if anyone was with me and attempting to separate me from Kierra.

She wouldn't budge. She continued holding on to me tightly, repeating, "Mommy, Mommy, I missed you."

I knew this wasn't a conversation we should be having outside. "Tyrone, let me in; I will explain it all," I said as I began crying. I didn't know what else to say. He hesitantly let me in. I followed him inside the house. Everything was still as I remembered.

Kierra was still wrapped around me. I held her close. I wanted to immediately explain myself, but I didn't want Kierra to hear. Tyrone just looked at me in disbelief, shaking his head. He sat across from me. I'm not sure if he wanted to lecture, hug, or hit me. Tears were forming in his eyes. I didn't know what to do or say. He just kept shaking his head. Tyrone looked at me as he picked up the phone and began dialing numbers. He said something fast and then hung up the telephone.

"Your children are on their way." Then, not able to hold it in anymore he repeated, "Tanisha, what the hell is going on? Where have you been?"

"I'm going to explain everything," I said as I patted Kierra's back; it was fifteen minutes later and she wouldn't let go. The excitement and me patting her back finally knocked Kierra out. Tyrone picked her up and took her upstairs.

He came back downstairs and yelled, "Tanisha, where the hell have you been?"

"Listen, Tyrone, I can explain everything. There is a lot I didn't tell you."

He got up and said, "Have you called Kevin yet?"

"Kevin?"

"Yeah, Kevin. Your son's father?"

"Okay, hold up. Let's not call Kevin yet."

"Why not? I'm sure he wants to know that you are here," he said as he dialed his phone.

"Hey, Kevin, this is Tyrone. Um, man, call me as soon as you get this message. It is an emergency." Momentarily I forgot the fact that I had been missing for a year. I just wanted to know how the hell Kevin and Tyrone knew about each other. I never talked about my ex-husband to Kevin and Tyrone didn't know Kevin existed.

Tyrone sat down and said, "I don't now what is going on with you. I just filed papers to declare you legally dead, and now you just come waltzing back in here. What the fuck, Tanisha? What the hell is going on?"

I stood up and said, "Tyrone, I killed a woman in the park last August. I was on my way home from the hospital visiting my baby, and this woman jumped in the car with me and she made me drive to the park. She had a gun and before she could kill me, the gun went off and I killed her. And I didn't want to go to jail, so I ran away."

"What woman?"

"I don't know. I think she was Kevin's ex-girlfriend."

"What, Tanisha? Kevin's ex-girlfriend is in jail."

"In jail?"

"Kevin's ex-girlfriend is in jail for shooting Kevin, and she was about to be charged with your disappearance. Your murder."

"My disappearance. Huh? She's alive?"

"Yeah, she is alive."

"I didn't kill her?"

"No, Tanisha. You thought you killed her?"

"Oh my God, she is alive. I didn't kill her." My body started getting warm. "I ran away because I thought I killed her. I thought I was wanted for murder. I'm not wanted for murder?" I asked, still confused.

"No, we thought she murdered you," Tyrone said. It took me several minutes to digest what he just said. He said that the girl in the park was shot, but she didn't die. If what he was saying was true, I ran away for nothing. I was on the run for nothing. Everything I had experienced was for nothing.

"Are you sure, Tyrone? I saw her die. She was bleeding and lifeless."

"She is not dead. Her name is Dionne Matthews and she is in jail." I was about to pass out. I couldn't understand. I thought she was dead. I took a seat. I heard Tyrone ask me if I was okay and to have a seat. I felt a little dizzy and then I heard the front door open; it was my nineteen-year-old daughter, Alexis. She stood at the front door and screamed and jumped up and down in one place, her hands covering her mouth as tears streamed from her eyes.

"Mom, you're alive? You're alive? You are here—what happened? Where were you?" Alexis said. I walked over to her and began hugging her. She hugged me. Then she separated from me. "Mom, you dyed your hair?" she said, touching my blond and brown short hair.

"Yeah."

"I like it," she said, giving me a slight smile. "Mom, what's going on? We have been worried sick. We thought you were dead."

I repeated the story again and then Tyrone's phone rang. He stood up and walked into the kitchen and said that Jamil was on his way.

In a few minutes Jamil ran through the door. He was looking at me like he had seen a ghost. He had facial hair and a more manly look to him. I stood up to embrace him. He stepped back and asked, "Mom, where have you been? I've been going crazy. I thought I lost you. I thought you were gone. Couldn't you have called? You couldn't pick up a phone in a year?" he sobbed. I pulled him into my chest and then began apologizing to him and trying to explain what happened.

For two hours I went back and forth with Alexis, Jamil, and Tyrone about my entire ordeal. For the most part they understood. They pulled up Internet articles for me to read off the computer. When I saw a newspaper article that showed the woman who tried to kill me, I began crying. I prayed for her every night. I prayed to God that she was protected and I didn't go to hell for ending her life. And there she was in the newspaper, being led in handcuffs, walking toward court. My family also showed me missing person articles about me. In one of the articles, there was a picture of a distraught Kevin alongside my picture. They said he had offered a reward for me, and took my disappearance really hard. I almost couldn't believe all of this was true. I had hurt so many people. My children, my ex-husband, my boyfriend. My life was upside down because I didn't think. Oh my God, I shouldn't have listened to Adrienne. I needed to rest—I felt my chest getting tight again. I really couldn't take anymore. I thought I was dreaming all of this and that I would wake up and realize that I was still in Detroit.

Tyrone wanted to call the police to let them know I was okay, but Alexis said we should probably call an attorney first and let him advise me. And she was right. I was so glad I didn't turn myself in downtown. Tyrone kept trying to get in touch with Kevin. I didn't know how to tell Tyrone I'd had enough for today. I couldn't deal with Kevin. I had so much regret. Seeing my children should have been the hardest. Facing my ex-husband was difficult enough. Now knowing I had run away in vain, I couldn't face Kevin and my baby boy. I didn't want to see him. I owed him so much, and I couldn't bear to look in his eyes.

Chapter 14

Adrienne

I got a call from Tanisha's daughter and I was scared to answer the telephone. I looked down at my cell phone nervously. I didn't know what kind of news she had, so I didn't answer. Hopefully, she would just leave a message saying what was going on. She didn't though. She just kept letting the phone ring over and over. I finally answered.

"What's wrong, Alexis?" I questioned.

"My mom is home."

"She is? Where was she? Is she okay?" I asked, trying to act surprised.

"Yeah, you should come over."

"Okay, I'm going to come over now," I said as I hurried and dressed myself and Asia.

I didn't know what to expect when I reached Tanisha's house. Should I cry and run up to her, or act calm? I didn't know what would be the right way to react to seeing a missing friend. But I did have a lot of real questions for her. What was she doing? How come she didn't call me so we could match up our stories? I had no idea what I should say or not say. Her ex-husband Tyrone answered the door. Tanisha was sitting on the sofa. She had cut her hair, and looked different.

She gave me a very slight grin. I sat next to her and said, "Hey, Tanisha."

"Hey," she said as I reached out to hug her, and I got this real cold look and feel from her. She kind of pulled back.

"Look at Kierra. She got big," I said as her little girl ran past me and got on her mother's lap.

"Yeah, she did."

"So what's up? How you feel?"

"Fine, I guess," she said, but her eyes revealed tiredness and worry. I asked her a few more questions and she gave me very short, one-word answers. I didn't understand why she was acting strange and had an attitude. I mean, I literally ran over there to make sure she was okay and to see if she needed anything. I asked her where she stayed, what she was doing, and she said she didn't want to talk about any of it. I asked her to go outside and talk with me several times. I guess when she was ready to talk to me she would. I didn't stay for too long.

When I called her later, her daughter said that Tanisha said she would call me back. I guess she forgot I was the one who kept her secret for this last year. All I made was a suggestion. I didn't force her to leave, so she shouldn't be mad at me.

I wasn't sure why Tanisha was being so distant, but her being home was one less thing for me to worry about. The other thing I just wasn't sure of was if it was possible to meet my next man in a club. I've only been off the scene like a year or two, but it just seems like this new batch of guys are just so disrespectful. This young guy I met texted me a picture of his dick and asked me what I could do with that. What the hell? I think I need a little older, settled-down type of man. Maybe a coach or agent or even a retired player. I need someone who is tired of running up in everything and can show a little respect. I don't know. I've been to a few parties and already I felt like I was seeing the same people. I really needed my ring finger to get rocked. But at this rate I don't know how. I was just happy today was my last day at work and then I had the next four days off. I didn't know how I was going to spend them yet. I didn't feel like hanging out. Angelique had left me a message about going to another party. I wasn't up for it. I think I just wanted to relax and take Asia somewhere.

On the way home to my mom's house, I saw DeCarious's number come up. I was about to not answer, but decided to pick up.

I answered and he asked, "Can you bring Asia down? I really miss her."

"If you buy us a ticket to Atlanta, I'll come."

"I'll buy your ticket. My parents want to see the baby. So can you do that for me, please?"

"I guess I can bring her down there."

"You going to order the tickets now?" he asked.

"Okay, we are going to come tomorrow. When I get home, I'm going to book my flight, but I need my money back as soon as I get down there."

"I got you. Thanks, Adrienne."

"Yeah, just have my money, DeCarious," I said as I ended the call.

As soon as I came home I searched for a flight. The only ticket that was available was $429.00 and that was for coach. To upgrade to first class was only $60.00 more. So I bought it. I didn't care; I didn't have to pay for it. Me and Asia are first class ladies anyway. I was going to pack our clothes later on after I got up. I needed a little getaway; maybe I'd let DeCarious babysit while I went out and had fun in the "A."

* * *

Our two-hour flight to Atlanta went fast. The plane ride didn't bother Asia—she slept the entire ride. Once I had my luggage, I called DeCarious to tell him I had arrived. But all this dumb-ass could say was that he forgot I was coming.

"What do you mean, you forgot, DeCarious? You the one who begged me to come down here yesterday."

"I know. Um, hold tight, my mama will come and get you," he said. Then he called me back and told me to catch a cab.

"A cab is going to be way too expensive. What are you, out of your mind, DeCarious? You better come and pick your daughter up now! You the one asked me to bring her. So you better come and get us!" I demanded.

"All right, calm down. I'll be there, but it's going to be a minute, though. I'm on the other side of the city."

DeCarious's minute was almost an hour, and then he had the nerve to pick me up with that flamethrower in the car, his cousin Rock. I hated Rock. He was the reason we weren't to-gether. Rock spoke to me and I rolled my eyes. I couldn't wait until Asia was old enough to travel on her own. Then I won't have to look at DeCarious or his cousin's face ever again.

DeCarious opened up the back door for me and I sat Asia down on the seat. As I was getting in the car, DeCarious's big-ass muscle-head self said, "Damn, Adrienne, you getting thick."

"Whatever, I'm not thick," I said as DeCarious got in the car.

"If you say so, but a gym visit might not hurt you." I could already tell what kind of weekend I was in for.

We pulled up to DeCarious's house in Alpharetta. It was a newly built mansion that sat at the end of a long cobblestone driveway. He had it built as soon as he was drafted. There were tall trees all around that divided his house from his neighbors farther down the road.

We walked inside where everything was bright and open. Miss Anne was sitting on the large black sectional watching the huge 55-inch television.

"Surprise, Mom!" DeCarious said. She jumped up when she saw us and came over and took Asia from me. Asia was still a little sleepy and wasn't that excited. Miss Anne smothered her with kisses and took her to go have a seat with her on the sofa.

"What are y'all doing here?" she exclaimed. "You know you can leave her—I'll tend to her."

"Yeah, Mama, I knew you and Daddy wanted to see the baby. So I got Adrienne to bring her down."

"Are you staying at a hotel, Adrienne?" Miss Anne asked.

"No, we are staying here until Monday."

"So you came all the way from Philadelphia to stay a couple of days."

"Yes."

"Oh, that's wonderful. I can spend some time with my grandbaby."

While his mama got comfortable with Asia I put my hand out to DeCarious for my money.

"How much did it cost, Adrienne?"

"Seven hundred."

"You're lying."

"No, I'm not; it was a last-minute flight," I lied. I needed the extra money and he wouldn't miss it.

"Okay, here," he said as he handed me seven crisp one-hundred-dollar bills. I thanked him and placed them in my bag.

Miss Anne kept Asia busy all weekend. She took her to the aquarium and to visit her friends and family all around town.

And I did absolutely nothing all weekend and it felt good just to sit back and do nothing. While I took long naps and chilled poolside, DeCarious was in and out. Him and Rock had a studio now at some house. I wasn't impressed; Rock had been trying to get him to invest his money in a studio for years. But what impressed me was DeCarious. There was something different about him. I couldn't explain it exactly. He just looked kind of handsome. He just had this new energy and glow about him. He was almost sexy to me, and I didn't even think I liked him. However, everything was very clear to me: I wanted a man who had money, a big house, a big car, good looks, treats me good. And I already had all of that in my baby's father. The only problem was, I didn't know how hard it would be to get DeCarious back.

But if I got him once, without even trying, I'm sure I could do it again. It had to be easier to get him to fall back in love with me than to start from ground zero with someone else. I didn't have months to build trust and fall in love and weed out other chicks. With DeCarious, I just had to work my way back into his life. And when I did, this time I was not going for just a baby. I wanted the full Monty. I wanted security for life, so I was going to need him to wife me. If I did, my daughter could have her father and I could have the good life.

First plan of action was to get this extra weight off. The next time he saw me, I was going to be thin. I was going on an extreme diet. Maybe I'd just drink lemon water and eat lettuce, combined with some kind of workout plan. I only had a few weeks before I saw DeCarious again, and this time the weight had to be off.

Chapter 15

Zakiya

Sometimes I still couldn't believe I was living in LA. I got up some mornings and was still amazed by how beautiful the sun and palm trees were. LA was the most beautiful place in the world, but it was also the ugliest. People here were so different than back home, especially the women. The women were so very materialistic and only cared about trying to stay skinny and look young. Most of them had everything and yet they still weren't happy. Out here if you didn't have money, then you basically were a nobody. That's all people talked about was money, money, money. If the conversation was not about money, it was about becoming an actress, model, or stuntman, or knowing someone who was one. But all in all, it was still a great place to live.

However, I couldn't live with my aunt Vicky and Jade forever. I'm getting a job and my own place. I went with Jade to her job and while she was at work I filled out applications all throughout the mall. Hopefully someone will hire me, because my aunt and cousin are some moody-ass people. I'm convinced that there is something wrong with all the women in my family. Like this morning, my aunt Vicky just got up and started yelling and carrying on about the neighbor's dog barking, and how she couldn't get any sleep. She went in

Jade's room and began fussing at her, telling her to clean up the damn house. Jade ignored her and told her to close her door. I think she was just upset about her boyfriend, Martin, not coming over like he said he was. And by the way, I think he is either married or has another woman, because he never spends the night and they don't really seem like a real couple. But whatever the case, I didn't want to ever give her a reason to fuss at me, so I just began cleaning when she left. I wanted to make sure the house was nice and clean when she came home. I did the dishes, washed and folded their clothes, vacuumed, and cooked dinner.

It took me a couple of weeks, but I got a job at a dress boutique in the mall. The store wasn't a really big store, but it was full to capacity with evening gowns, pants suits, hats, and purses. Everything was big, bold, and very tacky. The woman, Raquel, who owned the boutique was Portuguese and spoke broken English. Sometimes I would understand her; sometimes I would not. The only employees in the store were myself, Raquel, and another girl, Elena. She was a pretty Mexican-American girl with dark brown hair and light brown eyes. She was always nice and smiling at customers even when they were rude. Raquel mostly stayed behind the register and rang people up and supervised while Elena and I waited on and greeted the customers.

It was easy to sell to people who came in the store because they already had money. All you had to do was tell them how good something looked on them and they would buy it, even though everything in the store was overpriced by thousands of dollars. Most of our customers were retired or older housewives with fake boobs and a lot of bad plastic surgery, who had money for days.

Today Elena and I had to do markdowns in the store. Any item that wasn't sold after ninety days was reduced. I had to read the SKU number to her and she had to tell me how much to retag the dress for.

She looked at the list and said, "Those maroon sequin-and-feather dresses over there for two thousands dollars—they need to be marked down to fifteen hundred."

I laughed and said, "Oh, only fifteen hundred. Why do these people waste money on these ugly dresses? Do you know what I can buy with fifteen hundred dollars?"

"A lot. I say the same thing all the time. She is crazy for selling this ugly stuff."

"No, the people who buy this mess are crazy." I laughed.

"Where are you from with that accent?" Elena asked.

"Philly. Are you from here?"

"No, I'm from Texas."

"How long you been out here?"

"A year. I go to school and my brother works for the airlines. I live with him, his wife, and their four kids."

Because the buses didn't run fast or often, Elena gave me rides home after work and in exchange I would fill her tank up. Me and Elena became fast friends. She was silly like me and she showed me the city. She was a year older than me and she was down-to-earth. It was nice to have someone normal around. Jade wasn't anything but normal but was always too busy with her boyfriend to be bothered with little old me. I think she didn't like the way her mother kept saying, *Why can't you be more like Zakiya? Do you see how hard she works? Look how clean she keeps her room. She is filling out college applications, where are yours? She did more here in one month than you've done in a year.* Everything Aunt Vicky said was true, but I didn't have a choice. I knew I couldn't be all the way out here and fail.

Chapter 16

Cherise

The first few weeks of being a sports reporter weren't so bad. The e-mails and viewer feedback were mixed. I was forwarded some of the e-mails. Some of them were downright racist and others laughable. One man wrote he didn't want Kisha and her sistah-girl attitude covering his sports. Another asked for my phone number and asked if he could propose to me on air. One critiqued that what I wore each day in detail, saying my colors were off and I needed to enunciate more. But overall, Paul said I was doing well, but that I should be less pink on camera. He said for me to remember I was covering sports and not pageants. All I could do was my best, and that had got me this far.

I wanted to do the story on Tim Hughes, the football player I had met at TL Zone. I did a little research on him and he was a decent player, but off the field he was known for having a lot of issues. He'd been arrested three times for drunk driving in a six-month period two years ago. And a few months later he was charged with driving with a suspended license and received a firearms charge that he was later cleared of. In the past the interviews he did always made him look like a bad, ungrateful rich guy. So he stopped giving interviews altogether and just focused on his game. From what I read and could see he seemed like a good guy who was misunderstood. On his organization's Web site I read that he was paying for ten students to go to college and was employing a staff of five to run his various programs.

I was going to bring the story idea to Paul today. I tapped on his halfway-open door and asked if I could have a moment of his time.

He acknowledged me and said, "Come in, Cherise. Please have a seat and close the door." I closed the door. He had his legs on the desk, hands propped behind his head like he was stretched out on a recliner in his living room.

"Paul, do you know Tim Hughes of the Falcons?"

"Yeah, the asshole who stays in trouble but doesn't do interviews."

"Yeah, him. Well, he is trying to be more open now, and he has a real good organization that he wants to discuss. He wants to rebuild his relationship with the media."

"What kind of organization does he have?"

"It's called Brothers Helping Themselves. It's like a neighborhood resource center slash community center. He is doing job readiness training and he is even paying for ten students presently to attend college. He is just doing everything right now on his own dime, and wants to get donations and sponsors to help out with his organization."

"Really? Sounds interesting, the bad guy trying to do good. I like it, Cherise. I like it a lot," he said as he stood up and looked out the window.

"So, is it a go?"

"Yeah, just make sure it is an exclusive interview, though."

"Okay, I will."

I thanked Paul and walked out of his office. On my way out I saw Richard Hall. He winked at me. Great, let the rumors continue. I couldn't imagine what rumor Uncle Tom was going to come up with next.

Once I was back at my desk I called Tim and his publicist. We scheduled the interview. I was thrilled. It was my first exclusive and interview that I got on my own.

On the day of the interview, I was so excited to help out the organization and to do a news story with a sports twist. I met Tim and his friend DeCarious at the Brothers Helping Themselves house. Tim shared that all the young men who came to the program were at-risk youth between the ages of fourteen and twenty-three. He gave me a tour of the big building. There was a computer lab, full-size music studio, small boxing gym, basketball court, tennis court, and weight room. It was a nice place and a lot was going on.

After the tour, Gary went around to take extra shots. A few young men were working out in the weight room. I told them to act natural and do what they would be doing on a normal day.

When it was time to do the one-on-one interview, I could tell Tim was a little nervous. I told him to relax and just talk to me about the passion he has for seeing the young men succeed. And how he needed more mentors, donations, and what it would take for his organization to be a success.

In all I got a lot of good footage and the interview went very well. After we completed everything, they thanked me and I told them I would contact them once everything was ready and let them know when it would air. Tim thanked me as Gary packed all his cameras and lighting up.

The guy DeCarious came up to me. "Thank you for coming out."

"You're welcome."

"So where does your driver take you to next?" DeCarious asked.

"That's not my driver. He is a photographer, and I'm headed back to the station and then I'm done for the day."

"Oh, okay, I was wondering if maybe I can take you to lunch, maybe get a quick bite. I just wanted to thank you for doing the interview. It means a lot to Tim. He gets a bad rep from the media and this interview will show what kind of guy he really is."

"When?" I asked.

"How about now?"

"Now? Um, okay."

I agreed to meet DeCarious at a Cuban restaurant not far from my office. It wasn't very fancy, but it had a lot of ambience. It was family owned and the food was amazing.

"I just wanted to thank you again for the story and wanted to see if you needed any other information."

"So you asked me to lunch to thank me again?"

"Yeah, and to ask you, where is Mr. Long?"

I laughed. "There is not a Mr. Long."

"Why not?"

"I'm not sure."

"Okay, I'm going to leave that one alone. Do you have any children?"

"No, of course not. Without a Mr. Long that is not possible. How about you?"

"Yes, a daughter. She is a year and a half and lives in Philly with her mom."

"Baby mama drama?"

"No, not really. We got our kinks out of the way for the most part. I love my daughter."

"That was a very politically correct answer."

He laughed and then said, "But my family seems to think my daughter's mom got pregnant on purpose."

"Why? To keep you?"

"Yeah, and to get money from me for eighteen years. You know, gold-digger stuff. I don't know. I don't think so, but what you going to do? I'm going to take care of my daughter regardless. And like I said, we don't have any problems."

The waitress brought our food over. DeCarious had black bean soup, fried tamales, and rotisserie chicken. I just had a Cuban sandwich.

"So how do you like covering sports? There's not too many lady sports newscasters. You must be a really big sports fan."

"No, not really. I kind of just fell into the job. Eventually, I'm going back to news."

"Oh, did you always want to be on television?"

"Yeah, since I was kid."

"That's how I was with football. Me and my dad used to watch the game every Sunday."

"So how do you like Atlanta? Where are you originally from?"

"Charlotte. But I've lived in a few cities since college."

"Me too. I went to school in Florida and I played in Seattle when I first got drafted, then I just traded to the Falcons. Most people hate trades, but when I heard the Falcons were interested in me, I was happy. I couldn't wait to play for my home team."

We had a nice conversation and I agreed to have dinner with him later in the week. He seemed nice. He was only twenty-four, but he was very mature. I couldn't see anything serious happening, but he could be a friend.

Chapter 17

Tanisha

Ever since they informed me that I was not a killer, the scene at the park keeps replaying in my head. I've imagined that I was back in that moment and time, and I did the right thing. I helped the woman to safety and then I called the police and came home. I was ecstatic about not being a murderer. All of that burden of guilt had been lifted off of me—but I did shoot Dionne Matthews, and I could still be charged. With what, we weren't sure yet.

I wasted a year of my life. All of that hiding out and being on the run for nothing. All I had to do was stay, and everything would have been okay. I could have called the police and they would have handled everything. I really wish I could go back and do it all over again.

Kevin was still very distant, but he was being so helpful. I purposely had not spent one moment alone with him. I already knew the minute he had me all to himself he might go off on me, and he had every right to.

Tyrone and I met Kevin at his attorney's huge downtown office. The entire floor belonged to the law firm Saul, Hippell, and Ballard. The office was located in the Comcast Center on

17th and JFK. It was a stunning high-rise. There was a majestic, panoramic view of the entire city skyline.

We were greeted by a receptionist and led to a conference room. Two attorneys came in and introduced themselves and took a seat. One was young and favored the actor George Clooney, and the other was older and plump with glasses and gray hair. We all took a seat and the older attorney began speaking. His name was Mr. Ballard.

"Now, we are familiar with the case, Ms. Butler, but we need you to start from the beginning and tell us what happened." Once again I repeated what happened in detail. Both attorneys took notes and asked questions throughout my explanation.

"More than likely they are going to charge you with attempted murder."

"But she tried to kill me!" I screamed.

"Yes, we understand that, but you left the scene of a crime, and by leaving that automatically implies guilt."

"But I was protecting myself." I was so confused. I fell onto Tyrone's shoulder.

"We understand that, and we are going to assist you as much as we can, but we are going to need more information." I gathered my thoughts and they began asking me more questions.

"So you say the victim came to the hospital where you worked and then was writing you letters. Where are the letters?"

"I threw them in the trash."

"Why did you throw them in the trash?"

"I don't know. At the time I thought they were groupie letters."

"The letters said they were going to kill you and Kevin, and you dismissed them as groupie letters. Is that correct?" he said as he jotted a note on his yellow notepad.

"Yes," I said, nodding. "I just thought it was a groupie."

"So let's talk about the part when you got to the park and she attacked you."

"She pulled out a gun and told me she was going to kill me."

"She specifically said 'I'm going to kill you'?"

"Not exactly. She said 'You're not going to make it' or something, or I wasn't going to live, something along those lines," I said as my eyes began tearing up. Tyrone handed me a napkin and I wiped away my tears.

"So you scuffled for the gun, a shot goes off, you think you killed her, and leave town?"

"I told myself no one would believe me."

"How did you get to the station?"

"I caught the trolley after I left my car over at my girl-friend's." I lied because I didn't want to get Adrienne in-volved in this. I continued to tell him how I spent the last year in Detroit and why I decided to come back. Tyrone just kept his face down as he listened to the hard details about what I had to endure.

The George Clooney look-alike and the older attorney said they would take the case, but it was going to be very ex-pensive.

"How expensive?"

"Just to start, you are looking at eighty thousand."

"Just to represent me on something I'm not really guilty of?"

"Yes."

I told Kevin about the money I had saved. Tyrone said he would take out a second mortgage on the house and Kevin said he would put up the rest.

Mr. Ballard explained what was going to happen next. I was going to go to the police and surrender and they would process me. I would be arraigned and formally charged and bail would be set, then from there we would go to trial. He also said there may be media attention, because of the coverage the shooting received before. Plus, I was the mother of Kevin's child and his former girlfriend.

Two days later when I turned myself in at the Central Division of the Philadelphia Police Department, there were swarms of reporters waiting. As soon as we got out of the car, the bright camera lights started flicking and flashing. Kevin, Mr. Ballard, and Tyrone pushed me past the media frenzy. I heard different voices shouting out, "Why did you run?" "Where were you?" "Why did you come back now?"

Once inside the building, I felt tears begin to roll down my face. I hugged Tyrone and said good-bye to Kevin. I walked toward the officer, turned around, and they placed handcuffs on my wrists and walked me through an open door into the jail.

I was processed. First I was fingerprinted, then I had to have my mug shot taken. I had to look directly into the camera and then turn to the side. It was so humiliating. Mr. Ballard said the entire process should not take more than twenty-four to forty-eight hours for my arraignment and bail hearing. It was my first hour, and already I was ready to go home. They took me to my cell. It held a small, moss green metal bed and a toilet. It smelled, and I noticed I would be sharing my cell with a big giant water bug.

I was only in the cell for a few minutes and already it felt like an eternity. I stood up and walked around and then tried to look down the hall. I knew I had to get all of this over with in order to move on, but already I wasn't sure if I had made the right decision.

Another half hour went by and they brought in a woman with a short haircut like a man.

She said, "What's up?" I gave her a faint *Hey* back.

"I'm Keisha," she said, trying to shake my hand.

"Tanisha."

"So what are you in here for?" she asked.

"Um, a gun charge and shooting."

"Yo, for real. You don't look like you have gunplay. I'm in here for busting a bottle upside a stupid bitch's head. Stupid bitch works for me and came short with my money," she laughed.

"Oh, so you are like a madam?"

"No, a pimp. They have women pimps. I have better hoes than most men. Someone is always hating. Like whoever called the cops. But they ain't got nothing on me. They couldn't find her or the bottle I hit her with, but still booked me."

Keisha wasn't really that gangsta. After an hour or so she started telling me about how her mother left her and her father—and her father's mother—beat her, so she left home at thirteen. She shared a lot, so I opened up about what happened to me. She told me I had nothing to worry about and that it was self-defense and I would get off. She was real knowledgeable. I told her I already had an attorney, but she still wanted to recommend hers—an attorney named Stephanie Westcoat.

"If I put you down with this bitch, she is going to get you off. She is a bad bitch. You feel me? I mean, you could have had the gun right there, fingerprints on the gun, eyewitnesses see you pull the trigger, and she can still get you off. You should call her." I took her information as if I would call. I continued to make small talk with her. She looked very scary, but after getting to know her I could tell she was just a product of her environment.

I lost track of time. I knew every time I fell asleep, I was startled awake and felt like I was going to fall. I would look down at my watch, thinking I had been sleeping forever, and had only been sleeping for forty-five minutes. Keisha was on the floor, back against the wall, sleeping soundly like she was home. I told her I saw a few roaches down there. She said it didn't bother her and the only time she got good rest was when she was in jail.

Roughly two day later, Keisha, me, and everyone else who was waiting to be arraigned were led into the courtroom. I saw Kevin and Tyrone. They both looked very concerned. Just seeing the judge I got a little nervous. Keisha turned into a gangsta boo when we got in the courtroom. Her attitude changed. Her case was the first to be heard. I was waiting to see her high-profile attorney, but she was not there. The only person there to represent her was a public defender.

Her charges were read by the court. "Keisha Hardison is being charged with aggravated assault and possession of an instrument of crime."

"Your Honor, she has several priors. And she is a danger to society. She has two pending cases for aggravated assault. She should not be released on bail, Your Honor," the district attorney said. Her public defender didn't object, and she didn't get bail. I looked over to her to see if she was upset. She just stood up straight and gave the courtroom a mean poker face. Then the next three ladies after her were denied bail. There was a real chance that I was going to be stuck in jail.

The DA began to read off all my charges. "Tanisha Butler is being charged with attempted murder, aggravated assault, simple assault, unlawful possession of a firearm, and leaving the scene of a crime." He read off so many charges, like I was a really bad, horrible criminal.

"We are asking for bail, Your Honor," Mr. Ballard said.

The district attorney interrupted and said, "We request that bail be denied because the defendant is a flight risk, Your Honor."

"My client is not a flight risk. She willingly turned herself in."

"I will grant bail. Bail is set at two hundred thousand dollars."

As we were led out of the courtroom I began to tear up. I knew no one had two hundred thousand dollars readily available and I was going to be stuck in jail.

"What are you crying for? At least you made bail," Keisha said.

"Who has two hundred thousand?"

"You only have to come up with ten percent of that. That's only twenty thousand. Just make sure that your people get down here before five, or you are going to have to spend the night in the county jail. And you are a nice person. I wouldn't want to see you up there. Not even for one night. You know I gotcha—wouldn't let anyone fuck with you."

Keisha was scaring me, telling me how bad the jails were. I didn't want to go there at all. Luckily, I didn't have to. Kevin paid my bail in full and I was released.

It will be a month to wait before we go to preliminary trial to see if this case will stick. In the meantime I had to just sit and pray and hope that everything would work itself out. There was so much I wanted to do and start. Everyone was getting used to having me around again. I've been making dinner and spending time catching up with my children. The other day when Kierra came home from school and I wasn't there, she went screaming and hollering around the house. Tyrone didn't know what was wrong until I came through the door and she said, "I thought you left again. Mommy, please don't ever leave me again." It was going to be hard to get everyone to forget that I was gone for a year.

Chapter 18

Adrienne

I was tired as hell. I had just worked a double and I just wanted to get in the shower and go to sleep. I didn't feel like working out at 12 a.m., but I had to get my one hour in. Losing weight is an essential part of my plan to get De-Carious back.

Dina told me about these Chinese diet pills that her sister-in-law took to lose sixty-three pounds. She brought them into work, and I looked at the bottle and couldn't understand anything that was written on it. All of the writing was in gold Chinese letters.

"I am not taking pills when I don't even know what the bottle says," I said.

"I'm telling you, she took them and she is so skinny now— and she was really fat. All you're trying to lose is a few pounds. They work and they are safe. She got them right from Chinatown," Dina said, then she pulled up her sister-in-law's before-and-after pictures on her Facebook page. It was a big improvement, but I wasn't taking them.

Another week went by and I only lost two pounds. That was good normal weight loss, but I needed fast results. I needed to lose like eight pounds a week. I thought about the

Chinese diet pills, but I didn't want to ask Dina to bring them to work again. So I drove to Chinatown in search of the magic pills. There was a big red, gold, green awning with yellow dragon heads, I parked and then I stopped at what looked to be an herbal store. I went in and asked for diet pills. The woman shook her head and spoke in her language, and a young Chinese girl came out and said, "Hi, may I help you?"

"I'm looking for diet pills."

"What kind of diet pills?" she asked.

"I'm not sure. I just know they are in a white bottle with gold writing."

She walked over a few aisles and said, "Are you talking about these?"

"Yes, that's them," I said as I studied the bottle. "Do you know if they work? And what does it say on the bottle?"

"They're just diet pills and they work. I haven't taken it, but I heard about girls who have. You need this tea also. You take the tea right after you eat dinner. You only need the tea once a week." We walked up front, she talked to the other woman in Chinese, and then the lady rang me up.

I was so excited. If that big fat lady lost all that weight, I was sure to get skinny fast. I needed to be Mrs. Simmons, so I had to get this excess fat off my ass before my next trip to Atlanta. Therefore I was going to do anything and everything, including taking pills that I couldn't read the ingredients of. They couldn't sell me anything that would kill me.

I went home and made some of the tea so I could get ahead of the game. I was going to start the pills tomorrow.

Taking the tea was not a good decision. The tea did something crazy to my insides. My mouth was watering and I was weak. It felt like a little man was inside my stomach bouncing around. Let's just say I had to make half a dozen trips to the bathroom. The next day I had to call out of work and call my mom to come and get Asia to take her to school.

However, later that evening I felt much lighter. I felt like I lost twenty pounds in one day. I didn't lose twenty pounds, but I was down five pounds already. I felt energized and was going to head for the gym.

Chapter 19

Adrienne

In two weeks my clothes were falling off. Everyone at work had noticed the thirteen pounds I had already lost. It wasn't time to buy a new wardrobe just yet, but I did look nice. The Chinese pills jump-started everything, but they made me jittery, so I stopped taking them. However, now I was a regular on the elliptical and treadmill at the gym. I'm just a few pounds away from my slim-fitting size sixes. I just hope DeCarious takes notice. I was going to do everything in my power to show him I was the woman for him.

I had DeCarious before and I can get him again with careful planning, hard work, and dedication. All I have to do is be extra nice to him, kill him with kindness, and let him believe I've changed.

I flew into Hartsfield and picked up my rental car. I didn't want to rely on DeCarious and I didn't want to be stuck in the house again.

"Hi, Miss Anne," I said as I came in the house with Malaysia in one arm and my suitcase in the other. She took Asia and said, "Oh, look at my precious baby. You down here to visit Ma-Ma again." Asia smiled back at her as she took off her jacket and said, "How you doing, Adrienne? DeCarious, I guess he will be back. He went out a few hours ago."

"Okay," I said.

After I settled in I sat at the kitchen island and watched as she prepared dinner and played with Asia. We didn't really talk that much during that last visit. I was going to make it my business this time to get her to like and understand me. "You need any help, Miss Anne?"

"No."

"What are you cooking?"

"Macaroni and cheese and a roast."

"That's Asia's favorite food."

"She looks like her daddy. That's for sure," Miss Anne said, smiling.

"I think she acts like DeCarious sometimes. Nice, but sometimes she is stubborn."

"Yes, she does get that from her daddy. He can be mean and stubborn if he wants to be," she said.

"And that's all Asia is saying right now too—Da-Da. All day long."

"Oh, wait till DeCarious hears her say Da-Da. He is going to be so happy."

"Oh, let me show you the pictures, Miss Anne, that were taken at her day care."

She wiped her hands on her apron and then put her reading glasses on. "Oh, she looks so pretty. You are definitely a Simmons baby," she said, tickling Asia. "Which one can I have?"

"All of them. Oh, and I brought something for me and Asia to wear to church with you on Sunday."

"Oh, you did. You're really going to come out?" She got so excited and her demeanor changed drastically. "You will enjoy it. My pastor is a young, dynamic pastor. He knows the Word, but he brings new life to it for the younger generation.

You are really going to like it." *I don't really care about her pastor,* I thought. I just was trying to win points with her, by any means. Her being one of my supporters was essential to getting DeCarious back.

I heard DeCarious come in the house accompanied by Rock. Malaysia saw her daddy and became excited, extending her arms to go to her father and trying to run to the door. He came in and picked Malaysia up, gave his mother a kiss on the cheek, but barely spoke to me, even though I was dressed and looked beautiful.

"Where are you coming from?" Miss Anne said.

"The studio, Aunt Anne," Rock said.

"You staying for dinner, Rock?"

"No, I have to go back to the studio and make sure everything gets handled." *Thank God, good-bye,* I thought as Rock headed for the door. Now that Rock was gone DeCarious could pay attention to me. I hoped he noticed my new shape. I sashayed over to him.

"DeCarious, I got Asia's pictures taken," I said as I reached over his shoulder, letting my breast come in contact with his forearm, and handed the pictures to him.

He glanced at them and said, "These are nice. Why didn't you call me when you got to the airport?"

"I figured you might be busy, so I rented a car—and I can go out if y'all go anywhere this weekend."

"Makes sense," he said, not looking up at me and still giving Asia all his attention. So I walked back past DeCarious again and over to the sink.

"Girl, what are you doing? Why are you so skinny again?" Miss Anne said.

"I'm not so skinny." DeCarious looked over at me. He still didn't say anything, but I could tell he noticed, too.

"You are skinny—you better get some food."

"I do eat."

"Well, not enough. I don't like skinny. It makes you look like you're sick. Like you got problems."

"No, I don't."

Over dinner I smiled and was attentive to DeCarious and Asia. If he needed more juice I got up and got it. I laughed at all his jokes and smiled at him. I was very complimentary. When he walked past me in the kitchen to put his plate in the sink, I poked out my butt slightly, just so, so he could get a little feel of what he was missing. I thought I got a rise out of him. I'm also certain I did. He wants me, he just doesn't know it yet.

As promised, I went to Sunday service with Miss Anne. She was dressed in her big, black-and-white polka-dot hat and this black pleated dress. Her church was a mega church. We had to catch a bus from the parking lot just to get to the front door. Once we entered, I saw rows and rows of stadium-like seating. There was even a balcony. I felt like I was going to see a concert or something. Miss Anne must be important at the church, because the usher sat us in the third row.

The preacher was young and dressed in a burgundy suit. He stood behind the pulpit hyper and screaming. I had no idea what he was saying, but the crowd was excited. My mom was Catholic and the few times she took me to church, they didn't do all this. His preaching was electrifying. I felt like he was talking to me and he made me feel like I could do anything. He talked about how I was born with a purpose and I had roadblocks and things that needed to be lifted, and in order to get it done, I had to let God in and believe in Him to see change. After the preacher finished speaking, the large choir took over and began singing a bunch of songs. It was very interesting.

After service everyone walked up to Pastor Sneed like he was a rock star. Everyone was vying for his attention and wanted to be able to say just one word to him. As members of the congregation walked out, they patted him and said *Great service.* I was ready to go, but Miss Anne had to be one of the hangers-on. We had to wait damn near fifteen minutes so she could speak with him.

"Sister Anne, how are you doing today?" he said with a gigantic smile.

"I'm great, Pastor Sneed. I want you to meet my granddaughter and her mother, and say that service today was awesome, praise God." He thanked her, and I was mad because she waited all that time just to tell him that.

When we came in from church, I changed my clothes and helped her clean the greens, chop the cheese for her macaroni and cheese, and season her baked chicken and put it in the oven. She would have to cook and clean the ham hocks and pigs' feet on her own. I was not touching it.

After several hours of preparation there was a nice Thanksgiving type spread on the table. All Miss Anne seemed to do was cook, eat, and sleep, and then get up and start cooking again. And she got a little bit of church in between.

DeCarious walked in with the same clothes on from the night before. He picked some of the chicken off the bone and said, "Where ya'll go today?"

"They went to church with me."

"Church?"

"Yes, church. And stop touching my food when you haven't washed your hands," she said as she slapped his hand.

After dinner, I left Asia downstairs and went upstairs. I closed the door to my room and turned on the television. I was bored and tired of playing with Miss Anne. I called Angelique and caught up with her. She said that she dropped Nytika from the inner circle 'cause she was making her look bad. I laughed at her usual animated convo. I then called my mom and took a nap.

I was awakened by DeCarious knocking at the door. He came in and said, "What's up with all this church stuff?"

"What do you mean?"

"Come on, Adrienne. If you don't want to go to church with my mom, all you have to do is say no. Don't go with her just to be nice."

"I wouldn't do that. I wanted to go. Your mom gave me this Bible and everything. She is teaching me some things I didn't know," I said, grabbing the Bible off of the nightstand.

"Wow, and you're reading it." He chuckled.

"Yeah, like why are you laughing? I'm really trying to make changes in my life. I'm down here, right? I'm learning a lot. My mom never took me to church like that. And I've never been to a Baptist church, so it's good. And I want Malaysia to know about religion and stuff." I was saying anything and everything that sounded good and DeCarious was falling for it.

"Yeah, that's true. That's nice. That's real nice. I like that, Adrienne. Well, I'm outta here. I'll be back before you leave to go home."

"All right."

"Oh, if y'all going to be coming down on a regular basis, what I'll do is fix this room up for y'all."

"Yeah, that will be cool."

Tuesday morning DeCarious dropped us off at the airport. He gave Asia a kiss and then just said good-bye to me. It wasn't a bad visit, but the next visits had to be better. It seemed like it was taking him forever to warm up to me. This was going to be so much harder then I expected.

Chapter 20

Cherise

DeCarious has called and texted me a lot and we went on two dates. Right now I was just taking it slow. I liked him, but I didn't want our relationship to interfere with my job. There wasn't anywhere written that I couldn't date De-Carious, but it was a conflict of interest. As a reporter I was supposed to be objective, and that's hard if the person you're covering is your boyfriend. I wasn't sure how this would work out yet. Then there was the athlete factor that worried me. Even Toni said he probably had a lot of women, because of what he does. She told me to have fun with him, but not to take an athlete seriously. But it didn't seem that way. He came off as a genuine good guy. DeCarious was always helping out his parents or he was at the studio helping out.

Toni and I were about to go to Charlotte to visit our granddaddy. He was sick and Auntie Rose said the doctors said he could go either way. So we had to go and check on him.

"Toni, be ready. I will be at your house in the next half hour."

"I can't go," she said.

"What? You are the one who convinced me to go. So now

I have to go all the way Charlotte by myself? Auntie Rose is cooking a big dinner because she thinks we are coming."

"I know, but I can't go."

"If something happens to Granddaddy, you are going to be so upset with yourself."

"He'll be all right, until next time. Give him a kiss and tell him I love him. Dave wants to have a talk with me. It is real important. He is trying to save our marriage."

"Okay, whatever." I sighed.

"So are you still going to go?"

"I really don't have a choice, Toni." I hung up on my sister. Sometimes she made me so angry. I hated going home to visit or deal with my family. For the most part, I didn't deal with our family because of our cousin Patrick. Patrick was right between Toni and me. We all were close because our parents were always on the road, and his mom was on drugs.

My grandfather and grandmother took care of us all. Uncle Duke was my father's youngest brother. And when I was about nine and Patrick was eleven and Toni was fourteen, Patrick confided in us that Uncle Duke was molesting him. We convinced him to tell on Uncle Duke. He did, and we all swore that Duke was going to go to jail and they would kick him out of the house. But when he told, no one believed him and they said Patrick was crazy.

All the adults in the family said Uncle Duke would never do anything like that because he had so many women. But I knew what Patrick was saying was the truth because he repeated the same story over and over to us. And every time he would see Uncle Duke he would tremble and get scared. But every time he said that Duke touched him, my granddaddy beat him until he stopped saying it. Like it wasn't true. Right then and there is when I lost respect for all the adults in my family, and we all plotted to get out of Charlotte and never return. Toni and I did it, but Patrick is still there, and he was the one who needed to leave most.

By the time we were teenagers, Patrick was on drugs, a runaway, and a male prostitute. And then our family shunned him altogether. But Uncle Duke was still allowed to come around and no one ever said anything.

I tried to keep in contact with Patrick, but he was always moving around and changing cell phone numbers. I even tried to get him to move to Atlanta with me. Once I got to Charlotte I was going to see if I could get in touch with him.

I was mad that I had to drive to Charlotte on my own. I turned the radio on to V103. This was a time I wished I had invested in satellite radio. I hated when the stations changed. I heard the phone ring and I turned down the radio. I thought it was Toni calling back.

"How you doing, Ms. Long?" I recognized DeCarious's voice.

"I'm fine, Mr. Simmons. How are you?" I giggled.

"I'm fine. What's up with you?"

"Right now I'm starting my long journey up I-85 to Charlotte."

"By yourself?"

"Yes, unfortunately."

"You should have told me. I would have rode with you."

"That would have been nice."

"I still can go. How far did you get?"

"I actually just got on the road. My sister was going to drive with me, but her and her husband have to take care of something."

"Do you want me to ride with you? I'll drive and that will give us a chance to talk some more."

"You'll drive up there with me?" I really didn't want to drive four hours by myself.

"Yeah."

"Okay, I can meet you off the highway at the Exxon."

We met at a gas station. I parked in a supermarket parking lot and turned the alarm on and jumped into his big truck. I would normally not take anyone home to Charlotte, but it was only my aunt and sick grandfather.

My auntie Rose was sitting on the porch in her big blue-flowered dress when we pulled up in front of my grand-daddy's house. My auntie Rose was my father's older sister. She never moved out or married, she just took care of my grandfather and the house. She stared at the truck, trying to see who was in it.

She stood up and said, "Cherise, I'm glad you made it." She gave me a great big hug and then turned to DeCarious and said, "How you doing, young man? What's your name?"

"DeCarious."

"Nice to meet you, DeCarious. Come on in and have a seat."

Granddaddy was in a hospital bed, by the steps. I walked over to his bed and said, "Hey, Granddaddy."

He looked up, saw me, and called me by my nickname. "Ju Ju Bean."

"Granddaddy, it's me, Ju Ju Bean. You okay?" I asked him. He didn't have enough energy to sit up so I leaned over and hugged him. I always had mixed feelings about my grandfather. He treated us good, but allowed everyone to treat Patrick like he wasn't his grandson.

"Yeah, doin' as best I can." He coughed and paused and then said, "Where Sweet Pea?"

"She couldn't make it, Granddaddy, but she told me to give you a kiss and tell you that she loves you." I sat next to the bed and talked to him for a while and then went back to the sofa where Auntie Rose was talking DeCarious's ears off.

"Why Toni ain't come? What, she too good?" she asked.

"No, Auntie, she had a meeting she had to go to."

"Oh, 'cause I know how y'all spoiled girls be thinking about us and coming home," she said as she went into the kitchen and came back with a few glasses and a pitcher of lemonade. She poured us both a glass and then asked, "You talk to your parents?"

"No, I hear from them twice a year. They send me a big gift on my birthday and Christmas. You know."

"Yeah, your father does the same thing to me."

I looked over at DeCarious. He was being friendly, but he looked bored and so was I. I felt like I did—what was I supposed to do? I checked on my Granddaddy and chatted a little with Auntie Rose and now I could leave.

"Well, Auntie Rose, I think we'll be getting back on the road soon. I have to be to work early."

"Ya'll not staying for dinner?" she asked, disappointed.

"No, we can't. I have to get back and so does he."

"But I made all this food y'all better eat up. Toni was supposed to come. So was Duke, Duke's girlfriend, my friend Josie, and her husband. You know Duke is ill, too! Got cancer."

"I didn't know that."

"He got some other things going on with him, too. Good thing he has a good girlfriend now. She takes good care of him."

"Auntie Rose, I would love to, but we have to get back on the road." Just as I said that as I was leaving, there was a knock on the door. It was Patrick. I walked out and saw this skinny frame—he looked like a fraction of my cousin. I screamed as I gave him a hug. "I didn't expect you to get my message and just come."

"Yeah, as soon as I heard my favorite little cousin was in town, I got a ride over here. Look at you looking all pretty," he said. I couldn't say the same for him. He always stayed on top of his wardrobe and looks. But everything on him looked raggedy. His tan shirt had a few grease spots and his jeans were loose, like he wore them too many times in a row. His appearance made me a little concerned.

"I was just about to have dinner. Why don't you stay for a little bit? Come in and get yourself something to eat?" I said as I changed my mind about having dinner. Patrick looked like he needed a meal and someone to talk to.

"No, my ride is waiting. Plus you know I don't mess with them," he said, looking over at the running pearl-colored Cadillac and the older man driver.

"I'm here. I'll take you home. Auntie Rose is cooking dinner and Granddaddy is not doing so good."

"Then I'll stay." He went and told his ride he was staying.

Patrick came in and sat with our grandfather as Auntie Rose began making our plates in the dining room. Auntie Rose was never a good cook, but the ham, mashed potatoes, string beans, and biscuits and gravy looked edible. I introduced Patrick to DeCarious and he gave me a thumbs-up sign when DeCarious wasn't looking. We all talked a little and went to sit at the dining room table to eat. I picked at my food and so did DeCarious. However, Patrick was eating the bland food like he hadn't had a hot meal in months. Auntie Rose didn't mind—she was happy to take his plate and serve him seconds. Just as Auntie Rose placed Patrick's plate in front of him again, Uncle Duke came walking through the door. Auntie Rose gave him a big king's welcome. Damn. I saw Patrick's eyes go down and his whole attitude changed once Duke entered the room. Duke was in his late forties, tall, dark brown, with a thin mustache. He always dressed like he was on his way to church somewhere, even when he was just going to the corner store. His girlfriend looked like she was in her late twenties and her son looked to be about ten. I couldn't wait to hurry up and eat my food and go. I knew something was going to happen, I just didn't know what. I should have left when I had the chance.

Uncle Duke's girlfriend, Francine, sat next to me and Duke had the audacity to sit directly across from Patrick. I could feel the tension building. So to break up the uneasiness in the room I made small talk with Patrick. Then in the middle of the conversation Duke asked Patrick to pass the gravy to him. Why would he do that? I saw how Patrick looked at him, but I was surprised that he just passed it across the table.

He finished answering my question and then out of nowhere Patrick said, "I know you're not going to sit across the table from me like nothing happened, like you didn't used to come in my room and touch me."

"When are you going to stop telling lies?" Uncle Duke said.

"You mind your manners, boy," Auntie Rose said.

"I don't have to mind shit. I'm grown now. I told y'all that motherfucker touched and raped me and y'all ain't do shit about it. Y'all always taking up for him and he is the motherfucking devil." He turned to my uncle's new girlfriend. "If you know him like I know him, you better watch your son."

"You going to keep on lying. Why are you trying to talk that crazy shit?" Duke asked.

"I ain't lying shit. You know it's true. When you look in the mirror you should see Satan because you the fuck are him."

"You little faggot, you better be quiet."

"I'm a faggot? How did I get this way, you fucking asshole?" Patrick said as he lunged across the table and punched Uncle Duke in the jaw. Once they got in contact with one another no one could break the fight up. It was total chaos and happening so quickly. They knocked all the food off the table, and the fight was going all around the house, from the dining room table to the living room, where my grandfather was sleeping comfortably. It was just a mess. The best thing for everyone was to just move out of the way. DeCarious attempted several times to break it up, but Patrick was just throwing wild, fast punches. My aunt was crying and rocking back and forth. She kept saying she couldn't believe he would keep telling a lie for all these years. I couldn't believe that she still didn't get that her brother was a child molester. Uncle Duke was trying to stop fighting, but Patrick wouldn't let him. He didn't have enough energy to punch him anymore, so he began kicking him, screaming, "That's why you got cancer in your ass and you going to get AIDS in your dick, bitch. 'Cause of what the fuck you did to me." Patrick finally stopped hitting and went back to the table and began trying to salvage what was left of the food to make another plate. Uncle Duke's girlfriend picked him up off the floor. He stood up and wiped down his clothing and left out the door.

Moments later, the cops arrived. One of the neighbors must have heard the commotion and called. The police came in the house and saw the damage. They questioned Patrick and then put him in handcuffs and interviewed everyone else. They were going to let Patrick go, but he kept talking trash.

"Patrick, just shut up. They are going to let you go," I said as I walked over to the police car.

"Man, fuck that damn cop."

"Don't say that. If you get locked up right now, Duke wins. Don't let him have that kind of power over you." I walked over to the police officer and tried to reason with him. He said since Uncle Duke had left, he would let Patrick go if he was quiet. I finally was able to get him to be quiet and the police let him go.

We calmed my aunt down and then began trying to

straighten the house up. Everything was everywhere. I looked over at DeCarious, sweeping up pieces of glass, and thought, *What a great third date.* I was so embarrassed. I couldn't even imagine what he was thinking about. All I kept telling myself was, this is why I never go home.

I didn't have much to say on most of the ride home and I think DeCarious understood. We dropped Patrick off and I closed my eyes and tried to forget what just happened.

DeCarious woke me when we were at my car. I couldn't believe I slept the entire ride. He got out of the car, opened my door, and helped me out of the car.

"Don't worry, because everyone's family has drama a couple of times."

"Please, I know every family has drama. But not like mine."

"You know what, you might be right," he said as he attempted to hold back a laugh. I started laughing, too. "Cherise, it is not funny, but when your cousin started cussing your uncle out, I said to myself, it is about to go down."

"I knew it was, too, but I didn't think Patrick was going to hit him." I was happy he could make a joke out of the situation.

"Yeah, he fights like a man. He got him good, and it seems like it was overdue."

"It was, but I'm still sorry you had to see that, and thanks for helping to clean up."

"I told you it was not a problem. You going to be okay?"

"Yeah," I said as he walked me toward my car. He leaned me up against my car and began passionately kissing me and wrapping his warm arms around my core, which gave me the biggest rush. I had to push him away from me. He stopped momentarily, but then he moved in again, holding me even tighter. I had to stop, because right now the way I felt I would take him home and let him have his way with me and it was too soon for that.

"You sure you're okay? Do you need me to follow you home? I can sleep on the sofa," DeCarious asked.

"No, I think you might try to come in my bed."

"I promise I will stay in the living room."

"No, good night, DeCarious. I'll call you."

"Make sure you do," he said. Even if he could control himself I wasn't sure if I could. I wanted DeCarious to spend the night with me and reopen every space that hadn't been touched in two years.

Chapter 21

Zakiya

I came home from work tired as hell. Working a lot of hours is hell, but it was the only way I would have enough money to buy a car and save for an apartment. I was going to start school with Elena at LACC, LA Community College, by December and we were going to try to get a two-bedroom apartment. Her brother's wife and kids drove her crazy, plus I just didn't want to overstay my welcome at my aunt's house.

As I came in from work, I saw Aunt Vicky in the middle of the living room filling boxes. I said hello to her and walked straight back to my room and noticed Jade packing, too.

"Why are y'all packing?" I asked.

"We are moving to San Diego."

"You are?" I asked.

"Yeah, Martin just bought some property down there and he wants to be able to watch it better. My mom said she doesn't want to leave him down there by himself. So she is going with him. And I'm going with her because I'm not trying to be in LA by myself. So what you going to do?" The way she said, *So what you going to do,* was like, *You can't come with us.*

I wasn't sure if I was reading her wrong, but Aunt Vicky confirmed that I was not invited. She came in the room and said, "So Jade told you we are moving. So I'm thinking you can probably find your own place, right?"

"I guess," I said, surprised.

"Okay, good. We're moving tomorrow. You can stay here until the end of the week."

"This week?" I said as I began to become alarmed.

"Yeah, you should be able to figure something out," she said like she was just saying we were out of milk.

I was so confused. This was so crazy. As soon as everything was getting good, here was another damn problem. I only had a few days to figure out what my next move was. I called Elena and she sounded her usual happy self.

"Hey, chica, why you up so early?" At first I couldn't answer her because I was still trying to understand why this lady would let me move three thousand miles only to tell me two months later I have to move out.

"You there, Zakiya?" Elena asked.

I whispered, "My crazy aunt is kicking me out."

"What happened?"

"They are moving to San Diego. They basically looked at me like, *What you going to do? You have until the end of week.*"

"Oh my God, so where are you going to live?"

"I don't know. Do you know anywhere with any cheap apartments that I can afford? I wish we could get our own place now."

"I know, but I won't be ready to move for a few months. I'm going to ask around."

"All right, do that and then call me back."

Chapter 22

Cherise

I wasn't comfortable with anyone knowing about my relationship with DeCarious yet. I wanted to be cautious and plus right now it was hard to define anyway. We weren't exactly boyfriend and girlfriend, but we spent a lot of time together. We were taking things slow, but I really enjoyed his company and the way he made me feel. I felt like I had to talk to him a few times a day, and if I didn't I would miss him. I was in the middle of trying to figure out what I was going to wear to Tim's house. DeCarious and I were going there to watch the segment I did on Brothers Helping Themselves.

I was so disappointed when I looked in my closet. I really needed to go shopping. Almost everything I owned was black, and what wasn't black were suits and professional work clothes. I really needed to go shopping and get more fun clothes. Especially because DeCarious always dressed and looked so nice. My phone rang in the middle of my search for something cute and sexy. It was Gavin. I didn't really have time to talk, but I answered anyway.

"Hey, Gav. What's up?"

"So you must have got yourself a little boyfriend, because you never answer your phone."

"Yeah, I'm kind of seeing someone now."

"Too bad. Well, you have the number. Call me when you get some time."

"I will."

DeCarious showed up at my house forty-five minutes early. I hadn't been in the shower yet, and I still hadn't decided what I was going to wear.

"You're early," I said as I opened the door.

"I know. I was already in the city."

"Have a seat and let me get dressed. The remote is on the table," I said. I went back to my closet to see what I could wear. I decided on a pair of dark blue jeans and a black, short-sleeved ruffled shirt. It was cute. Just as I was getting ready to change into my clothes, I heard DeCarious walking toward my room. He tapped on the door.

"I wanted to see if you needed help picking something out to wear."

"No, I can find something on my own."

"You sure?" he asked. He looked so handsome. His shoulders were so broad, and I felt like I wanted to just go over to him and jump on his lap and throw my tongue down his throat.

I must have gazed a little too long, because he said, "Why are you looking at me like that?"

"I wasn't looking at you any type of way." He must read minds, because I was so attracted to him and it had been a very long time since I had a man in my personal space. All types of thoughts ran through my mind.

"I can't help you pick something out," he said as he came toward me, cornered me against my closet door, and began sucking and blowing on my ear and neck. His hands reached over, opening my robe to expose my naked body as he grasped my breasts and massaged my nipples in circles. His lips were moist, and I liked the way his tongue and lips nibbled my shoulder.

He was ready for it, but I had to push him off me or we would never have made it to Tim's house. "I can't—let's wait."

On the ride over to Tim's house, DeCarious asked me to go on a trip with him.

"I wanted to tell you next weekend is our bye week and see if you want to take a trip, maybe fly to the Bahamas or something."

"I can't. I have to work."

"Can't you just take off?"

"No, I can't just get up and take trips whenever I want to. I don't have that kind of job."

"Okay, my bad. So what do you want to do for your birthday?"

"It doesn't really matter. I'm not a big birthday person. I'll probably be working."

"Well, now that we are together we are going to celebrate birthdays, so we are doing something. I'm going to take you somewhere and surprise you. Can you try to take off now for your birthday weekend?"

"Okay, I'll try."

They were so excited about Tim being on the news. I couldn't understand it; he was on television every Sunday.

"It's coming on, Tim," Tim's wife Mari said as she used the remote to turn up the volume on the huge wall-unit television. We all had a seat. I wasn't normally nervous, but seeing my face on the screen and everyone watching intently, made me a bit uncomfortable. We all watched for the next five minutes, silently. I tried to study everyone's face to get a reading of what they were thinking.

They all clapped after the segment went off.

"My baby did good, didn't she?" DeCarious said as he

hugged me and grabbed my waist and kissed me on my cheek. I hated PDA, but I didn't push him off of me.

"That was so good," Mari said. I thanked her. I was becoming a little embarrassed. I had to switch the praise back over to Tim.

"No, Tim, you did all the work."

"But you provided the outlet, and thank you, girl, for that," Mari whispered. "Because he can't put in another dollar of ours."

Within minutes Tim's phone started ringing and people wanted to help out the organization. Mari turned on the music and began serving dinner. DeCarious was so loving, and it was fun being around him and his friends.

Chapter 23

Tanisha

There's been so much to catch up on, but my life is still in limbo. Kierra was the only person who opened her heart back up to me, no questions asked. She slept in the bed with me every night. Tyrone gave me my bedroom back and he moved into the back room. I didn't want Tyrone to think that we were going to be together again.

Mr. Ballard was trying to work out a deal for me so that I didn't receive any, or at least not a lot of jail time. The media attention was gone. After a half dozen nos to requests for interviews, all of the media attention stopped. Alexis, Kierra, and I have been out on mommy and daughter outings. We went to the movies and had lunch at Red Lobster. Jamil is busy with his job and his girlfriend. I really don't want to meet her, either. Alexis told me she is only twenty-three, with four kids, and she is using my son as a replacement father.

Kevin brought Jarell, our son, over twice, but when he came there was always a houseful of people and he never really seemed comfortable, plus when he visited he was never alone. There was always someone waiting in the car for him. Last time it was a blonde, this time a chocolate beauty. Both times the women got tired of waiting outside and began calling him, saying they were ready to go. I guess his only preference now was pretty with little patience. It made me a little angry that he was even bringing these random women to my home and around my son. But what could I say? I wasn't with him any longer and I had run away.

Mr. Ballard finally called me and said that he had reached a deal with the DA. I was petrified. My entire life was on the line. He had told me I could walk away with community service or I might have to do a few years. I walked into the dining room and grabbed Tyrone.

"It's Mr. Ballard. He said he has some good news about the plea." We sat down at the dining room table. I put the phone on speaker. "Yes, Mr. Ballard."

"Hello, Kevin is on the line, too. Tanisha, I believe I have some pretty good news for you guys. I was able to get all but one of the charges dropped. The only charge that is going to stick is the simple assault, which is a misdemeanor and no jail time."

"No jail time!" I exclaimed. All my prayers had been answered. I screamed out, "Thank you, God. Thank you." I had prayed and prayed and prayed some more, and it had worked.

"Hold up, Miss Butler, I'm not done. There is no jail time, however you will be on probation for a year, and three months of that year will be under house arrest."

"House arrest?" Tyrone repeated. I looked over at him, then back at the phone to hear the rest of what Mr. Ballard had to say.

"Yes, you will be able to leave the house to go see your probation officer once a week, but you will not be permitted to go outside of your home for three months. But under the circumstances, I think this an excellent deal and the DA is being very lenient."

"Will I have an arrest record?" I questioned.

"Yes, but after a few years we can try to get it removed. It will only be a misdemeanor." It sounded like a good deal to me. I got to be with my family, I wouldn't have a permanent record, and I could put this entire situation behind me.

Chapter 24

Adrienne

I hit my goal weight and I was making progress with De-Carious. Last week after the game I massaged his shoulders and gave his side a deep massage until he fell asleep. When he awoke, me and Asia were in the bed with him like a happy family. I poked out my butt slightly, just so, so he could get a little feel of what he was missing. I thought I got a rise out of him. He didn't say anything—he just positioned his body to the other side.

I was always happy, docile, smiling, and very attentive to DeCarious and Asia. I sent him pictures of us all the time and let Asia talk baby talk to him. I tried to laugh at all his jokes and I was very complimentary. I knew DeCarious was on his way back—he was calling me all the time like he used to. He deposited money in my account *just because,* he said. I like *just because* money, especially when it is a couple of thousand dollars. He was definitely coming back, and I just had to let him think it was his idea. If he thought that I was manipulating him even a little bit, he would run away.

And hopefully DeCarious came to his senses soon, because I was tired of being Miss Anne's praise pal. She had me going to other churches now, and she was even calling me too much. But I thought—no, I knew—all my hard work was eventually going to pay off. It had to, because I couldn't wait to quit my job and move back down to Atlanta. Then my life would be one big vacation again.

Chapter 25

Cherise

DeCarious was on his way back from a West Coast game against the San Francisco 49ers. I couldn't wait to see him. Tuesday had become DeCarious's and my unofficial day to be together. We both had very busy schedules, so we had to make time for one another. We did everything together, from doing nothing to watching episodes of *The First 48* on television. It was strange that we were so close and we hadn't had sex yet. We hadn't done anything more than hug and kiss. However, I felt an emotional connection to him like I just can't explain. We cuddled, hugged, and kissed a lot. He said several times that he had never felt so strong about someone so fast. I felt the same way. He was definitely what was missing from my life and we were making our way to the next level. He was everything I ever wanted. DeCarious had looks, personality, and intelligence. Plus, we had so much in common it was like I'd met the male version of me.

I wanted to be with him. He kept jokingly calling me a prude, but he had no idea. I am anything but. I didn't tell him about my two years of celibacy, because it was really none of his business. I was just scared that when I finally had sex I might go crazy on him. Before I had a man around I was

WHAT'S HIS IS MINE   151

good—never thought about sex. But now I felt myself always thinking about it. I knew I wouldn't be able to hold out too much longer. And I knew it was going to be so good.

DeCarious asked me to go to a few parties and I wouldn't go. To me, our relationship was just too new to put on display. He said this was the first time in his life he had to be a secret—people usually wanted to show him off. It was not that at all. I actually really liked him and couldn't wait to have sex with him, but I was a little scared. Then he kept offering me money. I told him I didn't need his money. If I needed it I would gladly accept, but I was happy with him just picking up the tab when we went to dinner.

I was at work and I got a text from DeCarious—lyrics from a Jamie Foxx song, "She Got Her Own."

I texted back,

CUTE :) SMILE

He texted me,

WHEN YOU GO HOME CHECK THE FRONT DESK.

I texted him,

OKAY. HAVE A SAFE FLIGHT.

The next day DeCarious called right before I went into my meeting, I remembered that I forgot to check the front desk as he had instructed me, and I hadn't called him back even though he had left several messages.

"Cherise, did you get your gift?" DeCarious asked.

"No, babe, I'm sorry. I forgot, but listen—I will get to it as soon as I get home."

"Okay, I miss you. Am I going to see you later on?"

"Probably."

"Cherise, I need to see your face. Send me a picture or something. Something sexy."

"DeCarious, I'm at work. Plus, I don't take those kinds of pics. I can't, not right now. I'll call you later," I said and turned my cell phone off.

When I came out of my meeting, I turned on my phone and was about to call DeCarious back when I got several crazy text messages from him.

U'RE NOT PAYING ME ENOUGH ATTN. U WANT TO KEEP ME A SECRET AND YOU COULDN'T EVEN PICK UP A GIFT I LEFT YOU AT THE FRONT DESK OF YOUR BUILDING. I'M DOIN' EVERYTHING TO MAKE THIS WORK, BUT I DON'T KNOW HOW LONG I CAN WAIT FOR YOU TO CALL ME BACK. I'VE CALLED YOU THREE TIMES & YOU HAVEN'T EVEN CALLED ME ONCE IN 2 DAYS. I GUESS I'M JUST USED TO A WOMAN WHO HAS TIME FOR HER MAN. OTHER WOMEN WOULD BE HAPPY A MAN WAS TRYING TO BUY THEM THINGS AND TAKE THEM ON TRIPS. AND MAYBE THERE IS SOMEONE ELSE. IF SO, KEEP IT REAL AND STOP PLAY-ING. YOU CAN'T BE WORKING THAT HARD ALL THE TIME & I KNOW YOU REALLY CAN'T BE THIS SHY PRUDE WHEN IT COMES TO SEX. MAYBE YOU GO ELSEWHERE.

I reread the text several times. I didn't have time to have a text war with him. Gary and I were on our way to do a pregame shoot around interviews with the Hawks. I didn't know how to handle DeCarious's stupid long text. At first I wasn't going to respond, but then I found myself sending him a bunch of texts. I must have sent about five.

BEFORE I START, I NEED TO APOLOGIZE FOR NOT RE-TURNING YOUR CALL YESTERDAY. I DON'T BELIEVE IN SCHEDULED CALLS. IF YOU SAY YOU WILL CALL AND DON'T, I SIMPLY PICK UP THE PHONE BECAUSE I WANT TO TALK TO YOU. I DON'T KEEP A TALLY OF WHO HAS TO CALL NEXT. YOU SAID IN YOUR MES-SAGE THE KIND OF WOMAN YOU PREFER. I FEEL THE NEED TO PROVIDE YOU WITH A LITTLE FEEDBACK. I PUT MYSELF THROUGH COLLEGE. I AM A YOUNG BLACK WOMAN IN A WHITE SOCIETY. I HAVE NO CHOICE THAN TO WORK HARDER, STAY LATER, AND CONSTANTLY KEEP MYSELF AHEAD OF THE GAME. I'M SORRY I CAN'T JUST GET UP AND TAKE TRIPS WHEN-EVER I FEEL LIKE IT. I PAY ALL MY OWN BILLS, ALWAYS HAVE, ALWAYS WILL. YOU JUST TEXTED ME THAT YOU LIKE A WOMAN WHO HAS HER OWN, BUT YOU HAVE A PROBLEM WITH HOW HARD I WORK. MAKE UP YOUR MIND!

AND AS FAR AS HORIZONTAL ACTIVITIES—I VALUE MYSELF AND DON'T JUST GIVE IT AWAY TO ANYONE. NO PRUDE, BUT JUST NOT EASY, LIKE THE WOMEN YOU USUALLY DATE. I JUST BELIEVE IN COMMITMENTS AND WHEN I'M READY I ENJOY ALL 3 HOLES!!! I WANT TO BRING SOMETHING TO THE TABLE, NOT JUST AN OVERNIGHT BAG. . . . WHY WOULD I WANT MY MAN TO HAVE THE STRESSES OF BEING A SOLE PROVIDER? I WANT A MAN TO KNOW I'M THE KIND OF WOMAN WHO—GOD FORBID SOMETHING SHOULD HAPPEN TO HIM—I CAN HOLD DOWN A FAMILY, BUSINESS,

AND POSSIBLE LIFESTYLE . . . I BELIEVE IN GIVING FOOT MASSAGES, BACK RUBS, AND, YES, COOKING IF NECESSARY. I WOULD LOVE TO TAKE GOOD CARE OF A GOOD MAN.

He didn't respond to my text. I was thinking maybe I had said too much. I wasn't sure if I should call him or not. I was scared of his reaction. However he shouldn't have sent me all those crazy, insensitive texts. Whatever I thought, once I was home I retrieved the box he left at the front desk.

I opened it as soon as I entered my house. It was just a teddy bear. A stupid teddy bear. I couldn't believe DeCarious was so upset until I looked down at the teddy bear's ears. Both ears had beautiful marquise diamond earrings. *Wow*, I thought. The earrings were nice, but they still didn't excuse DeCarious's behavior. I was about to text him back, but before I could call, he texted me.

DAMN, I GUESS YOU TOLD ME. SORRY, BABE. CAN I MAKE IT UP TO YOU?

I smiled down at my phone and texted him back.

SURE.

I smiled.

TONIGHT. YOUR PLACE AT 7PM, he texted.

OKAY, I typed back

Promptly at 7 p.m. DeCarious was at the door. He had two bags with him.

"What's in all the bags?"

"Dinner. My baby is working hard, and I have to understand. She can't take off to go on a trip with me to the islands. I have to bring the islands to her." He started putting out tropical drinks and food all over the table. Then he put his iPod in my dock and began playing reggae tunes. I had a seat and he served me dinner and drinks. He poured a coconut drink and made me a plate of red beans, curry, and jerk chicken.

The food was good and DeCarious had really thought the evening out. He served me like a queen, then made a cute toast.

"To us for you being the perfect woman. I wish I would have met you years ago. Maybe this is the beginning to our forever," he said.

"Our forever," I repeated. I looked into DeCarious's eyes. It scared me how serious he was at times. We hadn't been together that long, but I believed him.

"I know, Cherise, but I've never fallen for anyone this fast. I really feel like you are the one. To meeting the one."

"I am the one what?" I asked.

"You know—the one for me."

"What are you talking about, DeCarious?"

"I just like everything about you. I like how independent you are. Cherise, you are perfect. I love everything on you, from your gorgeous face to your pretty pink toes." I smiled. I was blushing. "I don't know, we are going to have to go ring shopping."

"We will see about that, but right now, thank you for the earrings. They are beautiful."

"You're welcome."

Our night was perfect. It wasn't because he was talking

about marriage or because he bought me earrings. It was perfect because DeCarious was just the sweetest man I had ever met. I was really falling for him, and fast. So when he held my hand and walked me into my bedroom and laid me on my back, I didn't stop him. We both quickly undressed. His body was so warm and firm. I wanted to attack him and could not get undressed fast enough. I was undressed and he still had his boxers on. He climbed on top of me and began kissing my navel and letting his tongue follow an invisible path up to my breasts. He unhooked my bra as I lay still. I wanted to relax and just enjoy every moment. Then he followed that invisible line back down past my pelvis. Just from his kisses alone, I felt a flash flood about to emerge from my body. It all felt so good I didn't know if I wanted to hold it in or release everything. We then switched positions. He lay flat and I got on top of him and placed his body inside of me. Our flesh connected and again I almost exploded. DeCarious made my entire body tingle. I felt every jerk of his body from my spine to my toes. It was an incredible, indescribable feeling. I felt like I wanted him to stop but keep going at the same time.

There was more pleasure than pain as we pleasured each other for hours straight. Two years of waiting was worth it for this moment.

Chapter 26

Tanisha

"We need to discuss what address you'll be using for your house arrest, Tanisha. I need to fax the information over."

"Here at my house. The Tioga Street address."

"Okay, Mr. Wallace gave another address. Let me give him a call and then I will call you back."

A few moments later Kevin called me, screaming and really upset. "Tanisha, did you just get a call about where you're going to stay for your house arrest?"

"Yes," I answered, confused.

"Okay, I was willing to pay for an apartment so you could get yourself together. I already discussed this with Tyrone." It was the first time he had showed any emotion toward me in months. But it was crazy because he was arguing with me about something we hadn't discussed.

"Yeah, Kevin, Tyrone told me about that. Thank you, that's very nice of you, but I'm going to stay here, where I'm at. My children are here."

"Your children are there. Do you know you have a son over here, too? I tried to make it easy for you. I can't believe you—so now you are worried about your children? I don't get you."

"What do you mean by that, Kevin?"

"You leave for an entire year, without thinking about anyone but yourself. Then you come back. I paid your bail. I paid for your attorney. I tried to provide somewhere for you to live, all the while I have my own career and I'm raising our son."

I interrupted him and said, "I did say thank you, and one day I will be able to pay you back. I appreciate everything you did, Kevin, but I just want to stay here. This is my home."

"Before you left, your home was with me. I guess you forgot about that. Maybe you want to stay there so you can play house with your ex-husband."

"No, that's not true. He is just helping me through all this and we are not getting back together."

"You think I believe that, Tanisha? You're nothing but a liar. I thought you were dead, Tanisha. You let me think that for a year. All the emotions I went through, and now you are going to walk back into my life like nothing ever happened. No explanation. After all I've done for you. You haven't even had a one-on-one conversation with me. I figured it was because you had so much going on, but now there is no excuse. How about this? Why don't you go on the run again? This time make it seventeen years, so our son won't ever have to know you. And you know what? Just stay out of my life, Tanisha. You hear me? Just stay out of our lives." I was speechless. I knew Kevin was too damn calm. I didn't know how to respond. He had so many things wrong.

"And you still are not going to say anything?" Kevin asked.

"Kevin, it is not like that at all. Let me explain," I said, confused.

"You don't have to explain anything to me. You don't

know how much you hurt me by leaving, and then you come back in town like nothing."

"I'm sorry! Kevin, I'm so sorry," I said as tears streamed down my face and I paced back and forth in the living room.

"You're sorry! All of this, and that's all you have to say is you're sorry. You fucking ran away! How pathetic is that? You ran away!"

"Well, maybe if I didn't have your crazy, stalking ex-girlfriend chasing me, I wouldn't have run away, Kevin."

"So every time something crazy happens, you're just going to run. If that's the case, I don't want you in my son's life, Tanisha," he said and disconnected our call. I tried to call him back several times and he didn't answer.

All I could do was pray on all of this. I just wanted my life to go back to normal. I just wanted to redeem myself, be a good mom, and get a job.

I went upstairs to take a shower. I needed to de-stress. I took my clothes off, and got in the shower. No sooner did the hot water hit my body than my phone rang. I knew it had to be Kevin, so I grabbed a towel and raced to retrieve my cell phone from my bedroom.

"Hello," I said frantically.

"Hey, Tanisha, it's Adrienne."

"Hey."

"I was just checking in on you, making sure that everything was okay."

"Yeah, I'm fine. I just got in the shower—can I call you back?"

"Sure." I wasn't going to call Adrienne back. I didn't really want to talk to her. Her voice was irritating and she just seemed like she still didn't get it. She didn't get that she gave me bad advice, I took it, and now my life was in shambles. All I wanted was a hot shower, a long nap, and a regular, drama-free life.

Chapter 27

Cherise

Iwas covering the Falcons game, sitting in the press box with all the other reporters. Every time I saw number 65 run down the field, I held in my excitement. I couldn't exactly scream, *Go baby,* but I wished I could. They were playing the Buccaneers and had just won. I wanted to hurry up and go say, *Good game* to DeCarious. As I was coming out of the press box, I saw Tim's wife, Mari. I went up to her and spoke. She looked very pretty and was speaking with two other beautiful women. They all had big designer-monogrammed bags.

"Hey, Cherise. I didn't know you covered the games, too! Wow, look at you," Mari said.

"Yeah, let me hurry and get to the locker room. I'll see you later."

I spotted DeCarious coming off the field. I could tell he wanted me to hug him or do something like couples would do, but I couldn't. I just said, *Good game* and told him I would be at his house after I got off work.

I was meeting DeCarious to go meet his family. I hadn't met anyone's family since college, and hadn't been that serious about anyone. I had had offers, but I said no. That to me was a very important step. He was everything I ever wanted. I tried to hold back a little. I don't know, I'd never fallen for someone so fast, so quick, in my life. It was scary. I didn't want to think too hard about it or overanalyze. Everything was going so well. I was just trying to make sure I didn't mess it up. I called Toni to get a pep talk.

"Ton—nee," I sang.

"Why are you all happy this afternoon?"

"I'm about to go meet DeCarious's parents and daughter. And I am so confused and scared."

"Why?"

"Because it is so soon. We've been dating what, six weeks?"

"Yeah, this is fast."

"Can you believe it? Who would have seen all of this coming?"

"I don't know—this is fast. But stop being silly. This is happening because you deserve it. You are right."

"But I'm still nervous a little bit."

"Don't be nervous. You will be fine."

"I know, Toni. He makes me so happy. Oh my God, I said it. I am so happy."

"This is so wonderful. You are going to get your hyphenated name after all." I thought about what Toni said and then told her she was silly and I would let her know how everything went.

It took me a while, but I finally found DeCarious's house. It was a big mansion and the next house was down the road. He greeted me at the door and gave me a kiss on my cheek and held my hand and led me inside his home. His mom was sitting on the sofa with his daughter. DeCarious said, "Mom, this is my girlfriend, Cherise."

She stood up and said, "Nice to meet you, Cherise."

"You look so familiar, like I've seen you before," Mr. Joe said.

"Because she is on the news, Dad," DeCarious said.

"You are? What channel?"

"Channel 7."

"I love FOX 5, but since I know you now, I'm going to have to change my station."

Then a woman entered the room. She was holding a precious little baby girl. DeCarious took the baby out of the woman's hands and then introduced his daughter, Malaysia, to me.

"Cherise, this is my daughter's mom, Adrienne."

"Adrienne, this is my girlfriend, Cherise." The woman looked a little shocked. We shook hands and I told her it was nice to meet her, but she just rolled her eyes and retreated upstairs.

Chapter 28

Adrienne

It was loud and festive at the Georgia Dome. Everyone had their red, black, and white Falcon colors on. DeCarious invited me, Asia, and his parents to his game. This was a major step for us. Being at the game was wives' and girlfriends' territory. Every now and then jumpoffs get tickets, too, but if DeCarious had anyone he liked she would be sitting in section 117, row 3, seat 2, instead of me.

And I was happy to be here. My plan was working. One step at a time, I was reeling him back in. And I don't know why, but DeCarious looked extra sexy and powerful in his uniform. I dressed Asia up real pretty in cute jeans and she had her red, black, and white Falcons colors on like everyone in the stadium. We were playing the Buccaneers and we were winning. I hadn't realized how passionate Mr. Joe was about football. He was screaming at the plays and calls. It was the most I had ever heard him speak.

Mr. Joe stood up and said, "Get them down! Take them down, son," every time DeCarious took down one of the Buccaneers players.

After the game was over, I had to show a special pass to get on the elevator and get into the family room. And with all the security they made us go through, there were still groupies galore in the room. They must have paid security to get down here without a pass. And I could tell they were groupies because of the hunger they had in their eyes. They looked so desperate and you could just tell they were on the prowl. Every time someone with a duffel bag walked through the doors, they tried to make eye contact and get their attention. Then I saw one groupie trying to make conversation with a player's parents, I guess with the hope that they could introduce her when the player came out of the locker room. They were disrespectful, but hey, every girl has to eat and get hers. They just better stay away from DeCarious or I'm going to kick someone's ass.

After the game we had a beautiful dinner at Nakatos, this hibachi-style Japanese restaurant. There was me, Asia, De-Carious, Miss Anne, Mr. Joe, and even Rock and his girl-friend, Shaundra. Asia didn't like the high flames and noise, but we all had a good time.

I told DeCarious what a great game he'd had and he said thanks and I thought we were all happy, but then when we got back home DeCarious invited some woman over and in-troduced her to me as his girlfriend. What the hell is really going on?

So here I am, thinking I'm making progress with DeCari-ous and we are a few steps away from being a couple and a family again, and he has the audacity to bring a chick home—what the hell? She spoke to me and I spoke back to her, but as soon as she turned her back, I wanted to kick my foot in her ass. I couldn't show how upset I was, so I left and went upstairs until they left.

I thought Miss Anne was my friend. I went to church with that bitch, and she knew about a *real* girlfriend, and didn't tell me. I said aloud to Miss Anne, "I didn't know DeCarious had a girlfriend."

"Me neither. I honestly thought you two were getting back together, because you've been spending so much time here. But anyway, she seems like a nice woman. And she is on the news on Channel 7," Miss Anne said.

"Oh, that's nice."

"Yeah, that's what DeCarious needs—a nice girl."

I knew I had to take action immediately. I didn't know what I should do. This slow and steady was not going to work. Tonight I was going to take matters into my own hands. I would have to turn up my pace on getting DeCarious back.

I was waiting for DeCarious to come home. He showed his girlfriend, now I had something to show him. I had it all planned out. I was going to walk out of the shower with my towel on. I then was going to knock on DeCarious's door, drop my towel, and show him all the sex tricks I knew. He was not going to be able to resist me. He was going to forget about whatever her name was, and life would be great.

Seducing DeCarious into obedience would have worked. I know it would have, but I didn't get a chance because he never came home. I even texted him first thing this morning to tell him we had an early flight, so he could see us before we left. But he didn't call or text back. This was mind-boggling and crazy. I couldn't believe I missed the fact that this dummy had someone. I hate DeCarious's sucker-for-love ass. I just wanted to get on my flight and go home. I needed to just go home, find a babysitter, and go to work every day, because it didn't look like I was going to get DeCarious back. I didn't know what my next step was going to be. I needed some rest so I could come up with a plan B.

*   *   *

At the airport it took forever to get through security. I was lucky enough to make the machine go off, even though I had my shoes off, belt off, and everything out of my pockets.

Asia and I arrived at gate A 27 with just forty-five minutes to spare. It was crowded and there was nowhere to sit. I was surprised they weren't boarding yet. I walked around, trying to find a seat when I heard that my flight was going to be delayed. *Great,* I thought.

Chapter 29

Zakiya

Elena was dropping me off at the airport. It was bitter-sweet. I wanted to go home, but I wanted to stay and do more in LA. I'd lived so much life in such a short amount of time, and wanted to stay, but I couldn't.

As Elena pulled up to the terminal, we both began to tear up.

"I can't believe you are leaving. I'm going to miss you. I feel like we've known each other for years. I don't know what I am going to do without you," Elena said.

"Girl, I'll be back. I need to check on my sister, make sure everything is okay with her and my nephews. And she doesn't charge me any rent, so I can definitely come back with enough money to get our apartment and buy a car."

"You promise? You think you can come back by January?"

"I'm going to try," I said as I exited the car and retrieved my bag from the backseat of the car.

"Thank your brother Enrique for me, for this ticket. I'm so glad I'm not taking the damn bus back home."

"He thanks you. He gets buddy passes all the time. He needed that hundred dollars for his cell phone bill."

"Well, still tell him I'm so thankful." I laughed. I gave Elena another quick hug and then said good-bye again.

The airport was empty. I got through security with ease and went to my gate and waited for my flight. The gate agent began calling sections to board the plane. My ticket was standby so I had to wait for everyone to be seated. When she called my name I walked up and asked her if she called my name.

"Yes, Zakiya Lee, we have one seat open. Give me a moment—step to the side, please, and I'll check you in," she said. I stepped over to the side and waited as she multitasked, tearing the tickets of all the other passengers and typing into her computer.

This man ran up, out of breath, in a business suit, with a briefcase and computer bag, and said, "They told me to tell you downstairs that I'm here."

"Are you Mr. Turner?"

"Yes, I am," the man said as he adjusted his travel bag on his shoulder and tried to catch his breath.

"You just made it, sir. Have a good flight," she said as she printed and tore his boarding pass. Then the gate agent looked over at me and said, "Miss Lee, I'm not going to be able to get you on this one. I'm sorry. Let me see if we can get you on the next flight."

"What time does that leave?" I asked, peering over the counter.

"In two hours."

The last four flights to Philly had been booked and I was getting mad. I knew my ticket was standby, but I didn't know that meant stand by until all the people who paid for their tickets got on the flight and if there was an extra seat we would let you on. It was not like I really had somewhere to be, but I did want to get out of this crowded airport. The only good thing was that the agent was being really nice about everything. Every time I came up to the counter she was pleasant and didn't act like I was bothering her.

I walked back up to her to see how the next flight looked. She looked at the computer screen, shook her head, and said, "I feel sorry for you, sweetie. Let's see how we can get you out of here. There are no more flights leaving to go to Philadelphia for a couple of hours." She then sighed and said, "Today these storms in the Midwest have just screwed everything up. How about this? I'm going to see if I at least can get you to the East Coast, and once you get there, it will be much easier to get to Philadelphia. You want to do that?"

I was becoming restless. I didn't care how she got me there. I just wanted to get home. "That's fine," I said.

She concentrated, looking at the screen, and then said, "Honey, you are in luck. There are a lot of open seats going to Atlanta. Then you can connect to a flight going to Philly. The flight leaves in thirty minutes. Go down to gate D 10. I already checked you in. You don't have to wait—you can just board." She printed my boarding pass and handed it to me.

I boarded my flight without any problems. There were plenty of seats. I didn't even have to sit next to anyone. I stretched my legs out, laid my head on the window, and slept the entire flight to Atlanta.

I arrived in Atlanta five hours later, only to I learn my flight to Philadelphia was delayed two hours. I wasn't complaining, but traveling by plane so far hadn't been that great, either. I went to the store and bought a few magazines and a bag of Gummi Bears and sat and waited. I was so bored. I wished I had music to listen to or a movie to watch. I just looked around at all the other angry passengers. I was nodding off until this cute little girl who was playing peekaboo with her mom ran over to me, touched my leg and wobbled, giggled at me, and then ran back over to her mom. She came over to me like three times, so finally I extended my arms out for her. She acted like she was going to come to me, and then she ran back over to her mother's lap again.

"She is so cute," I said to her mother, who was dressed nice. She was real pretty and was splitting her attention between her daughter and her phone.

"Thank you," her mother said, barely looking up at me.

"How old is she?

"She is eighteen months."

"What's her name?"

"Malaysia. We call her Asia, though."

The gate agent made an announcement: "Attention all passengers for flight 3301, nonstop Atlanta to Philadelphia. Your flight has been delayed until ten-thirty. You may go to the customer service counter located at gate A3 to rebook on another flight. Thank you."

"Oh no . . . Damn it, you have to be kidding me. I'm tired of sitting in this airport."

"Me too, damn it."

"Well, I might as well go get her something to eat. Could you watch our stuff?"

"Sure."

"Would you like anything?" the woman asked. I told her no and that I would keep an eye on her bags.

When she returned with her food she ate, and asked me if she could read my magazines. Her daughter kept playing with me.

"She likes you."

"Yeah, kids always gravitate to me—I don't know why. I have two nephews."

"So do you go to school down here?" she asked.

"No, I live in Philly, but I'm coming from California. It's a long story. I just can't wait to get home. I hope I can get my job back and just enroll in school."

"So you don't have a job."

"No, but I think I can get my job back."

"Would you ever consider, like, being a live-in nanny?"

"No, I haven't."

"Oh, because I work a lot and need someone to watch my daughter."

"Like what hours? I'm trying to save money to go back to California. So yeah, I can watch her sometimes."

I thought about her offer, took her number, and told her I would call her. I don't think I want to be a full-time nanny, though. I would probably get bored. Plus I needed a real job.

Chapter 30

Zakiya

Philly smelled different and it was cold for October. I was spoiled by the warm Cali weather. I took a cab home, because I wanted to surprise Lisa and my nephews. I saw Lisa's Toyota Camry. A strange vanilla smell greeted me at the door. The house just had a different vibe. I called out to Lisa. She came to the top of the steps.

"What are you doing here?" Lisa yelled as she came down the stairs and hugged me. I placed my luggage down and said, "Aunt Vicky and Jade were moving again. I couldn't go with them, and the rent out there is so expensive, so I had to come home."

"Damn, I didn't even get a chance to come out there. I'm happy you are home, but now I don't know where everyone is going to sleep."

"Who is everybody?" I asked, looking around.

"Saundra from my job and her daughter moved in. She is going through a divorce. I finally left Mikey, so we're helping each other. They're staying in your room. But you know, we'll figure something out. I'll just tell her she has to find somewhere else to stay."

"No, you don't have to do that. I'll just sleep on the sofa, and I'm going to walk to my old job and see if I can get my job back. Where are the boys?"

"Over at Mikey's mom's house. Well, I got a date. I'm glad you're back and we'll make it work. Don't worry about it."

I peeped into my room. It was filled up with several ten-gallon-sized plastic bags.

I couldn't waste any time. I needed to get my job back, so I could get a place and then save money.

I showered and then walked to my former job. Nothing had changed in the three months since I had left. I saw Lenora and she gave me the one-minute sign because she was giving a cashier change. After she counted the change she came over to me and said, "What's going on? You visiting?" We walked as we talked and I followed her up the stairs.

"No, I came back home. I'm moving back. I came here to see if I could get my job back."

"Get your job back? Um, actually I just hired five people last week. Zakiya, you should have called me." She picked up a few boxes of popcorn that had fallen back on the shelf and said, "You still have the same number? I can give you a call if anything changes."

"Okay, Lenora, call me."

I needed a job. I knew I wouldn't be able to stay with my sister. I love my nephews, but them plus Saundra and her daughter, Yahnee, was unbearable. They all got up at seven a.m. on a Saturday morning, to play games, scream, and yell.

Several days went by and Lenora still hadn't called, so I was going to call the woman—Adrienne—from the airport. I didn't know her, but she didn't seem crazy.

"Hi, Adrienne, this is Zakiya."

"Hey, Zakiya. I'm on the other line—hold on for a

minute." She put me on hold and didn't come back to the phone for a very long time. I felt like hanging up.

"Sorry about that. So what's going on?"

"I wanted to know if you still needed someone to watch your daughter because my sister's friend has moved in with her and I wasn't able to get my job back. So I kinda need a live-in nanny job."

"Yeah, I do still need you. When can you start?"

"I'm going to come tomorrow."

The next day Adrienne came and picked me up and brought me to her home. She lived in a big three-bedroom town house and it was just her and her daughter. She gave me a tour of her home. Her daughter's room looked like it was never slept in—it was beautiful. It was lavender, with a rainbow and a white unicorn painted on the wall. There were toys everywhere. Dolls and blocks and things her daughter probably won't be able to play with for years. Even the guest room, where I was going to be staying, had a huge brass bed, a white dresser, and walk-in closet. And her room and closet were set up like a department store. There were all types of perfume and jewelry and she had so many shoes. And clothes.

I liked Adrienne. She had so much going on for herself. She was a nurse, had a nice car and home. I couldn't believe she was the same age as my sister, but she had so much more. She said she worked a lot of hours, but who cares? She had everything.

Chapter 31

Tanisha

I tried to call Kevin several times and he never answered. I tried him again. A woman answered and said, "Kevin is busy. Who should I tell him called?" I wanted to curse the woman out and tell Kevin to get his ass on the telephone, but I didn't bother. I just hung up on her. I wanted to see my child and I was becoming angry. There was nothing I could do until he decided that he was going to let the hate he felt for me out of his heart. I wasn't going to bother or harass him, but by law he had to let me see my child. I was Jarell's mother. I knew eventually he would come around.

In the meantime I had to enjoy my other children. Alexis didn't have class on Tuesday and Thursday so she would come and visit with me while Tyrone was at work and Kierra at school. Today was going to be a very interesting visit. Unfortunately, she was about to witness me being put under house arrest. My probation officer, Robert Neal, was on his way over. He was young black guy who talked fast and was kind of funny. So far, he seemed nice, but stern.

He was at the door, clipboard and box in hand, promptly at noon. He wanted me to direct him to the phone line and he began setting up. He performed random tests on the box accuracy. Red and green lights flashed on and off. I made small talk with Alexis, trying to distract her attention off of the box. She stared at him as he began placing and adjusting the band around my ankle as he was running down all the rules I had to abide by while I wore the black box anklet.

Mr. Neal snapped the device on and then asked, "Does it hurt?"

I looked down at my ankle and responded, "No."

He got up off the floor and said, "Just so you know, I can pop in on you at any time, and the fastest way to land in jail is to not keep it real with me. If an emergency happens, call me. If I don't answer, leave a message. You understand?"

"Yes."

"Oh, and you need to try to distance yourself from whoever the people were that got you in this predicament."

"Okay."

"How is she going to take a shower and bathe?" Alexis asked.

"You can take a shower, but no baths because it can't be submerged in water. I have many people who think they are smarter than this box. They're not. My best advice—call me if something comes up. Do not try to deactivate or take this thing off." He spieled off more rules and then he left.

After he left, we caught up on Alexis's life. She had turned into such a remarkable young woman. Before, she barely wanted to get a job. Now she had a job and was going to school.

"Mom, you need your hair done. I'm going to bring my friend over to do your hair. She is in cosmetology school. She can give you a manicure and pedicure, too."

"I would love that. Bring her over," I said, trying to seem excited and enthused, but really I was becoming sad. I think the thought of three months in this one place was sinking in. I was about to be stuck. I felt myself about to panic, so instead I went into the basement and did a few loads of laundry. For a moment I was reminded of Detroit. I remembered how lonely, depressing, and miserable it was. How when I was there the only thing I wanted was to see my family. I have my family back, so I wasn't about to let an ankle bracelet upset me. I said a prayer and just tried not to get upset.

Chapter 32

Adrienne

Zakiya had been living with me for two weeks, and I already couldn't live without her. She made my life so much easier. I got three for one with her. She cleaned my house like a slave, cooked like a gourmet soul food chef, and took good care of my daughter.

When I came in from work, Asia was already dressed and didn't want to leave her to come to me. She was a godsend. She was like the little sister I never had. She was like a sponge, and I could school her on life. I told her every piece of advice I could think of. I gave her some of my old stuff and she was so grateful. She is just a real innocent nineteen-year-old girl and was like a sponge. I felt like it was my obligation to school her on life, because from what she told me, she had it very hard growing up without a mom. Her sister didn't seem like she knew that much herself. I told her every piece of advice I could think of. I gave her some of my old stuff, and she was so grateful. I told her to go to college, but still get a man with money. I told her that she wasn't going to be anyone's baby mother, and that she had to look pretty at all times. She was already a cute girl, but she just needed a little refining, and when I'm done with her, the world won't be ready.

My mom thought I was crazy when I told her I met a nice young lady at the airport and she was living with me and watching Asia. But she was the one who suggested I find a nice teenager to watch Asia. And now that I had my built-in babysitter, which she suggested, she was harassing me with phone calls, saying, "I miss my grandbaby. Bring her over." No, ma'am. I could get up, get dressed, and walk straight out the door. And then when I came home, Asia was already dressed, fed, and ready for school.

Chapter 33

Cherise

I wasn't going to hide my relationship with DeCarious from the world any longer. We were going to the pre-show activities at the Atlanta International Car Show. All the Atlanta elite would be in attendance. Every year, I heard the black-tie gala charity car show was one of the most coveted events. It was like DeCarious's and my unofficial coming-out party. I was so excited and wanted to look totally different tonight. I had my makeup done and hair styled at a salon in Buckhead that Mari recommended. The stylist did an amazing job seaming the long black flowing weave with my own hair. When she handed me the mirror I couldn't believe how my hair was moving back and forth so naturally.

From the salon, I went home, showered, and then changed into this crushed-fabric purple and silver cocktail dress. I looked in the mirror and was impressed. I felt beautiful and special.

The moment DeCarious saw me he stopped and whispered, "You look so beautiful." I thanked him.

We entered the car show arm in arm and there were cameras flashing, but I didn't mind. I was actually proud to say DeCarious was my man. Who wouldn't be? He was perfect. He looked so handsome in his black suit and silver tie.

The car show was huge. There were thousands of new and futuristic concept car models on display.

The entire event was very elegant. Servers were walking around with champagne and hors d'oeuvres as all the attendees mingled. We had a great time, but I couldn't wait to get home and get out of my dress and on top of my man.

When we got back to my place, DeCarious didn't let me get out of my dress. He just pushed me onto the sofa and began giving my warm insides a massage with the tip of his tongue. I brought his face farther in and glided my hips onto him, when the knocking at my front door interrupted everything. DeCarious looked at me like who was at my door at one in the morning? I didn't know. I threw on my robe and went to the door. He was right behind me. I opened the door and saw Toni. She barged in, walking right past me, hand and hand with Lou.

"Toni, is everything okay?" Why was she at my house at one in the morning?

She spoke to DeCarious and then said, "Yeah, I just wanted to tell you I parked downstairs, so if Dave calls here tell him I'm asleep. He is getting on my nerves. I had to get out of that damn house. Plus I needed my Lou fix," she said as she gave Lou's ass a slap.

I couldn't believe she was talking about cheating on her husband in front of DeCarious. I didn't know what else to say, but okay. As soon as they walked out the door, DeCarious started asking questions.

"What's up with your sister cheating on her husband?"

"I don't know. She said he cheated on her. And she can't forgive him," I said, trying to change the subject and get back to where we left off. I disrobed and wrapped my legs around him.

"Do you agree with that?" he asked, looking at me.

"No. I've tried to talk to her, but she doesn't listen. I stopped caring."

"Wow, that's really messed up. If her marriage isn't working, don't cheat, just leave."

"She can't. She has a house and family. I'm not going to argue about what she does. Just mind your business."

"Would you ever cheat or leave?"

"I wouldn't cheat. Now leave it alone and stop asking me silly questions." I didn't know why DeCarious was so angry about what Toni was doing. I reached over and grabbed his face and kissed him. "Babe, let's not worry about anyone but us."

"Okay. But I don't like that, Cherise."

"I understand, but that's not me and that's not us. Okay?" He calmed back down and we returned to our previous activities until another knock at the door interrupted us. Now I was mad. I was going to kick Toni's ass, but it wasn't Toni. It was Dave standing outside my door. I hurried and threw my robe on and answered the door.

"Cherise, tell Toni I'm out here." He wasn't even my husband and I was scared as hell. What was I going to tell him? I looked at DeCarious, who was now behind me. I just said the first thing that came to mind, which was she was here but she left. He accepted my answer and said if she came back to call him. I closed the door. I then dialed Toni.

"Girl, your husband is at my door. Where are you?" What the hell? I wasn't the one cheating, but my heart was in my throat.

"He is? Damn it . . . What time is it? Oh shit, I got twenty-five missed calls from him. I'm just going to come and get my car. If he calls back, tell him that I just called you and said I am on my way home, but my phone was about to die."

"Okay, I'll do that."

I went back and got in the bed. DeCarious was putting on his clothes.

"Where are you going?"

"Home. What are you doing? This is so messed up. Cherise, you're helping your sister have an affair."

"So you are leaving me in the middle of the night, because my sister is having an affair?"

"No, I have to get up early in the morning, but I think you are so wrong for covering for her."

"So what should I do—tell him she is cheating on him?"

"Do what you want to. I'll call you tomorrow."

Chapter 34

Cherise

I didn't get any sleep with all that happened last night. I was going to look crazy on camera today. I put eye cream under my eyes and put on a lot of concealer. But I still felt like I had the dark raccoon-eye thing going on. My sister and her drama were interfering with my relationship. I called her to see how she had made out.

"How did you explain everything to Dave?"

"I didn't. He didn't even really ask me anything. He knows he is getting paid back."

"So now are you going to leave it alone? You got him back."

"I'm not sure. I don't think I feel like being married anymore."

"DeCarious left last night."

"Why?"

"Because he had a strong opinion about the way you were treating Dave, and wondered why I was taking up for you when you were doing something wrong."

"Tell him to mind his business. Oh, and by the way, news lady, I like the picture of you and your defensive tackle boyfriend in the *AJC* today."

"What?"

"Yes, it reads, 'Now we know how Action 7 gets all their exclusive interviews with the Falcons.' "

"Does it really say that?"

"Yes."

"Ugh. I'll call you back." I logged on to my computer and pulled up the paper's Web site. And there were the pictures. We looked cute, but damn. I knew I was going to hear about it when I got to work. Oh boy, this was horrible. Not only had I been accused of sleeping with Paul to get my job, I was sleeping with the Falcons to get exclusives. I guess I was sleeping my way to the top. I was ready to call Gavin to see if he knew the gossip columnist. Maybe I could get a retraction. But you can't withdraw the truth, you just had to deal with it.

I received an e-mail from Mrs. Ellerbe. I hadn't seen her since the event. I guess that meant she'd seen the paper, too.

> *Cherise,*
> *Remember, we all have to have a social life, but as a respected journalist you have to make sure you don't become part of the news. You should always try to walk under the radar.*
> *Let's do lunch soon!*

DeCarious called and said, "I didn't get to recover from the e-mail before."

"You know our picture is in the paper."

"Yes, and I'm not happy."

"Why? You act like I'm an ugly broke dude."

I had to laugh. "DeCarious, it is not that. It's just I really don't need anyone in my—I mean our—business."

"Our business? I get it. You're ashamed of me."

"No, I am not. It is not that. It is just that it doesn't look good, babe. We know about us and everything else is not anyone's business."

"All right, Cherise."

I knew his feelings were hurt, but I didn't want to tarnish my reputation.

Chapter 35

Tanisha

I hated being under house arrest. I couldn't wait to get off. I was only two weeks in and I didn't know if I could make it. This was a mess. It was so hard to deal with. I just felt like sleeping, but then I couldn't sleep and my heart was racing and I was restless. I was gaining weight because I was cooking anything I could possibly think of. I wrote my grocery list and Tyrone picked it up. He was so happy to have home-cooked meals and me around. I could tell that he was thinking there was a future for us. I gave him subtle hints that there was not. I loved him for everything he had done for my children and me, but I was not in love with Tyrone.

I was not in love with being in the house, either. I was bored out of my mind. I felt like I was living the same day over and over again. Repetition is the devil's relative. I did the same thing every day. I got up off the right side of the bed, walked in the bathroom, turned the radio on. I swear the same song was playing. I awoke Kierra for school. While she was in the shower I was ironing her clothes and making her breakfast and packing her lunch. Then I cleaned up the living room and did the dishes. After that I took a shower and then got ready to watch all my shows. I loved *Cheaters*, *The Wendy Williams Show,* and *Maury*. And every day I be-

lieved the women when they said they were a thousand percent sure that the man was the father. I almost screamed at
the television: *Take care of your child, you deadbeat dad.*
Then I was always shocked when Maury read, "You are not
the father." However, even my favorite shows couldn't com-
bat my boredom.

After my shows I tried to work out. By working out, I
mean running up and down the steps, jumping in place, and
shaking my arms wildly. I have two workout DVDs but I was
tired of them, too! I had to move around. I was becoming a
real coach potato and my butt was hurting from sitting so
long. Then after my around-the-house workout, I pulled out
something for dinner, waited for Kierra to get home, helped
her with her homework, cooked dinner, waited for Tyrone to
come in, talked to him, watched a little more television, talked
to Alexis on the telephone, and got Kierra ready for bed and
then tried to fall asleep.

I was at the try-to-fall asleep part. Everyone was asleep,
but I couldn't close my eyes. I felt like screaming really loud,
because I felt like I was gradually going insane. My chest got
tight again and I was sweating. I had this overwhelming feeling like I was trapped and I needed to get out of the house. I
felt like snatching the ankle bracelet off and throwing that
stupid box and running for my life. Each time I felt like I was
going to lose it, I had to count to ten and take long deep
breaths. This couldn't last forever.

In the morning I called my probation officer and told him
about the tightening of my chest and throat and heavy
sweats, and I said I thought I might need to go see a doctor.
He got me a medical pass to go see a primary care doctor.
The doctor said I was physically fine, but recommended that
I go and see a therapist.

*   *   *

My therapist, Clare Sturgis, diagnosed me with panic attacks and mild anxiety. I had to go to her office, which meant I got to get out of the house once a week. Being able to leave the house was therapy enough. She was a very petite white woman. Her hair was short and red. She had a slender ballerina frame. She spoke to me in a very low, almost childlike tone. Her office was on Rittenhouse Square in a picturesque office space in the front room of her home. At first I didn't think I needed counseling, but it felt good to get everything out. I let her know about all the sweating and the tightness in my chest when I was excited. She said that I might also be depressed. I might have been depressed before I came home, but I definitely was not depressed now. I was actually happy. Even though I told her this, she still prescribed three different medications. I took them home because I just might need them, but I was determined to fight it on my own. I didn't want to become an addict relying on pills just to sleep. I just wished my life would start moving forward. I was going to be so grateful to walk my daughter to school, go to the market, have a job, and just live my life. I couldn't wait to do everything I used to take for granted.

Chapter 36

Adrienne

I had to do something about DeCarious, and fast. My time was running out. I thought I was gaining on DeCarious. I guess not. I had to get him away from this news reporter woman. I looked this bitch up and she's very successful. I read her bio on her station's Web site. She was okay. I don't care how pretty or educated she was. She wasn't going to mess my plans up of being a family with my baby daddy. I was about to call DeCarious and tell him a little white lie so he would rush to Philly and I could get him out of the range of that woman. I was not going down to Atlanta anymore. I needed him to be isolated so we could be one-on-one.

I called DeCarious's phone several times before he answered. As soon as he picked up I dramatically yelled, "De-Carious, Asia is sick."

"So y'all not coming down here this weekend."

"No. Why don't you come up here? She might feel better if she sees her daddy. She hasn't seen you in a few weeks. But I don't really want to put her on another plane. I think it is becoming too much for her."

"Yeah, you're right. Okay, I'll be up there. Let me check and see if I can get a flight."

DeCarious called me back and said that he would be in

town by 6 p.m. That was good, but the only problem was that Asia wasn't really sick.

Luckily, when I picked him up she was already asleep in her car seat. I could tell he was very concerned. He sat in the back with her and stroked her face lovingly. So I had to let him know his visit was not in vain.

Looking at him through the rearview mirror, I said, "I'm glad you came. Her temperature was like a hundred and two when I picked her up from day care. But now I just checked it before she took a nap and it is going down."

The next morning Asia was running all around. I had to act like it was a miracle that Asia was up and full of energy.

"Let me see if I can get an earlier flight."

"There is no reason to run home. We can take Asia somewhere and we can go grab something to eat later on. If you want to go home, I can check on the flights for you, but you're here now, so you might as well stay."

"You're right."

We took Asia to the Please Touch Museum, which had a bunch of exhibits for children. Asia really didn't know what was going on, but it gave us time to be a family. After the museum I told DeCarious my mom wanted Asia to come over and asked if he minded, since his flight left first thing in the morning.

After we dropped Asia off at my mom's, I asked if he wanted to stop and get something to eat. I had already made a reservation at a steak house. DeCarious wasn't aware of it, but the seducing into obedience had already begun. I was going to get him nice and drunk, feed him, then fuck him and send him home.

We were seated at a red leather booth in the restaurant and I could tell he was a little nervous and uncomfortable. He kept checking his phone, but I had something for all of that.

When the waiter came to our table, I ordered two Belvedere and cranberrys.

"You're going to drink both?" DeCarious asked.

"No, you are going to help me." I laughed.

"Oh, I am?" he said, looking down at the menu. "What's good here?"

"We are in a steak house, so I think you should order a steak."

"Okay, that's what I'm having then."

Our food was good. The evening was going as planned: I was feeding his belly and getting him relaxed so he felt good, safe, and secure, and then I was going to attack.

After our meal, DeCarious asked, "What happened to the old Adrienne? You're going to pay for dinner?"

"Yes," I said. "As I told you, I have changed. I'm a different person now." I looked down at the bill. It was one hundred and six dollars. I didn't want to pay it, but it would make me look less selfish, so I pulled the money from my wallet. This was nice.

When we arrived home, I played it cool and acted as if I wasn't going to attack DeCarious. He had no idea I was preparing for war. I told him, "You can sleep in my bedroom. I'm going to sleep. I'm tired."

I waited until I thought he was sound asleep. I opened the door and it creaked. He was snoring loudly. I slipped into the bed with him and pulled back the sheets. Damn, he still had his pants on. So I unbuttoned them slowly. I didn't want him to wake up and say, *What are you doing?* Once they were down far enough, I pulled his flesh out and placed it in my mouth. I took long pulls. It was thicker and sweeter than I remembered. His veins were widening with every kiss. He wasn't even awake, but his body was cooperating. When he finally opened his eyes, his dick was still in my mouth and it must have been feeling good to him because instead of stopping me, he grabbed the back of my head and brought it down farther. Perfect—I had him. He was palming the back of my head so hard I felt like I might choke, but I just relaxed my throat and kept going. Right before he was about to climax, I came up from under the covers and shoved his dick into my moist, accommodating pussy. He refused to look at me or kiss me. It was as if he was at war with himself for fucking me. He wasn't sure if he hated or loved me. He tried to resist, but my rippling, pulsating insides won. He furiously turned me around, pushing my shoulders down, which made my ass poke up at him. He slammed his erect dick in me and then he pulled my hair. He was ramming his body into mine so hard, my face was being mashed into the mattress and I bounced up and down. I was out of breath and didn't think I could take any more, but I had to keep going, so I got back on top of him like a reverse cowgirl. I brought my body down as he popped his up. With each jerk and rock I knew he was one step closer to being mine. Whatever he wanted, I was going to give him. Before long he couldn't control himself and he let his dick's moistness rupture all inside of me.

DeCarious's little reporter girlfriend had something to worry about now. A whole lot to worry about. My insides hurt from how hard and long I fucked DeCarious. Now she had competition on her hands. I knew better than to ask about her. I had to let him come around to the subject on his own. We wouldn't even discuss what happened, but change had come.

Chapter 37

Zakiya

I was determined to get into school. Adrienne was at work and me and Asia took the bus down to the community college. I finally was able to register for spring classes. When January rolled around I would be in school. California was on hold—I called Elena and told her and she said she was thinking about moving out here. I told her to come out and we could still get an apartment, and she could go to Temple or Drexel. That was one thing crossed off my list. The other thing was to call my aunt Tina. I wanted her to know that I was still doing the right thing and I wasn't going to be a failure.

"I just registered for school."

"That's good, Kiya," my aunt Tina said cheerfully.

"Yes, I start at the end of January."

"Okay, I am so proud of you. Don't let anyone stop you. I know you had to come back because of Vicky moving and everything, but that is just a minor hurdle."

"I'm not. I'm babysitting and living with this nice lady. She is a nurse. I'm going to do what I'm supposed to, Aunt Tina. I just wanted to say thank you again for sending me to California."

"You're welcome. Call me and keep in contact."

"Okay, I will."

After calling Aunt Tina I called Lisa. She was at work and couldn't talk, but told me to stop by over the weekend and visit her and the boys.

I came home and began cooking dinner and doing the laundry. I wanted the house to be nice for Adrienne. She had really been so nice to me.

I would watch Asia for free, because I loved living there and watching Asia was not a problem at all. Adrienne was teaching me so much. She took me with her when she got her manicures and pedicures. She always looked so nice and put together. Even when we just went to the market she was dolled up. And I saw how men treated her differently, because of how nice she looked. They were always speaking, asking for her number, wanting to pump her gas, or helping us carry something to the car.

She even took me to the Sephora store and bought me all this makeup and taught me how to apply it. It was a lot to keep up with, but she knew what she was doing and every man she met was nice and had so much money. I wished she would talk to my sister and help her so she could meet someone nice.

Chapter 38

Cherise

I looked at the phone all day at work, something I usually didn't have to do. Usually I had missed calls—today no calls. DeCarious had been so unavailable lately. The season was over and I should have been spending more time with him, but I was spending less. Last weekend he had to rush to Philadelphia because his daughter was sick, and I understood that. I was so confused. It was like he was trying to pull himself away from me. He had not called me all day. I really thought he was still mad from the entire Toni thing and our picture being in the paper and me not being excited about it. I did not want to call him out on his sudden change of behavior, because I didn't want to come off as insecure. But I didn't now what was going on with us.

I picked up. "What's up, DeCarious? You have been acting strange. Does this have anything to do with Toni?"

"Of course not."

"Why does it feel like you have been pulling back from me in the last few weeks?"

"I'm not pulling back. Babe, I'm just real busy lately. Okay, one week Asia was sick so you know I had to run to

Philly. Then the week after that I was handling business with my daddy."

I didn't want to ask him about my surprise trip for my birthday, but I needed to know. "Are we still taking a trip for my birthday?"

"Yeah, of course."

"Okay, can I get a hint? Bikini or boots?"

"Yeah, I'm not sure yet."

"But you're going to let me know."

"Yeah."

Everything felt normal. I guess I was overreacting.

Chapter 39

Adrienne

I didn't know what was up with DeCarious. He had sex voluntarily with me a couple of times and he was making an attempt, but I wouldn't exactly say I had him wrapped around my finger yet. I don't know, maybe I couldn't compete with his girlfriend. Maybe they were already in love. Either way, I wasn't going to worry about it. I tried. In the meantime I needed to get out and have some fun. Angelique was in town and we were about to go to a Christmas toy and coat drive. It was being held at this restaurant called Swanky Bubbles in Cherry Hill, NJ. I knew it was going to be so nice, and some potential money would be in attendance.

My mom had Asia because ever since I hired Zakiya, she has wanted to keep Asia more, and for free. I still paid Zakiya her salary, because she washes my clothes, folds up everything—even socks—and has my windows and mirrors sparkling. She doesn't even go anywhere, really. So I was going to let her get dressed up and go out with us. She was cute, could pass for over twenty-one, and had earned a night out with me.

On the way to the party we shared men tidbits with her. I wanted Zakiya to be on her job.

"Listen, Zakiya, any of these dudes want to talk to you, they have to spend money first. Like make a man chase you, make him wait, play games, be evil. Don't answer the phone every time he calls you," I said.

"And never, never, ever come home with a wet pussy and dry, empty-ass pockets," Angelique cackled.

I looked over at Angelique and said, "Don't corrupt her mind. She is not into any of that. But she is right. Don't give it up for free."

"Okay," she said, confused.

"Guess what? Shavone is writing a book," Angelique said.

"About what?"

"About all the athletes and rappers she dealt with. She is so serious, she is trying to find an agent or something," Angelique said.

"Tell her no one wants to read *The Hoe Trick Chronicles*. I don't know why every whore with a story, who has slept with a few celebrities, thinks she should write a book now."

"That's what I told her. She is the worst, but that's on her."

The party was the best, but it was a mistake bringing Zakiya. She kept asking questions and following me around like a little lost puppy. She looked mature and grown-up, but was acting like an excited teenager. She didn't know how to glide through the room and mingle on her own, and I didn't have the time to teach her.

Angelique spotted everyone. "That's a rookie. He is young—only like nineteen or twenty. He was just drafted by Oklahoma."

"Oklahoma College?"

"No, they have an NBA team. I think they used to be the Seattle Supersonics, something like that."

"Damn, wow. My radar is off. He is cute, too." He was

cute and he was worth so many millions, and I couldn't go after him, or let him go to waste. I waved to Zakiya to come here. She was sitting at the bar.

"What's up?" she said.

"Zakiya, there goes a rookie for you. Go sit over there next to him. Go say something," I said as I pushed her a little. Her chances were fifty-fifty. She was cute enough, but she didn't have any game.

Chapter 40

Zakiya

They pushed me over to talk to this tall guy. They said he was a rookie and that I should introduce myself to him. He was tall and had a baby face but a grown man's body. He had light brown skin with light chestnut brown eyes and a dark fade haircut and he towered over me. He was very tall—at least six-foot-five. Me introducing myself to him went against everything Adrienne schooled me on. She said I should never talk to a man, chase one, or let one disrespect me. She said men love it when you are evil to them and play. Now she wanted me to go up to this guy and introduce myself. I must not have moved fast enough because I felt her push me, and I stumbled into him.

"My bad," I said, trying to regain my composure. He held his long arm out so I wouldn't fall.

"You all right?"

"Yeah, I'm fine."

"I'm Jabril Smith," he said.

I almost forgot my name, but I managed to get it out and said, "My name is Kiya . . . Zakiya Lee."

"That's a pretty name."

"You want to get a drink?" he asked.

"No, I'm not much of a drinker."

"I'm about to go downstairs to the lounge. It's a little loud up here. You want to go down there?"

I told him yeah. We had a seat in the quieter lounge downstairs. He asked me where I was from.

"From across the bridge in Philly. I just moved back from LA."

"LA. I was a Bruin at UCLA until I got drafted."

"You did? That's nice. Did you like college?"

"It was cool."

"I want to go to college. All my friends went away to school."

"Why didn't you?"

"I didn't really have the money and I didn't want to leave my sister. Then I moved to LA and lived with my aunt."

"It's just you and your sister—no brothers?"

"Yeah, my mom died when I was eleven."

He looked at me. "You for real."

"Yeah."

"My dad died when I was eleven. My uncle Wendell raised me. My mom was working all the time, so Dell had me on the court practicing my game. He went to college, then he got kicked out. He didn't want me to make the same mistake."

"That's nice you had him in your life."

"Yeah, I was lucky."

Jabril was interesting and he seemed nice. We talked a little more and then I saw Angelique and Adrienne coming down the steps.

"Those are my friends. They are probably ready to go. It was nice meeting you," I said as I stood up.

"Oh, y'all leaving?" he asked as he stood up. "Zakiya, you have a number or something?" I gave him my number and he put it in his phone.

As soon as we left the party Adrienne asked if I got his

number. I told her I did and she screamed out, "I'm raising her right! Yeah, my rookie then snag the million-dollar rookie."

"Girl, you are about to be rich. When you get him in bed, turn him out. Suck his toes first, then suck his dick so hard your inside cheeks touch each other. Okay?" Angelique said.

I said okay, but I wasn't paying her any attention. How did she figure I was going to be rich just because I met someone with money? His money wasn't mine.

Jabril had already texted me by the time I was taking my clothes off and getting in the bed. He wanted to know if I was still up. I texted back that I was, and a few seconds later my phone rang.

Jabril's conversation was nice. He played for a team in Oklahoma—the Thunder, or something. They were new, and they were a team trying to build a franchise by drafting him to help this player named Durant. They were supposed to be the next Kobe and Shaq. He had a house in Cherry Hill, New Jersey, for his mom and had a house in Okalahoma City where his team was. We talked on the phone until I saw the sun come up. It had to be like 5 a.m. I told him I was going to sleep and he said he was about to go and get breakfast with his friends, but he said he wanted to take me out later on.

Adrienne made a big breakfast for me and her, and was about to go pick up Malayasia. Angelique had already gone home.

"Did you speak to that rookie yet?" she asked.

"Yeah, we are going out around three."

"You are?" Adrienne said as she got real excited and said that I needed to start getting ready after I ate. I didn't think that it was that serious, but Adrienne insisted it was. She curled my hair in big curls and painted my nails for me. She looked in her closet and pulled out cute fitted jeans and a pink and black shirt.

Around 3:20 p.m. I heard a horn beep twice and looked out the window. I saw Jabril, so I told Adrienne I would see her later. I was on my way out the door.

"Don't you dare run to the door. Let him get his ass out of that car and ring the doorbell," Adrienne yelled. I didn't see what the big deal was, but I said okay. "Also, have him open every door for you. If he doesn't do it automatically, just wait by the door until he opens it." I told her okay.

A few minutes later Jabril rang the bell and I answered. The first thing he said was that I looked so pretty. I said thank you and we walked to his car and he was a gentleman and opened my door. His car was nice—it was black with silver rims and detailing all around. I didn't even know what kind of car it was, but I saw a big *B* on the hood with wings. I think it was a Bentley.

"So what's up? What kind of food do you like?" he said as we got in the car.

"I like seafood."

"Okay. I know this place we can go to on Columbus Boulevard."

We pulled up in front of a restaurant called the Chart House. It was located on the waterfront. When we went in, a hostess came up to us and sat us at a table right by a window looking out over the water. I looked at the menu and decided what I wanted to eat.

"So when do you have to go back?" I asked him.

"Tomorrow. Enough time to have a little fun and then go back home before I get in trouble."

"Why would you say you would get in trouble?"

"Because I grew up in the worst part of Camden. I know

so many people who were murdered or in jail. I just feel lucky to be alive at nineteen."

"My sister and aunts told me to stay away from trouble and go to school, but I know people who were getting in trouble, too. I just walked in the other direction."

"Like I was telling you when I first met you, I just listened to my uncle about things because if it wasn't for him, I don't know where I would be. Because of him I'm getting paid millions of dollars to do what I love to do."

"Yeah, that has to be nice."

"It is. I think I like you, Zakiya."

"Why do you say that?"

" 'Cause like you're not trying to impress me, and you don't care about any of this. I like that. That's what my uncle told me—to find a regular girl."

"Oh, so I'm regular," I asked with a playful attitude.

"No, not regular like regular 'cause you're real pretty— but like a girl who's not fake or after your money. Hold up, let me answer this," he said as his phone began ringing. "Where y'all at? . . . I'm near y'all. . . . I'm about to eat. When I'm done I'll come through there. All right." He turned his attention back to me and said, "That was my friends. They want me to meet them and get another tattoo. How many tattoos do you have?"

"I don't have any."

"Oh, we are going to have to change that."

After dinner we met up with some of his friends at a tattoo shop on South Street.

"This is my family—LJ, and that's Chris," Jabril said. I waved and then he said, "And y'all, this is Zakiya." They said what's up and began to show him all the tattoos they were thinking about getting.

"Y'all have any pictures of a phoenix?" Jabril asked. The

tattoo artist, who was a stocky guy, brought a tattoo book over. He flipped through the book and then found a big bird with all these colors.

"That thing is huge. Man, a phoenix?" LJ asked. I took one look at that picture that he was about to get on his back and told him it was really big and maybe he should get something else.

"I know, but I like it. It represents a bird that rebuilds itself over and over. That's me. I had to rebuild so many times." He got the outline of the bird drawn. Then he looked in the mirror and said, "Yes, I want it just like that." He asked me if I wanted one, too, but I told him I was good.

Chapter 41

Tanisha

I knew Kevin would eventually stop being mad and let Jarell come over. He brought all his things over. I just stared at my child—I had missed him so much. I didn't know how I was going to make it up to him for being absent from his life. He was walking and trying to talk. I turned on Nick Jr. for him and just watched it as he played.

By lunchtime I was wiped. Jarell had so much energy. He was pulling everything off the sofa and laughing and running around. But I was enjoying every moment with him. I missed him so much and just hoped he would never remember that I wasn't there for him.

Kierra and Jarell were looking at me like I was crazy when I was running all around the house and up and down the steps. Kierra was home from school and I was beginning to get antsy. I didn't want to have an attack in front of them, so I ran.

"Mommy, the phone," Kierra sang as I grabbed the phone, out of breath.

"Hey, Kevin. Jarell is fine. He is sitting on the sofa talking to Kierra now while I do my running."

"Running where? You are not supposed to leave the house."

"I'm not leaving the house."

I got a little claustrophobic sometimes so I just opened the basement door and ran from the basement up to the second floor a few times, and then I felt okay.

"You need a treadmill," Kevin said.

"Yeah, I do, but by the time I get one, I will be a free woman."

"How was your day?" I asked.

"It was good. We won. You didn't watch?"

"I don't think it was on here. To be honest, I am so television and movied out. When you get Jarell back he may be spoiled because Kierra has been hugging and kissing him all day."

"That's okay. Y'all are just making up for lost time."

We talked for three hours. It was like our old conversations we used to have, when we first met. We discussed everything. He liked being back in the States, but he missed the slow pace and serenity of Rome.

Chapter 42

Adrienne

I hadn't come down to Atlanta to visit, and DeCarious was texting me like crazy, asking me where I was and what I was doing up in Philly. He said he missed his daughter and me and that he wanted us to come down. I wasn't sure if he cared, but I guess he did. I know I had DeCarious right on the edge, and hopefully my next move would push him over. I was on my way to Atlanta and I was going to tell DeCarious I was pregnant. Hopefully me being pregnant would be a reality check to him, that we needed to be a family. If DeCarious got really serious with this woman, she was not going to continue to want me around, and I'd be stuck in scrubs for the rest of my life. I was running out of time and had to get everything into place. I drove over to Walgreens and purchased a few home pregnancy tests. I was looking around the pharmacy to see if maybe I could pay a pregnant woman to pee on the stick. Yes, that sounds disgusting, but whatever. I looked at the box—two pink lines if you're pregnant, one if your aren't.

I had four pregnancy tests. Some teenage boys were standing behind me in line and their mother shook her head. *If only you knew what was at stake, lady.*

The lady at the register counted my money slowly, each

time dipping her finger on a wet sponge. Then she said it only takes one test to see if you're pregnant. I didn't ask her opinion.

I intended on faking a pregnancy test. Somehow I was going to make the test positive. Once home, I stood in the bathroom and then tried to draw a straight line. The first one was straight and the second one was crooked. So I opened the second box. This time I used the edge of the marker and made two perfect lines. I held it up to the light. They were straight enough. They were perfect. When I got down there I was going to set everything up.

Miss Anne was out and I had a little bit of time to execute my plan. I had everything situated. I had placed the abortion pamphlet and the pregnancy test in the trash can at the top. I propped it up with a bunch of toilet paper. As soon as he went into the bathroom he would have to see it.

"Adrienne!"

"Huh?" I said as I entered the bedroom. I let him show me the test and pamphlet.

I ran to the bathroom and started making vomiting noises. I flushed the toilet, washed my hands, put water in the inner corners of my eyes. I came out of the bathroom like I was flushed.

"Yes, DeCarious."

"What's wrong with you? What's this?" He was holding the stick from the pregnancy test.

"Nothing."

"Are you pregnant, Adrienne?"

"Yes."

"Why didn't you tell me?"

"You have another relationship, we are not married, and I just don't want to ruin everything going on in your life."

"So you are going to get an abortion? When did you take this test?"

"Earlier today. My period didn't come on and I felt it."

"You can't do this, Adrienne. You can't do that to my child—he could be my son."

"I know, but I can't be a single mom with two kids. My appointment is next week. I'm sorry for ruining your evening. I didn't want to tell you."

He sat on the bed. "Listen, let's think about this for a moment and at least let's try to pray on this to see what else we can come up with. I think I'm going to tell my parents."

"No, DeCarious. No, your parents would be so disappointed in us. Especially your mom. You know I've been going to church with her and everything. And how would she feel if we go through with it? She will be so angry."

"You're right," he said.

DeCarious came back home and he was a little bit intoxicated, but he wanted to talk.

"Listen, I've been thinking. I don't want you to have an abortion."

"So what does that mean, DeCarious? I'm not doing this on my own anymore. It is too difficult."

"You won't have to. What will it take for you to keep the baby?"

"I'm not keeping the baby."

"Adrienne, you can have the baby and I'll take custody, and you can do whatever you want. It won't be a burden on you."

"No, our kids deserve a family, DeCarious. A real family. Asia already has to go through security checks and plane rides to be with her family. I won't do that to another child.

I'm not going to bring another baby into this world without us being married."

"So what are you trying to say, Adrienne?"

"I'm saying I'm getting an abortion. I'm not going to be a single mom again, and that's it. There is nothing left to discuss." I got up and walked out to the bathroom, and just for pure drama I left and went home, and let DeCarious marinate on my pregnancy.

Chapter 43

Cherise

This morning I woke up not thinking, but knowing that this is a man's world. They run it. People can say women secretly run the world, but I know we don't. We are the weaker, dumber, and loyal sex. Men are the faster, smarter, no-emotions-feeling species. They are hunters. They prey on us, take us down, rip out our hearts, and then leave us for dead. At least that's how I felt today. I hated men—all men. At my job, I hated Paul, I hated sports. I wished I could go back to the news. They needed to hurry up and get someone in this position.

Every day at work was a constant reminder that I was involved with an athlete. And DeCarious had been so distant. He had not been calling me. We hadn't spent any time together in a week, and something just didn't feel right. A bunch of crazy thoughts flooded my mind. Maybe he met someone—but he was in love with me. Maybe he met someone prettier, more successful—but he was always telling me how perfect I am. I could hear it in his voice right now. *Cherise, you are perfect. You are the best thing that ever happened to me.* I thought, *If this is true, where are you, DeCarious?* Maybe I was overanalyzing. Maybe he had a good reason not to call or be in touch. I don't know, something had changed in my relationship with DeCarious. I wasn't sure what it was, but it didn't feel right. I felt like we were stable, and now the lines were blurred. Honestly, right now I didn't know if I was taken, or available. And I didn't feel this way a few weeks ago. But what I was sure of was that he hadn't spent any real time with me in weeks. This was ridiculous; I called his phone, texted him, and left several messages. No response. I was so concerned.

I'm so confused. What did I do? Maybe he's really upset. Maybe he thinks I'm just like Toni. It is all Toni's fault. How did I fall for this man so quickly?

I've called him and got his voice mail several times. It even seemed like he was intentionally not answering my calls.

I couldn't concentrate at all, going over what I did wrong in our relationship. This was so juvenile. Waiting for him to call me to find out what was going on with him. I was tired of calling Toni, but she was the only person who understood.

"Yes, sistah?" she answered.

"Toni, I'm still so confused. Last night I had a dream that he came to me and told me that he had to break up with me because he wanted to have sex with another man."

"Maybe that's it. He's a gay football player. Makes sense."

"Do you think so?" I asked Toni.

"Maybe. I mean, he is around all those men all the time."

I thought about DeCarious being gay—no, that wasn't it.

"You know what I think? I think his baby mom's probably smelled another woman on him," Toni said.

"No, I doubt it. He introduced me to his daughter's mother. She doesn't care anything about him."

"Well, just think positive. You will find out what's going on."

Chapter 44

Zakiya

I was going to go visit Jabril. We had been keeping in touch. I was so nervous. I changed my clothes several times; I had to make sure I looked perfect. I was wearing this cute royal blue silk dress and black peep-toe pumps Adrienne gave me. She was going to drop me off at the airport. She came in the room and asked me if I was ready.

"Almost," I said.

"Let me see what you have on." She looked me up and down and said, "Take those shoes and that dress off and put on some flats and jeans."

"Why? I thought you said always look good. I'm confused."

"Zakiya, let him think you are not trying to impress him. You just look too dressed up for the airport."

"Okay, why am I not trying to impress him? I thought I was supposed to look cute all the time." Adrienne had so many rules it was hard for me to keep up and follow.

"You are, Zakiya, but you have to make it look effortless. And right now you look like a first-time flyer, all dressed up in the airport. And you don't need two suitcases. You are only staying the weekend."

I went and changed my clothes as I was instructed. As I

took off my cute dress and put on jeans and put everything I needed into one bag, Adrienne ran off some more do's and don'ts. "I want you to compliment him, not his stuff—okay? Men like for you to appreciate them, not what they have to offer. You have to show him that you are not a dumb young girl who is easily impressed. Okay? Also, whatever you do, do not give him any. If you give him some, or act all excited because he paid for your flight, this will be your last visit. When he tries to show you his house, act like his house is just okay. His car is all right and you've seen much better. Just act nonchalant all weekend."

I shook my head yeah and took a mental note of all the things I was supposed to do and not do.

Once I was inside the Will Rogers World Airport in Oklahoma City, five texts came through from Jabril. He said he was outside circling the airport and to call him as soon as I was ready.

I'm glad I packed light, like Adrienne said. I didn't have to wait to get my luggage. I called him and said, "I'm at baggage claim, level one."

"Okay, give me a minute. I'll be right there." I sat and called Adrienne to tell her I had made it. She didn't answer. I just sat and watched the people get picked up as I waited and waited. Then I saw a car pull up. Jabril had sunglasses on. He got out of his car and gave me a hug. He looked so handsome. I handed him my bag like Adrienne said, and he took it.

I wanted to take a picture of Jabril's house, but I had to act mature and unimpressed, like Adrienne said. He pulled around back where there was a huge pool and a brown and redbrick deck. Across from the deck were tennis and basketball courts. Inside he had trophies everywhere and pictures of him when he was a kid.

We went to his game against the Golden State Warriors at the Oklahoma Ford Center. It was the first live basketball game I'd ever been to. His friends were texting during the entire game like it was no big deal. It was a big deal for me. I was taking pictures and sending them to Lisa. Everything was so exciting and noisy.

After the game LJ, Chris, and I waited for Jabril to change. Then we went out to eat and a strange man came out of nowhere and pulled up a chair to our table. It was so rude. I was ready to tell him to get up but before I could he reached out his hand to Jabril and said, "Jabril, my man, how you doing? My name is Sam."

Jabril didn't shake his hand and said, "What can I do for you, Sam?"

"Well, I called your manager a few weeks ago because I have a great opportunity for you. I can triple your worth in six months. I want to talk to you about investing in my company. I have a few guys from the Browns, the Saints, and the Nuggets on board. This is a chance of a lifetime."

"Sounds good. You got a card?" Jabril asked. "I don't have a manager, but I can have my uncle call and talk to you."

The man hesitated a little bit and said, "I wanted to talk to you, but okay, have your uncle call me." He then got up from the table.

As soon as he left Jabril ripped up his card and said, "Wendell already told me they have these pyramid schemes they try to get you involved in and take all your money. I'm not falling for it."

*   *   *

When we got back to the house LJ had some girl, and me and Jabril went downstairs to watch a movie. When it was time to go to bed I was so tired, scared, and a little nervous. I didn't want him to get the wrong idea. I liked him a lot. We had fun—I was enjoying myself, but he wasn't getting any.

"Where am I going to sleep?"

"Right here with me," he said, patting the space next to him. I got in the bed and lay as far away as possible.

"You are going to sleep in your jeans?"

"Yeah."

"That's uncomfortable."

"I'm fine—it's okay. I sleep in my clothes all the time," I replied quickly.

"Um, I don't allow any jeans in my bed."

I looked at him and I took off my jeans, folded them, and placed them on the nightstand at the side of his bed. I didn't know if I should tell him now or later that he was not getting any. I decided to wait. He didn't attack, but he did start kissing me on my lips and neck, and I let him. Then his hands began caressing my breasts while they were still in my bra. Everything he was doing felt good, but I didn't want him to get the wrong idea.

I sat up and said, "Jabril, we can't have sex because I'm a virgin."

"Are you serious? A real virgin—so you never had sex before?" he asked, shocked, and began sitting up.

"No, I never had sex before, and I don't want you to get the wrong idea. So if you want me to, I can sleep in the other room or downstairs."

"No, you don't have to do that. Lie back down. I'm going to put the television back on and we are just going to relax. I understand. I'm not in a rush."

I sighed in relief.

I think me telling Jabril I was a virgin made him try harder to get some from me. All night he kissed me and sucked on my breasts and neck. But at the end, several times he pulled his ruler-length penis out and whispered, "Please, can I feel it just a little? I'm going to use a condom."

"It's not that. I'm just not ready," I said as I got out of the bed, letting him know that I really meant it.

After several more attempts, he finally stopped. I thought he would get mad, but he didn't. I was safe for now, at least.

Chapter 45

Tanisha

I was watching *The Young and the Restless* when I heard a loud diesel engine. I looked out the window and saw a UPS truck was in front of the house. I opened the door and a man dressed in all brown said, "I have a delivery for Tanisha Butler."

"Tanisha Butler—you sure?" I asked. "What is it?"

He looked at the side of the box. "I think it is a treadmill."

"A treadmill?" I repeated as the driver began unloading it off the truck. It was a nice big gym-size one. I looked around the living room. I had no idea where I was going to place it. There was hardly any room, I thought as I moved everything out of the way.

I dialed Kevin. "Thank you, that was really sweet."

"I wanted to thank you for watching Jarell."

"No problem. He is my son. I miss him. I wish I could spend every day with him."

"I'll try to bring him over more often. My flight gets in after midnight. I'll pick him up."

"It's no rush. I can just keep him over the weekend. He can stay until after your game."

The first thing Tyrone noticed when he came home was the treadmill.

"Where did you get that thing from?" he asked.

"Kevin bought it."

He twisted lips and said, "I'll try to set it up for you." I could tell he was angry. "So he's buying you gifts now?"

"It's a gift for watching Jarell."

"I knew he was going to want you back sooner or later."

"Tyrone, it is not like that. Trust me, he has girlfriends and my only concern is being a good mom and putting my life together." I thought I convinced him. I was really trying to convince myself. I wondered if there was any hope for me and Kevin. I didn't want to read into anything.

Chapter 46

Zakiya

Jabril was in town and I went to visit him at his house in New Jersey. He introduced me to his mother, Claudette. She was really pretty with big bright chestnut eyes like Jabril. She was thirty-eight and looked like her midtwenties. I would have easily thought she was Jabril's sister. She was wearing Gucci high heels with a Baby Phat sweat suit. I'm not really into fashion, but I don't think Baby Phat and Gucci are two designers that should be worn together. I don't know. She had a bunch of expensive things on, but she didn't really look real cute like Adrienne and her girlfriends. She didn't really have too much to say. She asked Jabril for his car keys and for money. He happily gave her both.

When she left, Jabril's jeweler came over. He had these black velvet displays with all these diamond chains and platinum bracelets. Jabril pointed to a bracelet chain and said, "I want that butterfly chain for my girl."

"For me?" I said, shocked. "How much is this?" It was nice, but I didn't want him spending a bunch of money on me.

"Eight thousand."

I looked at him and said, "Don't buy me nothing this expensive."

He said, "Man, put that necklace on."

The jeweler's assistant came over and put it around my neck.

I walked over to Jabril and said thank you. He smiled and said it was nothing.

"Do you have anything else? Not as flashy. My unc don't like flashy stuff, but I want to get him a nice ring."

After the jeweler left Jabril said, "I want to show you something." We walked into the garage where he had a red Lamborghini.

We went for a ride.

"Why would you buy this fast little car, Jabril? You are too tall for this car."

"I saw one on television."

"You don't want to listen to anyone, Jabril."

We were going down the highway so fast. I looked at the gauge and it read 105 m.p.h.

"Jabril, slow down," I yelled, but he didn't listen. We were weaving in and out of traffic until the red and blue lights were flashing behind us.

"Can I have your license and registration?" the tall police officer said as he approached the car and began looking in at us.

"Here is my license. I don't have my registration. I just bought this," Jabril said.

"Okay, let me see your license." Jabril handed it to him.

The officer looked at the license then back at him and said, "Nice car. Listen, man, take this car home and get your paperwork together. And make sure you make Camden proud."

"I'm going to try."

"That was nice. He didn't give you a ticket."

"Yeah, it was," Jabril said as the light turned green and he sped off in front of the cop.

*   *   *

We had done everything that we weren't supposed to do. It was like no one knew how to say no to Jabril except for his uncle Wendell. I was in Jersey with him the entire weekend and was about to head home, because Jabril had to go back to Oklahoma.

Just as we were leaving, Wendell came in. He looked mean. He had his Bluetooth in his ear. "Your accountant called me, Jabril."

"And."

"And do you know how much money you spent in the last week?"

"I don't care. It's my money. I buy what I want."

Wendell wasn't half as tall as Jabril, but still walked over to him and said, "I know whose money it is. Just because you have it don't mean you have to blow it. Nobody is going back with you. LJ and Chris just be sitting here chilling. They need to go get their own jobs and to be in college somewhere, making their own way. And you can't be missing practice.

"People who have had millions have lost it all. It is easy. I didn't bring you all this way to get you here to let you fail. That's not going to happen. The party stops now. The girl can come back, but you're not bringing any of them hoodlums to Oklahoma with you. You have a job to do."

Wendell left and I was scared to move, but what he was saying was right. "You should probably listen to your uncle."

"I do, but he thinks he's my father. Let me get ready to get out of here. I'll have LJ take you home. You going to come and visit?"

I told him I would and gave him a kiss good-bye.

*   *   *

I came in the house and Adrienne's eyes widened as she looked down at my chain.

"This is this nice. He bought you that?" she asked as she flipped the chain back and forth.

"Yeah, he had his jeweler come to his house."

"Wow, this is beautiful. He bought you that. Oh, you are going to give him some." She laughed.

"That's why I came home. I can't give him any, Adrienne. I'm a virgin."

"You are? He will probably marry you. There aren't many of them left."

Chapter 47

Adrienne

Home sweet home, I thought as soon as I touched down again in Atlanta. I was getting tired of flying back and forth. I was going to have to somehow get DeCarious to get rid of his girlfriend and get back with me permanently. He'd been calling me nonstop, begging me to come back down and discuss what I was going to do about the baby. I somehow, some way had to get him to marry me. When he married me I would have my family and security, and then I could really get pregnant with his baby.

When DeCarious picked us up, he grabbed my bags from me and surprisingly gave me and Asia a kiss.

"You all right, babe?" he asked, concerned.

"Yes."

"You hungry?" he asked as he opened my car door.

"No. You can stop and get Asia something, but I keep having morning sickness and I don't want to throw up again."

Instead of going out, DeCarious was all about Asia and me. He took care of me and my pretend sickness all weekend. I sent him to the store to get me a bunch of things that I didn't need, like saltines and ginger ale.

"I just hope I feel good enough to go to church." I sighed.

"So why don't you just have the baby? I will take care of you," DeCarious asked.

"Decarious, there are no guarantees in life. I need security, I don't have a job, the lady got me fired, and I have Asia. It is just a lot on me right now. I don't know what I'm going to do."

He came in the bed and made love to me. I didn't have to seduce him any longer.

Sunday, we all got dressed and went to church. DeCarious looked so nice in his suit. The preacher just coincidentally was talking about men being the head of the household and how men need to step up to the plate and stop leaving women out there. Oh, how perfect. The heavens were smiling down on me. I saw DeCarious shaking his head a few times. I caught him looking over at me. I watched the pastor attentively.

That evening, after dinner, I did the dishes. I gave Malaysia a bath and went into DeCarious's room. I knocked on the open door. DeCarious was sitting on the bed in deep thought.

"You okay. You have been acting strange since church."

"I'm fine. I've just been doing a lot of thinking," he said as he blew into his hands.

"What's wrong, baby? You okay?" I asked as I walked in the room and rubbed the center of his back. DeCarious looked up at me and took another deep breath. I had a seat next to him. "You look like something is bothering you." I said as I touched his face.

He stood up and said, "Listen, Adrienne. I know we have been through a lot, and well, I just had a long talk with the pastor. I told him about our situation."

"Why did you tell him our business?"

"Because you can go to God with anything. Anyway, he said what I already knew."

"What's that, babe?"

"He told me not to abandon my family and whatever problems we had in the past, leave them there and start over new. And just to pray on every single thing. So long story short, I want you to have our baby and I want us to get married."

"Married?" I repeated back to him like it was the most absurd thing I had ever heard. "DeCarious, you have a girlfriend and you think I'm going to marry you just because I'm pregnant?"

"I'm going to break up with her. Listen, we can plan it now," he said as he got on his knees and put his head next to my stomach. "Adrienne. That's my baby in there. You could be having my son, and I don't want to get rid of him." I didn't say anything at first. I acted as if I was at a loss for words.

"DeCarious, stop." I tried my best to push out fake tears. I couldn't believe it. He was ready to marry me. Yes! Okay, things were moving way faster than I expected. I tried to gain my composure as I walked to the bathroom. What was I supposed to say to that? *Shit. Focus, Adrienne,* I thought. Okay, he wanted to marry me. I had to get him to do it now before someone or something changed his mind. I heard him coming toward the bathroom. I put my head down in my lap. He picked my head up off my lap.

"You okay, Adrienne?"

I stood and left the bathroom. "No, I'm not. I can't let you marry me because I'm pregnant."

"I'm not marrying you because you are pregnant. I'm marrying you because I love you, my daughter, and my unborn child. Please, I want us to be a family. I know I haven't been the best, to you or Asia, but I'm willing to change."

"I know, but what will everyone think? I don't want to be walking down the aisle with a big stomach and people thinking you married me just because I'm pregnant."

"We can get married before you start showing."

"Like a city hall or Vegas wedding?"

"Yeah, city hall, Vegas, whatever you want, Adrienne. Set it up. We can do it this weekend. I'm going to call my mom now and tell her," he said as he went to reach for his cell phone. I stopped him by wrapping my arms around his waist and giving him a hug. I set his phone down. "No, um, babe, if we are going to do this, let's just surprise everyone. I'm going to go online now and find tickets."

I convinced DeCarious that we couldn't wait for the weekend and that we had to get married now. I booked us a flight to Philly. I had already made plans for us to drop Asia off with my mom. I promised her money and a few days with her only grandchild, no questions asked. She was going to meet us at the airport. I couldn't risk waiting for Miss Anne to get home. I knew she would start inquiring about what we were doing and why we were going to Vegas, and I didn't have time for that. We flew from Atlanta, met my mom at security, and got our connecting flight to Vegas.

As soon as Asia was secure, it was time to finalize everything.

DeCarious wasn't saying too much. I could tell he was getting apprehensive.

"Babe, you look tense. Relax. Let's turn off our phones and just think about us."

"You're right. I was just thinking about calling my parents, but I will call them afterwards."

"Don't worry, babe. We are making the right decision."

In the busy Vegas airport all I could see in front of me was a colorful rainbow of red, orange, yellow, and green. Irony is a motherfucker and I love her. I met DeCarious's ass in Vegas and now I was about to get married to him.

We checked into our room where I changed into an off-white, short cocktail dress. DeCarious put on a black suit. The Little Chapel house was across the street from the license bureau. I already had paid for our package, so we had our wedding all set up.

A cab pulled up. We were going to get our license first. The woman on the phone said it only took about twenty minutes. Then all we had to do was walk across the street and get married. There were only two couples ahead of us—a young Indian and Asian couple and an older white couple. We filled out our forms and then handed them in. Within a few moments we were ready to be married.

We went to the Little Chapel. It was empty. I guess most rushed weddings don't happen on Tuesday afternoons. I couldn't believe this was going to happen. I was about to be Mrs. DeCarious Simmons. In the room where our ceremony was taking place there was a fountain with water flowing, and green vines looped all around it. My feet could not get to that altar fast enough. DeCarious was all smiles. He touched my stomach once more and looked up in the air, I guess to say another prayer. We said our vows and the moment I said I do, I gave him a kiss. I was so ecstatic. All I was thinking about was that I had won. All my hard work and all my planning and plotting had worked. I was now Mrs. DeCarious

Simmons. I realized I really did love DeCarious and though I wasn't pregnant yet, that could easily be fixed. Our baby would just be a few weeks late. DeCarious had a game, so we had just enough time to have dinner, gamble a little, consummate our marriage, and fly home.

Chapter 48

Cherise

I had to find out what was going on with DeCarious. I hoped we didn't move too fast and now he was scared I wanted to tie him down. He brought up the marriage talk, not me. He kept telling me I was going to be his wife and I was the one—not me.

I hadn't talked to my man in two weeks now and I didn't know how to feel. I knew he had my e-mail address, my cell phone number, and my adress if he wanted to reach me. I tried to just blame it on our schedules, like maybe he was just caught up, but the football season was over. *What could he be doing? Where the hell is he, and why hasn't he answered my calls?*

I just wanted to go to work and listen to my friends Alicia and Mary sing. Yes, Ms. Keys and Ms. Blige are on heavy rotation. Those two are the only people who understood what I was going through, because Toni really didn't. Her only advice was, *Girl, I already told you. Forget about him. Why are you tripping over a few months of dating someone? Get over it. If he hasn't called, that's your answer. I told you from the beginning that you should not get serious with an athlete.* And all I could tell her was DeCarious was different. He really cared about me. He really loved me. I wasn't crazy. I knew how he felt about me. But to be honest, I didn't know if that was true anymore. I kept asking myself what I did wrong, but I came to the conclusion that I didn't do anything wrong. It wasn't me, it was him that made our relationship go at an accelerated pace. He gave me an all-access pass to his life, which I didn't ask for, but I was foolish enough to swing it around my neck. I'm so embarrassed he had me around his family and friends. Why would he do that if he was playing games? And then all that stupid talk of us getting married. He had me believing I was really going to be Mrs. Simmons because he said it in front of everyone. I thought he was the one.

I was about to be sick. I needed answers. I wanted to call him, but he should call me. I felt like screaming.

Instead I called my big sister. "Toni, DeCarious has not called or texted me in weeks. I called him and he didn't answer."

"So, the honeymoon is over. If he didn't call you, he is not thinking about you, so just go ahead with your life and have fun. A man who wants you calls you."

"I know. I know, but I was just thinking maybe he is busy or he is going through something. Maybe he thinks we rushed our relationship. I don't know. I'm really confused right now, Toni."

"Well, he hasn't returned any of your calls, so just go to his house."

"I just can't go to his house."

"Why not? You go there and you have him explain all this to you."

"You're right. I'm going to go there."

"All right, call me when you get there."

Toni was right. I needed a logical explanation for why he had not returned any of my calls. I got in my car and drove to his house. I was in a rush and I needed answers. I needed

234 Daaimah S. Poole

clarity. If he was scared about our relationship, I would understand. Maybe we could slow down a bit. If he wanted to date other people I'd be upset, but we could work through it. I don't know. I just needed to know.

As I drove up to DeCarious's house, I saw his truck. I was so scared to knock on the door. When I did, he opened the door and said, very frankly, "What are you doing here?" He slid out the door and started walking toward the driveway. I followed behind him.

"What am I doing here? I haven't heard from you, DeCarious. What's going on?" I looked at him. He looked bothered, like he hadn't had a lot of sleep.

"Nothing's going on, but I can't talk to you right now."

"What do you mean, nothing's going on? I haven't talked to you in about two weeks. You haven't returned any of my calls."

"Cherise, listen. Can I talk to you a little later? I have a lot going on. We need to sit down and talk, and right now is not a good time and you won't understand." He had this coldness in his eyes as he spoke to me, like he wasn't my DeCarious. He was talking to me like I was a stranger. I felt myself becoming emotional. I didn't want to cry and reveal how much pain I was in right now. I could not detect if he cared or not.

"DeCarious, can you please talk to me?" I begged and grabbed his arm.

He snatched it away and said, "No, you have to leave, Cherise. I'll call you later."

I didn't want to get physical with him, but I felt like I wanted to grab him and make him stand still and talk to me. I didn't know who was in the house and I didn't want to cause a scene, but I wasn't about to leave until we talked and he gave me some type of answer.

"No, I'm not going anywhere. Make me understand what I did wrong. Please tell me what it is." I felt weak.

And then he said the words that all people in love never want to hear from the person they love. "It's not you." *It's not you* means, one hundred percent sure, it was me. What did I do wrong? My face began to scrunch up as I tried to hold the flowing tears back.

"But you just . . . we were perfect. You told me you loved me and you cared about me and you never felt this way about anyone so soon."

"You're right, we were perfect. I care about you, but you are not going to understand and I can't tell you right now."

I tried as best I could to hold back the tears. I didn't want to feel like a crybaby, but I couldn't help it.

"Cherise, don't cry. Please, don't cry." He didn't reach out to me, to try to stop my tears or pain. He just seemed more frustrated by the sight of my emotions. He grabbed my hand and pulled me toward my car and said, "Cherise, it's not you. We had something good. You are perfect, but I got married."

Everything stopped. I mean, he just told me he got married. What the hell? To who, for what, how, when, why? My sadness instantly went to anger. I couldn't believe this BS. "DeCarious—to who?"

"My daughter's mother."

"Are you kidding me? You married that crazy gold digger you were always talking about? The one who everyone said had a baby by you to take your money? The one you just introduced me to?"

"It doesn't even matter, but she is not like that anymore. She goes to church and she is pregnant. She wants to be a family now. I owe her that and I want all my children by one woman. I don't have to explain anything else to you, and if you don't leave right now I'm going to call the cops on you."

"Call the cops on who? Me?" I stood in shock for a moment. I didn't know what else to do. I was hurt. I felt tears streaming down my face. I was so embarrassed. I had to walk away, I couldn't let him see me cry.

I got in my car and drove away. I don't know how fast I was going. But I knew I had to get far away from his house before I did something I would regret. As soon as I stopped, I put my face in my hands and began to cry. How could I have been so stupid? How could I have been so naïve? I thought they weren't together, because he introduced me as his girl-friend. I met his mother. He had me around his daughter. He told me I was the one. I was the fucking one. How could he do this to me? *Damn it, DeCarious. I believed you.*

When I left DeCarious's house I was so furious. How? Why? I guess it didn't even matter. How embarrassing was this going to be? I was glad I was smart enough to always deny our relationship. I was so glad I told everyone we were just friends. This was just all too unbelievable.

Damn it. I was just trying to block the last half hour out of my memory. I would go crazy trying to dissect what I did that was so wrong that DeCarious would run and marry a women he despised. And he said she was pregnant—when and how did that happen? It didn't make sense, and I couldn't try to understand it. I took a deep breath and told myself *no tears, no tears,* as more dripped from the corners of my eyes. I felt like I didn't want to go home and cry and play a victim. I didn't want to go to Toni's house and hear I told you so. I wished I had somebody—anybody—to talk to. Just as that thought popped into my head, Gavin called.

"Hey, you."

"Hey, Gav. What are you doing?"

"Nothing. Sitting here working on a story. I haven't heard from you in a while. Wanted to just check up on you."

"That's nice of you. Where are you?" I asked.

"I'm home. Why? What's up?"

"I'm coming over."

"To my house? What for?" he asked in a high voice.

"Yeah, I'll be there in about fifteen minutes."

"Why now? What, you and your man having problems?"

I was already upset. I didn't need him to ask me stupid, but very accurate questions. "No, I'm not having any problems, but if you don't want my company—Never mind, I'm not coming," I said as I ended the call. Gavin called right back.

"I didn't say that, Cherise. I want you to come. I just wasn't sure why you were coming, but whatever the case I would love to see you."

I didn't respond. He had irritated me already. I should just go home, get under the covers, and sulk until it was time for me to go to work.

"Cherise, are you there?" he asked in a panic.

"Yes, I heard you. I'll be there."

Gavin was waiting for me in the lobby of his apartment building. He was all smiles. He gave me a quick hug. When we got to his apartment, he opened his door and asked if I wanted anything to drink. Yes, I did—several of them. I came in and I had a seat.

Several drinks and movie later, I didn't feel any better, but I knew what *would* make me feel better. I scooted over to Gavin and pushed him down on the sofa and began kissing him. He was so shocked he pushed me off of him.

"What's going on, Cherise?"

"Nothing," I said as I stood up and stood two centimeters away from him.

"Cherise, what are you doing? Stop—let's talk. What's going on? What's happening?" He was asking too many questions. Maybe he was gay and didn't know how to say it.

"Nothing is happening. I want this and so do you," I said as I took off my clothes and began undressing him.

He stopped me again and said, "Hold up, Cherise. What does this mean?"

"It doesn't mean anything. I want this and so do you," I repeated as I placed my finger in front of his lips, silencing him. He was still in a state of shock, but became a participant anyway. He took off his shirt and began kissing me all over. He went from my neck to my navel in a matter of seconds. After several moments of heated kissing, Gavin went into his wallet and grabbed a condom. He tore the wrapper and placed it on his erectness. I couldn't wait for him to enter me. I couldn't wait for him to make love to me, to make me feel good. I needed to feel like a woman. I needed to feel desired. He turned off the lights and then his warm body entered mine. It felt amazing. I needed it. I needed all of what he was giving me. For a moment my mind was off of DeCarious and all that he had just said to me.

But all I could think about was DeCarious. How I missed him. How he was supposed to make me feel like the way Gavin was making me feel. I wanted my man. A tear fell. My body started to shake and I started to cry again. Gavin stopped and turned the light on. I pulled the covers over my face.

"Cherise, are you crying?"

"I'm not crying."

"Yes, you are. Am I doing something wrong?"

"No."

"You're making me scared. Did I do something? Talk to me, Cherise. Are you okay? You have me feeling bad, like a rapist."

"It's okay. You're not doing anything wrong."

"No, something's up. I really like you, and I want you, but not like this." He pulled the condom off and turned the television on. "Talk to me, Cherise. What's wrong?"

"Nothing is wrong. Why did you stop?"

"Because I want you to talk to me and tell me what's going on with you."

"I said nothing—now let's finish," I said, holding tears back.

"No, not until you talk to me." I wasn't going to talk to Gavin about what happened so I got up and walked into his bathroom. I began sobbing quietly in his shower.

I came out of the shower fifteen minutes later. I still didn't want to talk. I just got in the bed and lay beside him. I wrapped his arms around me and nodded off. I didn't want to be with Gavin, but I couldn't be alone.

In the morning I didn't feel any better about DeCarious. I wasn't sure if halfway sleeping with Gavin was a good idea, either.

I went to work, and as I entered my building Toni was ringing my phone. I didn't really want to talk, but I answered.

"Where have you been? The last thing I heard from you was that you were going to DeCarious's house. So what happened? Where have you been?"

"Gavin's house."

"What? You spent the night with Gavin? Oh no, I don't like this. What happened when you went to DeCarious's house?" Toni asked.

"He pretty much said he is married and told me to leave before he called the police on me."

"Married! To who? And he was going to call the police on you? Oh hell no!"

"Yup, he said he married his daughter's mother, because she is pregnant again."

"But didn't you say he said she set him up with a baby before, and all she wants is his money? See, I hate women like that—using babies for a paycheck."

"Well, her paycheck is going to be big, because she is pregnant again."

"Oh my God, are you okay?"

"Yeah, I'm fine. I'm just going to act like none of this happened."

"I'll be over there after work." I was going to tell her not to come, but she knew I needed her. I was devastated. And poor Gavin, he must have thought something had changed with our relationship. He sent flowers and left a few messages today. I don't know how I am going to tell him that everything that happened was just a mistake. And it would never happen again.

Chapter 49

Adrienne

Our honeymoon was short-lived. Rock and Mr. Joe were in the driveway when we pulled up to the house in Atlanta. We got out of the car and they didn't say anything. They didn't speak, so neither did I. I walked into the house and saw Miss Anne sitting, arms folded, like she had a problem.

I spoke to her and she said, "Adrienne, I need to speak to my son." She did not even look at me and kept her eyes fixed on DeCarious. It didn't matter what she said. We were already married and grown and there was nothing she could do about it.

"Okay, babe. I'll be upstairs unpacking," I said as I gave him a big kiss. Before I reached the second step, I heard Rock ask, "Bruh, did you at least get a prenup?"

"We don't need a prenup. She is the mother of my children, and y'all going to respect that. There's nothing else to be said. She's my wife now. She is pregnant," DeCarious said.

"How do you know she is pregnant?" Miss Anne asked.

"Look, all that doesn't even matter. Ma, she took a pregnancy test and was about to get an abortion because we wasn't together and she didn't want to raise another baby by herself.

So I stepped up and did what I was supposed to do. Which is be a man to my family."

"But you didn't have to sneak off and get married!" Miss Anne yelled.

"Mama, since when are you so against marriage?"

"DeCarious, your mother is not against marriage. I just wish you would talk to someone before you make irrational decisions," Mr. Joe said.

"All I have to say is that's my wife, she is having my baby, and we are a family. Whoever don't like it, I don't know what to tell you," my baby said, shutting them all down. I stood at the top of the steps eavesdropping . . . silently laughing. *That's right, take up for me, baby.*

"Okay. Fine. I can't take this. I'm leaving."

"Why, Mama?"

"You have a lot going on, and I just can't sit back and watch this unfold. You know what you did and what you're doing," Miss Anne said.

I came down the steps. Miss Anne was still my girl, but she shouldn't be talking against me. It's all good being her grand-daughter's mother, but not her daughter-in-law. Whatever. I walked her to her car.

"Good night, Miss Anne."

"Good night, I'm not going to say I'm happy that y'all got married, because I'm not. I think y'all are rushing, and if y'all are pregnant, a lot of things need to be discussed."

"I know, but we are working everything out now, and I'm working on myself."

"I hope so, for you, Asia, and DeCarious. Good night. I'll call you tomorrow."

I lugged in my luggage from the car. I was thinking about all the things I needed to do. I had to get everything from Philly. And call my mother and tell her the good news. I had to see what I was going to do with my house, if I was going to sell it or keep it. For the meantime Zakiya could take care of the house and I could afford to still help her out until she found a job. I didn't want to leave her with no job and nowhere to stay.

As I unpacked, DeCarious took a shower and his stupid family was still calling and texting.

Rock sent him a text and it read,

THINK LONG AND HARD ABOUT WHAT YOU ARE DOING AND WHAT SHE DID TO YOU. THINK ABOUT WHY Y'ALL PARTED WAYS THE LAST TIME.

Instead of DeCarious responding to Rock and his stripper-loving self, I responded. I deleted his text and typed,

ROCK, IT'S OVER. THAT'S MY WIFE. RESPECT THAT. THERE IS NOTHING ELSE TO BE SAID.

Then I deleted both texts and put DeCarious's phone back.

DeCarious came out of the shower and I grabbed him. I had to show him that he made the right decision and make him uber happy.

"I can't wait until the baby gets here."

I guess I better get working on that.

"I can't wait either, DeCarious. I am so happy to be your wife and to have our family," I said, hugging him but thinking I need to get pregnant ASAP. When I got pregnant with Malaysia it was totally a surprise, but before DeCarious I tried for a few months to get pregnant and it didn't work out. But I'm not on anything now. I'm going to go visit an ob-gyn and get this baby stuff happening.

Chapter 50

Zakiya

I really liked Jabril. We always had fun. We were silly together. He told me he could be himself with me, that I would play video games with him, but I knew how to be sexy, too. And as much as he liked me, I knew time was running out. I wanted to try it, but I was just so scared. The other night, when he just put the head of his long friend near the rim of my vagina I wanted to cry. But I was going to have to have sex with him soon. Like real soon. Like right now.

I was back in Oklahoma again, at Jabril's house. We were both naked and coming out of the shower. He began kissing the side of my face. I tried to relax. He inserted one finger and slid it in and out, then he tried two as far as his fingers would go. It didn't feel so bad. I pushed my hips down to meet the end of his fingers. He kissed me on my lips again.

"Please, Kiya, please can I try it now? You're wet. I know you are ready. It is not going to hurt, and if it does I will pull it out if you tell me to. I promise."

"Okay, okay. But we have to use a condom."

"Man, why? You are a virgin and I'm good. You're really going to make me use a condom? I don't have anything—you don't have anything."

"Jabril, I don't want to get pregnant," I said.

"You're not going to get pregnant, and if you do, so what? We should have a baby. We would make a pretty baby—all that long hair like her mommy, and light eyes like me."

"Jabril, I want to go back to school and do something with my life."

"I'll pay for you to go to school. I can buy anything I want in this world. I can. I don't know, I was just thinking, what if something happened to me? I need a little shorty to carry on my name. I'm going to call him J. S. the second."

"No junior." I laughed.

"No, junior is too back in the day."

"So—what, Jabril? I'm serious. I don't want a baby yet."

He sighed then and went to go grab a condom. I lay on my back on the bed. He began kissing my neck and rubbing on my breasts. I felt relaxed, and then I felt him fumbling around with a condom and then the head was pushing through. It felt like my entire body was ringing as he gently forced his body through mine. I knew I had to take the pain. He was huge, and I felt like he was tearing my body apart. He was taking real slow, deep, delicate strokes. He pulled me in closer and went in deeper. I just took it all in. I knew the pain couldn't last forever. Adrienne told me to think about something else.

"Zakiya, this feels so good. You feel so good. You're my girl, right?"

"Yes, Jabril," I whispered back.

"I'm the only one who is ever going to have this, right?"

"Yes."

"Forever."

"Yes. Forever, Jabril."

Chapter 51

Adrienne

My first order of business as Mrs. DeCarious Simmons was to treat myself to a new car. I couldn't decide if I wanted a Mercedes-Benz, BMW, or Range Rover. I really wanted a Bentley GT, but I'd wait on that. I walked out of the Benz dealership because they didn't have an E550 in white. So I went to the Range Rover dealership and bought a white-on-white Range Rover. It was beautiful. The insides smelled so new. My white leather was plush, buttery, and so soft. It only had five miles on the odometer. I cruised down the highway in my new car. I loved it.

I was so glad to be back and to have money. Having money is like . . . I can't describe it. Of course you want your health and family. But money is better than a best friend. Forget what they say, money doesn't make you happy. It doesn't, but you have less issues when all your bills are paid. The only problem I wanted to have in my day-to-day life was Gucci or Louis Vuitton, or Christian Louboutin or Manolo Blahnik.

Right after the car dealership, I went to the mall and went crazy. The sales girls—white, black, didn't matter—they just knew if they waited on me they were going to get a big commission. People just treat you differently when they see you coming. Like, *Hello, money, how you doing?* It is the sparkle in your eye and the way you carry yourself. People can just tell.

While on my spending spree, my phone rang. It was Angelique.

"Where have you been? I've been calling you."

"Girl, my phone has been off. I'm about to get this number changed so no one can call this number and get me in trouble, 'cause I'm married now."

"Shut up. You got your baby's father to marry you?"

"Yes, I did."

"Oh my God, you are my shero for real. How did you do it?"

"I told him I was pregnant again."

"Are you?"

"No, not yet. I'm working on it, though. At first I was going to act like I lost it, because I didn't feel like being all big, but I have to do it now because his family is hating."

"He didn't ask you to take a test?"

"No, I was a step ahead of that. I put my positive pregnancy test and abortion pamphlet in the trash so he could find it."

"That was good. Well, I know a real good fertility doctor down there. My friend was trying to get pregnant and had twins. I can get the number for you. And he can hook you up and you can be pregnant in weeks."

"I need that number, 'cause I think right now he thinks I'm like two months. I got to get pregnant fast so the dates won't be too off. I can just act like the baby is coming late. He is dumb—he won't know any better." I laughed.

"You married. Princess married. Damn, I gotta get married."

"Angelique, you always get someone with some money."

"I know, but I'm having a dry spell right now. And it is not about getting it. It is about keeping them for the long haul, not just be their girl for a few months. I'm tired of going city to city."

Chapter 52

Tanisha

I had two weeks until I got off of house arrest. I already knew what I was going to do. I wrote a list of everything I ever wanted to do. I wanted to run in the park on Kelly Drive, take the children to the beach, to the zoo and just enjoy my freedom. I could not wait.

I called my Mr. Neal. "How long before you get up here?"

"I'll be there."

When he arrived, he inspected the box and then took the ankle bracelet off and my leg felt so much lighter. I felt like a dog and someone left the door open. I was free. I walked around the neighborhood. I took in the sun and the cars passing by. I had been to hell and back, and now I was off punishment. I called Kevin.

"I'm outside!"

"That's what's up. So when are we going to go out? I promised the kids I would go out with them tonight, and then after that maybe you and I can go out."

Chapter 53

Zakiya

"Didn't I tell you to watch these fast girls? You just got in the NBA. Damn it! It didn't even take your dumb ass a year to get somebody pregnant. I told you one would try this on you. I knew I should have sent that girl home, too. Everything is at stake. All these years, all my hard work. For what? For this? I can't believe you, Jabril. What's wrong with you?" Wendell yelled as he paced back and forth in the living room.

"She didn't try to get pregnant by me. I got her pregnant. I wanted a baby by her. I don't care—I have enough to take care of her and a baby," Jabril said.

"That's not the point, boy. You are trying to get endorsements and everything else. Now you are just like any other player. You got tattoos all over your body and a baby mom. Why do I even bother? You are supposed to be a role model. You are not supposed to be a father yet. You are a young kid. Let me ask you—are you to ready to marry her?"

"No, not today, but when I'm like—when I'm old, like twenty-five or something."

"I can't believe you. You're so stupid."

I couldn't believe Wendell was accusing me of trying to get

pregnant. It wasn't my fault it was Jabril's. He wouldn't stop touching me. Bril would come in from practice, all energized and find a way to get me naked. It was Bril's idea for me to stay here. But now Wendell was acting like this was all my fault. I don't even know how I became pregnant. Almost every time we had sex we used a condom. The only time we didn't use one is when I would wake up and Jabril would already be having sex with me, or at least he would be trying to have sex with me. I'd be half-asleep. I told him to stop and he promised me that he never came inside of me. Now I know for sure that was a lie. I didn't even realize I was pregnant until my breasts became so sore every time he would touch them. I asked Claudette what did it mean, and she said my period was probably about to come on and took me to the doctor to make sure I didn't have the flu. That's when the doctor told us that I was expecting.

Jabril was scared to tell Wendell, but Claudette said if he didn't tell him, she would. So he decided to tell him this morning. All I know is I don't want a baby. I don't want to be stuck. I'm mad. I don't want an abortion, but I'm not ready to be a mom. I texted Lisa first and told her. I told her not to tell anyone. I didn't know how she was going to react, and she texted me back *Congrats*. Within a few minutes my aunt Darla was on my phone.

"Congratulations, little lady."

"Aunt Darla?"

"Yeah, it's me. I'm so glad me and Tina got you out of Philly. I looked up your boyfriend, and Vicky told me how famous and rich he is. We are all so proud of you." Was she serious? Why was she proud? She asked for tickets and wanted to know when I was coming to town.

Immediately after I hung up with Aunt Darla, Aunt Tina called me screaming.

"What is this nonsense. I hear you're pregnant?"

"He plays basketball, Aunt Tina."

"And that doesn't mean he is going to be a good father. All I can say is I tried, Zakiya. I wanted so much more for you. I don't have anything else to say." And she hung up on me.

I started crying and then I called Adrienne. I told her I was pregnant and I didn't get the reaction I expected. She almost sounded excited.

"Adrienne, I don't want to be pregnant. How am I going to take care of a baby? I'm not ready. I don't have anything. You even said 'don't be anyone's baby mom.' "

"Those rules don't apply in this situation. Look who your baby's father is—he is a millionaire. Zakiya, you are one of the most compassionate people I know. You are going to be a great mother. You took great care of my daughter and your nephews."

"But I don't know how I'm going to go back to school with a baby. I am so mad at him."

"Sweetie, the guy you are with has a lot of money. When you are ready to go back to school, you'll be able to go."

"But I don't want to be with him for his money."

"You are not with him for his money. Let me tell you something: Love will get your ass. Love is what your sister has. Your sister tried to commit suicide. He just walked away. That's love. You might not love him yet, but you will grow to love him. What you have is security, and security trumps love any day. You hear me?"

"Yes," I said.

"So I don't want to hear any more of this crazy talk. Forget everything I said about not getting pregnant and ruining your life. This is a different situation. You don't know how lucky you are. The rest of your life is already paid for." I couldn't listen to Adrienne talk. She kept saying I was lucky, but I didn't feel cute.

Jabril came in and said, "I don't care, I know the truth, Zakiya. I'm never going to leave you or our child. Can you stay here and live here with me? I don't want you to go back to Philly."

Chapter 54

Cherise

My condo was an official No Slow Music zone. I refused to listen to any more love songs. I no longer wanted to hear how good love was. How no one ever made me feel like this, I'm ready for love, it kills me you are not around. No, no, no. I couldn't tolerate any of that nonsense right now. I didn't care if it was praising or condemning love. Only hip-hop or party music like Black Eyed Peas or Lady Gaga. I would rather hear some hardcore rapper saying no one was better than them, forget the world, and the hell with everyone. Yeah, that was how I felt. Forget everyone.

My baby, DeCarious, was gone completely. He never called one time. Not one time, to say I'm sorry, apologize to me, anything.

It was just still so hard to believe that I experienced our relationship on my own. I was wondering, how did we fit a lifetime into four months? We weren't even together that long, but he left his mark on my life. Maybe the entire relationship was a game to him. It hurt because I felt duped. Like the months I spent with him weren't real.

I found myself going to sleep every night dreaming, wishing, praying that DeCarious and I were back together. I just hoped it didn't take another two years to meet someone else who I connected with. I think that's what made the sex even better, because we were connected emotionally and physically.

Oh, how I missed my man. I still called DeCarious my man. Him loving to just taste me, him sucking on my breasts. I needed him. I felt warmth growing in my pelvic area. I wished he was here, to take care of that feeling. I needed DeCarious.

I would have given anything to turn over and feel him on the other side of the bed. I actually felt so mad at myself for wanting him. He left me with no explanation and made me track him down to tell me he married his no good baby's mother.

It was the same thing every day, doing the best job possible. Come home from work and then have a glass of wine. Get in the bed and drift off to fantasyland. In my own little world. DeCarious and me—every night I went to sleep, I was thinking about DeCarious. When I closed my eyes we were still together.

I wished I knew what I did wrong to make him leave me, to just out of nowhere tell me he loves me and then go marry his child's mother. It didn't make sense. I wanted to reach out to him. I thought of calling him. But I couldn't, even if he was interested in me and he wanted to have a relationship with me again. I did not want to be his mistress. I was so close to having DeCarious to myself and I didn't know what I did.

I awoke and went to work. This was going to be hard. The best descision I ever made was to keep this relationship a secret.

Chapter 55

Adrienne

It had been a month and I was still not pregnant. How the hell did Zakiya get pregnant and I didn't? Go figure. I was so happy for her. I raised her right—she was going to be set for the rest of her life. I just had to get my own situation under control. I looked at the calendar, trying to see how off schedule my baby projection was going to be. I'd been fucking this dude nonstop and still nothing. I was so mad last week when my period came on. DeCarious was trying to touch me and feel all over me. I had to stop him and hide my tampons. In front of him I've been eating everything and trying to wear baggy clothes. Faking my pregnancy was a mess that was becoming a nightmare. I even had to act like I went to my first two doctor appointments. Most people waited for their period to come on—I wanted mine to go on a forty-week vacation. Shit.

DeCarious came in the house so happy. Asia and me were on the sofa watching television. "How are my girls?" he said as he kneeled down, kissed my stomach, and said, "Hopefully that's my son. Babe, when's your next appointment? I want to go with you. When are we going to find out what we are having?"

"I have to go every month, the same thing like with Asia," I said, changing the subject.

"Okay, because I just want to do everything right and be there for you."

"I know, babe," I said as I got off the sofa to answer my ringing phone. I didn't recognize the number but I answered anyway.

"Hello."

"Mrs. Simmons, this is Deirdre from Neiman Marcus."

"Hi, Deirdre. What's going on?" It was a shame all the saleswomen knew me because I had been there so much in the last month.

"I know you would like these shoes I have. I only have two pairs of size eights."

"Okay, I'll be right there," I said, ending the call. I told DeCarious I was running to the mall. They would be the perfect shoes to wear out with Angelique when she came to town tomorrow.

I was looking in the mirror getting dressed to meet Angelique. We were going to get drinks then hang out a little. Miss Anne was going to watch Asia while I was out. I was trying to leave before DeCarious came home and asked a million and one questions. I was almost out the door when DeCarious came in.

"Where you going?"

"Out for a little bit with my friend Angelique. She just came to town."

"I don't want you going out."

"DeCarious, kiss my ass," I said under my breath. My friend was in town and I was going out. I had been stuck in the house playing the good wifey.

"I'm only hanging for a little bit, DeCarious. I don't go out all the time. My friend is in town."

* * *

We went to the Key Club. It was so much fun. I had been in the house playing wifey and had forgotten about how much fun I have when I go out with Angelique.

I had one of the best nights of my life. I dropped Angelique off at her hotel. I was tipsy as hell. I didn't want to go home, but I couldn't stay out all night. I could blame being sick in the morning on my false pregnancy. When I got home, I tiptoed in the house, took a quiet shower, and got in the bed. I really overslept—it was one before I got up. I wiped my eyes and walked downstairs to the living room.

"Morning, baby. I'm hungry—you going to take me to get something to eat?"

"No," he said, looking straight ahead.

"DeCarious, why are you starting to act like you are in your little mood?"

"I'm not in no mood."

"Well, why are you being short?"

"I'm not being short with you."

"Okay, well, you said you were taking me out to get something to eat. I don't understand what your problem is. If you are going to start on your bitch shit again, let me know so I can leave and have lunch by myself. I'm hungry and this baby is hungry."

"Yo, you really get on my nerves sometimes," I swear he said slowly.

"Okay, so what—I'm your wife and sometimes I'm going to get on your nerves, but I want to go to dinner and you are going to take me."

"You are so immature sometimes."

"I am hungry. I want food!" I screamed.

DeCarious dug inside of his pockets, took out a few hundred dollars, and threw them to me. "Well here, take yourself to lunch."

"I hate you, DeCarious. I don't know what your problem is, but don't throw any money at me."

"Get the fuck out my face then."

"Okay, I don't have any clue what's going on. I'll get something to eat by myself. And then I'm going to the mall and I hope you like that," I said as I walked toward the door.

"Come here, I'm sorry," DeCarious said as he got up off the sofa and came to the door.

He grabbed me and I pulled away from him and said, "No, I don't understand. What's going on? You change from day to day."

"I don't know. I just be tripping sometimes."

"So you are going to take me to lunch?" I asked.

"Yeah, let me put my clothes on." He hurried and put his clothes on. We went to this steak house. I sat in the car and waited for him to open my door.

"Pull up to valet."

"They don't have valet here," he said.

"What? I don't want to eat somewhere that doesn't have valet."

"What?"

"You heard what I said. You think I want to eat somewhere where they don't have any valet?"

"You eat at restaurants without valet."

"If they don't have valet they probably aren't four stars. So you need to start this car and take me somewhere else."

"Yo, Adrienne, you tripping."

"I'm not tripping. Take me home," I said. DeCarious made a U-turn and began heading toward home.

"I can't believe you had me get dressed and ride all the

way down here for this. You asked me to take you to lunch and I did. I do everything in my power to please you, but you still want to act like a bitch."

"Oh, now you want to call me a bitch. Fuck you, DeCarious. What are you going to say to me? You are getting on my nerves. You have something you want to say, say it."

"Man, my mama was right."

"Your mama was right, what?"

"My mama said I shouldn't have married your ass."

"I don't get what that lady said about me. Your mother ain't nobody to be judging anyone. What the fuck did she mean, you shouldn't have married me?"

"She said you ain't nothing but a gold digger and all you want to do is take my money and that's the only reason you married me."

"That's not true, DeCarious."

"It is true. All you care about is yourself and how much money you have and can spend. Do you even love me? Do you even care about me? Do you even care about our daughter? What have you done since we've been married but spend money, go to the mall, go to parties, buy cars, spend money? I got my fucking Amex statement yesterday. You spent nineteen thousand dollars in one month. What could you possibly have spent that much money on in one month? I'm not rich. I'm doing okay, but the way you're spending my money, I will be in the poorhouse. I'm starting to think you're putting money to the side or something. I got the statement right here. Don't tell me no, because I see it. If you love me so much, y'all saying like tomorrow if I don't have any money I'm not going to have you. If it's all about the money, then I don't want to be with you."

"DeCarious, it is not all about money."

"But listen to what you're saying: If I don't take you to a restaurant with valet parking, then you can't eat there."

"No."

"You just said it. I don't know about this. I don't know if we should be married. I love my daughter and I love you, but I'm not sure if this could work out."

"Yeah, well guess what? We are already married and ain't nothing you can do about it. You don't give up on a marriage that quick."

The rest of the ride he remained silent. He was driving so erratically I put on my seat belt and closed my eyes. But even with my eyes closed I could feel him swerving lane to lane and going fast.

We pulled up to the house and I got out of the car and went in the house and slammed the door.

I said to myself as I went in the house, *How did he know I spent all that money? Nineteen thousand?* I tried to find receipts. I really had to get my spending under control. I couldn't believe it. It is just that I felt so powerful every time I swiped a credit card. There was just so much that I wanted. And since we've been married anything I ever wanted I have been able to buy. I loved DeCarious. I didn't want to lose him. *How can I make this up to him?* I asked myself as I paced back and forth in our room. His birthday was coming up—I could give him a party. I could give him a surprise party. I would call his mom and everybody would be happy and then he wouldn't be mad at me. I frantically wrote on a yellow notepad, plotting and planning DeCarious's party. *His party will be so nice, he won't think about divorcing me. I don't want a divorce. I like living this life. I like going into the store and buying whatever I want. I don't want to leave him and I don't want him to leave me.*

I was going to invite everyone to the party. All his friends and family, even though his family despised me. But I would smile and bear it because it was not about them. It was about me and my daughter and our happiness. I needed security. Who wants to go back to getting up every morning and going to work? Raise your hand if you want to go back to the nine-to-five job. Not me. I wasn't raising my hand.

I was going to start a company or some kind of business so I could have my own money. Nineteen thousand in one month? That is crazy. I can't do that anymore. That's too much.

Chapter 56

Zakiya

I was so tired and drained. I was getting fat and constantly throwing up. I got big fast. I was only three months and my stomach was poking out a little. I think I was gaining weight so fast because I didn't have anything better to do than eat and watch movies.

Oklahoma was so boring. When Jabril was not here, I had nothing to do and nowhere to be.

Me and Claudette went to the mall all the time and we ordered everything off the menu—lobster tails, shrimp, juicy steaks. Then we went home and had a buffet. I was trying to hold back, because I was so scared of getting stretch marks like Lisa. But I was really scared of how it was going to feel when the baby came out. I was looking online and they say it feels worse than any pain you ever experienced in your life. I read sex makes it easier. So I was having sex with Jabril a lot. I didn't want the baby to split my insides open. Claudette said I was going to have a real big baby, because Jabril was almost ten pounds at birth. I might have to get a C-section. I hope not.

Jabril traveled so much. They had eighty-two games: forty-one at home, and forty-one on the road. I thought about going home for a few weeks, but he wanted me to stay there. He called me or texted before the games. After the games, he was usually so tired he would go back to the hotel and sleep or head to the airport to go to the next city for the next game.

When he was away, I missed him, but he sent me flowers, teddy bears, and presents. That made me feel good, because at least I knew he was thinking about me.

But it wasn't all bad. One thing I realized is that people treat you really nice when you are pregnant. When I walked through the mall someone would always open the door for me, and Wendell and Claudette acted like I was carrying a baby king in my stomach. Jabril called the baby JS2 and talked about him like he was already born.

I missed being in Philly, but I knew I had it so much better here. I'd been calling Lisa, but she had a new boyfriend and was always out. Adrienne checked in on me and I called Elena, too. She couldn't believe I moved to Oklahoma.

Claudette knocked on the bedroom door and said that my phone was ringing downstairs. She had already answered it for me. She handed me the phone and left.

"Hello?"

"Hey, Cousin."

"Who is this?"

"Your favorite cousin . . . It's Jade."

My favorite cousin? What did Jade want? I thought. "What's up, Jade?"

"Cousin, I heard the good news. Congratulations. You are so lucky."

"Thank you. So what's up?"

"Nothing, really. I was calling you because I was on this Web site, SkirtsOnTheScene.com, and I saw your boyfriend hugged up with all these girls at some club in Miami called the 400 Club."

"Really?"

"Yeah, and there were girls all over him. But you guys are still together, right?"

"Yeah. Why do you ask?"

"Oh, nothing. Then I wouldn't worry about those girls. They are just groupies."

"Groupies? Let me pull up the Web site." I typed in the Web address and scrolled down, but I didn't see what she was talking about right away. The site had stories about Kanye West, Beyoncé, and Jay-Z. Then I saw a picture of Jabril with two model-looking chicks. They were kissing him on each side of his face. In the next picture he was sitting down with his arms wrapped around all these other girls.

"Do you see it?"

"Yeah, I see it. Let me call you back, Jade. Thanks."

"No problem. I saw it and was like, let me show my cousin. I think she needs to see this. You know, family have to stick together."

"Yeah, thanks," I said and hung up the phone and began looking at all the pictures. I scrolled down with the mouse and realized there were one hundred and fifteen comments underneath the pictures. It was just random crazy stuff like, *The rookie of the year can get it.* Then another read, *I met him in Miami. Mad nice, he was buying all the drinks. I wonder if he has a girlfriend* was the next comment. *Who cares? I know how to spend all that money,* someone answered.

While I was sitting here, pregnant with his baby in my stomach, he was in a club taking pictures and buying drinks. I didn't understand. He told me he was going to sleep when I talked to him last night, because he was tired. He said he had been to Miami so many times it wasn't a big deal. But that was a lie. He was having fun partying with all these girls. I was beginning to get angry, but then my anger became fear. How about if he liked one of these girls better than me? Or how about if they were prettier and really skinny, and he fell in love with them and broke up with me? I didn't know how to handle this, so I called Adrienne.

"Adrienne, Jabril is on a Web site with all these girls at a club in Miami, taking pictures."

"Huh, what are you talking about?" Adrienne said.

"My cousin called me about some Web site called Skirts on the Scene, and Jabril is on there with all these girls. I don't know what to do. Do you think he is cheating on me? What should I do? Should I break up with him and leave?" I asked as tears started flowing down my face.

"Zakiya, calm down. Let me see—I'll pull it up on my phone."

"The pictures are at the bottom of the page. You have to scroll down."

Adrienne didn't say anything for a few moments, then she said, "Zakiya, these are just club pictures. They don't mean anything. He just took a picture—no big deal. People always want to take pictures with famous people. He is not cheating on you, okay? You are pregnant and have to relax and don't let your emotions get the best of you."

"You think so?" I asked.

"Yes. Now relax, Zakiya. Don't get yourself all upset over nothing, okay? Don't bring these petty pictures to Jabril. It is not worth it. You have to pick your battles, Zakiya. This is not one worth fighting, okay? It's only pictures."

"I guess you're right. Thanks, Adrienne. I'm not going to say anything."

Chapter 57

Cherise

Michelle Hartley was out on maternity leave and I was at the news desk for the morning and weekend news. The weekend news stories were light and breezy. It was fun, and since I took over, the ratings had been great. I was just so happy not to be covering sports anymore. They hired this real energetic guy, Pete Seleciak, and he was a sports head. So life was going well, but I didn't have anyone to celebrate my promotion with. I guess, whether I liked it or not, I was on my way to becoming another Mrs. Ellerbe—a beautiful, successful woman with a great career but no man or children. I wanted to at least call Gavin back and talk to him. I felt like a man: I slept with him, used him, and now won't return his calls. I'm actually embarrassed about everything and I don't know if we can ever just be friends, so I'm avoiding him.

I couldn't decide what was worse—staying in my empty, lifeless condo or going out with someone I know I will never be with. Toni said I would never get over DeCarious if I continued to sulk and not move on. She was right, but I went out on a blind date she set up last week. It was awful. I looked at him across the table at the restaurant, aggravated. I wasn't even going to waste his time. Before he ordered dinner, I asked him to take me home. There was no need pretending. I

268 *Daaimah S. Poole*

wanted what I wanted, and that was DeCarious. I missed him so much it hurt. I wanted to hear his voice. I wanted to feel his touch. I thought as time went by it would get easier, but it didn't. I still felt like the biggest fool. I kept wondering what I did wrong to make him run and leave me and marry his daughter's mother. I don't know if I worked too much or was too independent. I should have stopped trying to fight him and let him treat me like a lady. I wanted to be Miss Independent and now look—I was single again.

Chapter 58

Adrienne

A woman knows when she is losing control. We might not want to admit it, but we know. But there are all kinds of signs that your relationship is going downhill. It is the way he looks at you; it's the way he doesn't look at you. It is the way he calls you; it is the way he doesn't call you. It's the way when you call him he doesn't answer the phone, or when you're trying to be nice and he still tries to pick a fight with you.

Basically, I knew I was losing DeCarious. If I had him under a spell it seemed to be deteriorating. I was doing everything in my power to make things work. I hadn't been to the mall and I even cooked dinner last night. But DeCarious's bitch shit didn't stop. I was hoping that after his surprise party everything would go back to being normal. I rented a hall a few miles from our house. Miss Anne invited everyone and the hall was going to decorate and prepare the food. The only thing I had to do was buy the cake.

I arrived at the hall and the decorations were set up nicely. The food looked delicious. I got him a big football-shaped cake that read "Happy Birthday, DeCarious."

Everything was fine, but I was still nervous. Miss Anne

and Mr. Joe invited a lot of DeCarious's cousins and relatives from Louisiana that I've never met. When I spoke to them, they gave me dead faces and didn't speak back. I got the impression DeCarious's entire family hated me, but that was okay. They didn't matter. The only people that I cared about were DeCarious and Asia. I took a deep breath and approached my mother-in-law.

"Miss Anne, do you think DeCarious is going to be surprised?" I asked.

"He should be. Everything looks nice. Good job. When are you going to call him?"

"I'm going to call him now and tell him that I have a flat," I said as I stepped out of the hall, but before I did that I was going to the bar to get a drink. I needed one to relax my nerves. I looked around to see if anyone was looking. I ordered a vodka and cranberry. Right after I set my drink on the bar, Mr. Joe tapped my shoulder and asked where the bathroom was. I wasn't sure if he could smell the liquor on my breath, but I spoke with my lips closed anyway.

"Over there, Mr. Joe. I'm about to call DeCarious now," I said as I pulled out my phone and dialed him up.

"DeCarious, I have a flat. I pulled into the parking lot near that hall on Old Mercer Road."

"Here I come," he sighed.

I went outside and put my hazard lights on and parked in front of the hall. Ten minutes later he pulled up and I forgot I hadn't figured out how I was going to get him inside without looking at my tire. He walked up to the car and inspected the tires.

"Adrienne, your tire is not flat. What kind of game are you playing?"

"It's not? I thought it was flat. The car was shaking and wobbling to the side. Well, that's a relief, but walk me inside real quick."

"For what, Adrienne? What are you thinking about? And what do you have on? Where were you on your way to, and where is my daughter? Something's not right. I'm leaving. I have something to do," he said as he walked back toward his car.

"No, DeCarious, I need you to come with me. I have something for you," I said as I ran and grabbed his arm. "I thought it was flat. Can you walk me inside? I just want to go to the restroom and I want you to ride behind me when we leave."

He finally followed me and I led him inside. He still had no idea what was going on until we walked into the hall and everyone shouted "Happy Birthday" to him. He was really shocked. He put his face down for a moment and then brought it back up and said, "Y'all got me." He smiled and thanked everyone and gave me a kiss on the cheek and said thank you.

The food was good; we danced and took a lot of pictures. I didn't spend a lot of money, but we all had a great time. Everyone came up and said how nice and beautiful everything was. I did it. DeCarious was very happy, or at least I thought so.

On the way home, I was so excited—I did it. I pulled it off. The party was wonderful and DeCarious was no longer angry with me. To top the night off, I was going to meet him at home and hopefully get a baby in my womb tonight.

I came in the door and DeCarious was downstairs sitting at the dining room table. I walked up to him and kissed him and said, "Baby, did you enjoy your party?"

"Yes, thank you. It was wonderful," he said as he thanked me again and gave me a hug and kiss. I had him, I thought. I gave him another kiss and then began to unzip his pants.

"Hold up, Adrienne. I need to ask you something," he said, backing away.

"Yes, baby?" I said looking up at him.

"Are you pregnant?"

"Yeah, I'm pregnant," I said, shocked.

"How many months?"

"Almost four months."

"If you're pregnant, why were you at the Key Club with bottles of champagne? And my dad saw you drinking tonight."

Shit, I didn't know what to tell him. Should I tell him I lost the baby? I couldn't tell him the truth.

"I was not drinking tonight, DeCarious."

"You weren't? Okay, but you're pregnant, right?"

"Yeah, I am. Why wouldn't I be?"

"Okay, we are going to see," he said as he went into the living room and came back with a pregnancy test.

"Are you serious? You want me to take a pregnancy test?" I said, looking over at him. I didn't know what to think or say. This shit was crazy.

"I do, right now. If you are pregnant, then we move on. If you are not, then we have a big problem."

"I can't believe you would actually doubt me," I said, shaking my head.

"That's what the test is for—to get rid of all the doubt."

"You are crazy. I can't believe your family got you thinking all crazy. This is madness," I said as I walked out of the dining room into the living room.

He followed me, grabbed my arm, and said, "Take this test, Adrienne. Our whole marriage rests on this. Are you going to take the test or not?"

"No, I'm not taking any stupid test. What does that test prove?"

"A whole lot," he said as he threw the test down and started to walk out of the house. "You don't love me. I tried—I really tried, and all you want to do is play games. You keep making me look like a fool and I'm tired of it."

I followed him outside as he got in the car and began pulling off. I jumped in the car with him. He stopped the car, pulled out the keys, got out, and yanked me out of the car. Then he got in and locked the doors before I could get up off the ground. He slowly began driving away as I banged on the window and yelled, "Okay, okay. I'll take the test!" I screamed.

He stopped the car and came back in the house and picked up the test off the floor. I knew the test was about to read "not pregnant" so I had to come clean. I walked over to De-Carious and said, "I lost the baby. I didn't know how to tell you, because you were so excited. And I was just hoping I would get pregnant again. Then I was going to tell you." I began holding him and hugging him, hoping he would hug me back.

"Adrienne, get off of me before I hurt you. We are over."

"I told you the truth, DeCarious."

"You've been lying all along," he said as he went to leave the house.

"No, I haven't," I said, blocking the door as he tried to leave.

"Move out of my way, Adrienne."

"No, we need to talk," I said as he pushed me out of his way and went to get in his car. I jumped in with him.

"Adrienne, I'm not playing. On my mama, I'm going to hurt you if you don't get out of my car."

"I'm not getting out of anywhere."

"Yes, you are. I'm going to ask you again—please get out of my car." I was not getting out of the car. He snatched the keys out of the ignition and came around to the passenger side and started yelling, "I married your ass for nothing. You haven't changed. All you want to do is lie and spend my money."

"That's not true."

"Yes, it is. You ain't shit, Adrienne. You not. I fell for your stupid lies and tricks, but it is over now. I'm leaving you." He grabbed my arm and tried to pull me out. I was getting tired of him talking about me and I was mad that he knew I wasn't pregnant. He kept trying to get me out of the car so I just attacked him. I began kicking, scratching, and swinging on him. I wanted him to hit me back, but he wouldn't. He just went to the driver side and opened the door and pushed me out of the seat and I fell to the ground and he pulled off.

When DeCarious left, I called Miss Anne to tell her that her son just pushed me out of his car. She didn't sound like she was that interested in hearing my side of the story. So I just hung up on her. I couldn't believe DeCarious was acting this irrational. I kept calling his telephone, but he would not pick up. I decided I would stop calling him and let him relax and calm down. He loved me and his daughter, and I knew he didn't really want us to leave. I wasn't going to worry about it. I went upstairs, took a shower, and got in the bed. When DeCarious came home I'd be ready to talk and forgive him.

I heard DeCarious come in the house at five a.m. It sounded like he was not alone. I didn't feel like dealing with anyone, so I stayed in the bed. But then I heard multiple footsteps coming toward the door and then the bedroom light came on. I looked up and I saw two police officers.

"Ma'am, we have an order for protection from abuse."

What? I must have still been asleep. I tried to wake up. I knew DeCarious's bitch ass got a protection from abuse on me. "So, what do you want me to do?"

"Ma'am, I need you to get all your belongings and leave."

"Huh?" I questioned the police officer who was putting me out. "Are you serious?" I asked.

"Very serious, and I need you to get out of bed and move quicker."

"What? This is bullshit. He put me out of his car. Arrest him for pushing me out of the car."

"Miss, your husband filed this paperwork on you. He has bruises and scratches. If he hit you, you can go file a complaint against him. But right now, I need you to get dressed and leave." I was ready to hit them for even believing that I could abuse DeCarious's big, okeydoke ass.

I packed a few things and the police told me I was not to return or have any contact with DeCarious and gave me a court date.

I had nowhere to go. I checked into a hotel and tried to figure things out. I couldn't believe how foul DeCarious was being. I called Miss Anne and told her I was coming to get Asia. I didn't know if they would try to keep my baby.

I picked up Asia and strapped her in her car seat. I drove back to Philadelphia and didn't know what I was going to do next.

Chapter 59

Zakiya

Jabril had the NTX Sports Network coming to the house to interview him. It was Claudette's job to make sure everything was organized and together, but she missed her flight. So I had to do everything. The house needed a quick clean and all the cars needed to get detailed. I was tired, but I got everything done.

The interviewer and his camera crew came to the house at exactly 3 p.m. I wore a white T-shirt, gray sweat pants, and my hair was pulled back in a ponytail. I didn't care, because I wasn't being interviewed. I had been rushing around the house making sure everything was right. I didn't have time to get dressed.

I welcomed the crew. I pulled out the fruit and sandwich trays. The interviewer was a young white guy with a blue-collared shirt on and brown khakis. Jabril took them out to the basketball court and they did the majority of the interview out there.

"So how is life in the NBA so far?"

"It's cool. I'm on the road a lot and I miss my home town. Camden."

"You miss Camden. Aren't you happy you left and got away from the rough streets?"

"No, Camden is a place that's my family. I love that city. I wouldn't trade it for everything in the world."

Jabril was handling the interviewer well. I didn't want to be on camera, so I stood on the sideline staying out of the camera's lens. Every time the camera turned in my direction I moved out of the way, until the interviewer asked about the baby and the camera zoomed in on me and my stomach. They asked me to come over and join them. I said no.

Jabril finished the interview, then it was back on the road. It was very hard to see him go. I felt like he was always leaving me. Claudette said I was emotional because I was pregnant.

A few weeks later I went back to that Web site that Jade told me about, just to check to see if Jabril had any new pictures up there. He wasn't in any pictures, but the Web site did have a clip of Jabril's interview with NTX and they had a big caption that read: Jabril Smith—Is That Your Baby Mama? I played the video and saw the clip of me when they zoomed in on me.

There were all these comments about how could I be on television with a rag on my head and not dressed.

The _#1 _Chick
That bitch is fugly
212Eyesdontlie
They are cute couple she is so pretty and he loves her
The _#1 _Chick
Who ever say they are a cute couple must be her friend LMAO

I logged on and made an account. I decided to post a couple of things myself. I stayed on the computer for three hours. I went back and forth with haters. Fuck these stupid bitches.

I read two hundred comments on how cute Jabril was and

how I was one lucky ugly bitch. There were comments from people who went to school with him who said he left his high school sweetheart when he got signed. I typed in his name and did a search, and the first page was all basketball stuff, but I kept clicking and then I started seeing all these pics. He had two girls on each side of him biting his bottom lip. He looked like he had been drinking. I didn't know what to think. I looked to see when the pictures were from. There were all these Web sites with girls on there saying they met him in every city and what hotel they stayed in. I went back to check the dates and they matched Jabril's schedule.

This time I didn't listen to Adrienne. I was so mad I called Jabril. "When were you in Miami, Jabril? Did you meet some girl in New Orleans?"

"No, what are you talking about?"

"Or how about last month, when y'all played the Wizards?"

"What are you talking about?"

"There are pictures of you with all these girls. They are talking about where you have your tattoos. First it was girls in Miami, then other girls in New Orleans."

"Man, I just took pictures when girls asked me. They have pictures with my tattoos everywhere."

"What about your high school sweetheart? You left her."

"What? Where are you getting this stuff from? She broke up with me in eleventh grade. Now she keeps calling me."

"All these girls are saying they mess with you."

"Who? Where? I don't mess with anybody. They are lying, Kiya. I don't want anyone else. What are you talking about?"

"You got me pregnant, fat, and ugly. You trapped me so I can't leave. But I'm still leaving. I don't need you, Jabril. I'm not going to be my sister. I'm not going to have a man cheat on me and keep getting me pregnant. When you get here, I won't be here. Jabril, you're not going to ruin my life." I ended the call.

Then Wendell came bamming on the door. When I let him in, he asked, "What's going on with you, Zakiya?"

"Nothing."

"What are you doing? Do not call my nephew, upsetting him. He has to stay focused."

"I didn't call him, Wendell."

"Yes, you did. Please don't call him with dumb shit. He is on the road and needs to concentrate. He don't need no bull-shit going on."

As soon as he walked out of the room, I called Jabril again. "Why did you tell Wendell on me? You have him cussing at me, Jabril. I'm really leaving now. You think you are going to take pictures with all these girls and then your uncle is going to yell at me like I'm his child? I'm not staying here."

"Kiya, just stay until tomorrow. I'll be back tomorrow and we can talk."

"No, I'm packing, and when I have the baby I will call you." I hung up the phone.

A few moments later, Wendell came in the room and apologized to me.

Claudette came in, too, and looked on the computer. "Girl, let me tell you something. Jabril loves you. You and this baby are all he talks about. Don't get me wrong, men do what they do. But you don't have anything to worry about. If Jabril cheated on you, I would kick his ass. Zakiya, forget these little stupid computer whores. Do you think if he was really dating them they would really have enough time to get on the computer and talk shit? He is on the road, and when he is not on the road he is here with you."

Chapter 60

Adrienne

My young prodigy, she was losing her little mind over blogs and Web sites. I was trying to make this girl roll with the punches. She was carrying a golden ticket in her stomach, but did she care? No. She was worrying about what people were saying on the Internet. She was driving me crazy trying to let people know he was with her. I didn't know how to explain to her that she was the main girl chick, the main woman, and all the sideline pieces didn't matter. She was number one. As the quarterback she ran the team, and all those other bitches didn't matter.

"Does he come home every night?"

"Yes."

After I soothed Zakiya, it was time to call DeCarious because he cut me off and sent me paperwork saying he wanted full custody of Asia. Our joint account had five dollars in it. I hated him. I was back home again, no job, and with almost no money. Of course I had ninety-five hundred on the side, but how long was that going to last?

It had only been a week and I already knew I wanted to stay with DeCarious. I wanted my married-woman life back.

This single mom shit was scaring me. I tried being mean to him, so I was going to try being nice again and call him and see if he wanted to talk. I dialed his number. He picked up on the second ring.

"What do you want, Adrienne?"

"I don't want a divorce, DeCarious. I want to be with you and I want our family. Please, let's give it another try," I begged. I clutched my phone against my face, hoping to hear a yes.

"No, I'm done. I gave it a try."

"Let's try again."

"No! Are you crazy? Why would I want to stay married to you? You spend money like it's nothing and my family hates you. Why would I come back to you? Tell me, why? You got me by acting like you were pregnant, and I was dumb enough to fall for it and marry you."

"DeCarious, I thought I was pregnant. I didn't act like I was pregnant. You saw the pregnancy test. I went to my doctor and he said that you can have a false pregnancy. Some women have their period and don't know they are pregnant."

"You are a liar, but it doesn't even matter. This is the second time you got me. There will not be a third. It doesn't matter, we are over. I'm getting this marriage annulled."

"I didn't get you. I love you, DeCarious. I'm sorry, baby. I want to be with you. I'm sorry. DeCarious, Asia needs us to be together, to be good parents. She needs to grow up with a family."

"I'm done. Your sorrys don't mean anything, Adrienne. We can love our daughter and be good parents. We can come up with some type of arrangement. I'm hanging up."

I hated him. I was steaming mad. I didn't want a divorce. I knew I had made a mistake, told some untruths, but this was not the way I wanted everything to end. I wanted to remain Mrs. DeCarious Simmons. I wanted to live in Atlanta, have my family and my good life.

I called him back six times before he answered. I'd show him the thug gangster in me.

"What do you want, Adrienne? Didn't I tell you, if it's not about my daughter, don't call me."

"DeCarious, all I want to tell you is that you are stuck with me. You want to get rid of me, then pay half."

"Half? I'm getting an annulment, and I'm going to be done with your ass."

"Not if I don't sign. Whatever, nigga, please. Get the fuck out of here. Okay, go jump off a bridge somewhere."

"Damn, I should have listened to my mom. She told me not to marry your ass."

"Maybe you should have. But if you really think you're going to get a restraining order on me, kick me out of the house, and I'm going to take that shit lying down, you must be crazy."

"No, you are crazy, Adrienne!"

"DeCarious, shut up. I think you just punched me in the eye and I need millions to keep quiet before I go to the media."

"So you would lie on me?"

"Why not? What do I have to lose? It is not a lie—you pushed me the other night."

"I pushed you off me as you attacked me."

"A push is a push. I'm going to need hush money."

"I should have known better. You are the dumbest bitch I know."

"I don't care. You're not going to see your daughter until you get that paperwork right."

"I'm gonna see my daughter. Watch. I'm gonna see her."

"I bet you won't, DeCarious. Fuck you. Pay me, bitch.

That house is mine. So are those cars. Everything you own is mine. I'm taking half, bitch! I am not playing. I will make shit up and get the media and say you beat me," I said as I hung up the phone. He kept calling back and I didn't answer. I had four voice mails. They were all hang-ups. The last one he must have been talking to Rock in the background because I heard him say, "She is going to make me kill her. I swear on my mama and daddy. She is playing with my life."

I called him back. "DeCarious, dumb ass, make sure the phone is off before you start running your mouth. I just got your message that you just left about killing me."

Chapter 61

Zakiya

Jabril invited me out to the Kyle Davis Jr. celebrity charity weekend in LA. If I'm with him then I can't accuse him of cheating. He was making up for all the rumors, and dumb blogs. Bril bought me a new Mercedez Benz and took me to Hawaii. He is just doing everything right. He loves me.

It was so much pressure being with him. I loved Jabril, but I was getting tired of people telling me how lucky I was that he was so good to me. I was good to him. Or how lucky I was that he was rich, or how my baby was going to have everything and I would never have anything to worry about in my life. Which was not really true. I was not going to live off Jabril. I was going to do something with myself as soon as I had the baby. I could at least take online classes. I couldn't just be Jabril's girlfriend or baby mom the rest of my life.

I didn't really think he was cheating on me. I knew he loved me, but it was just hard. Adrienne explained to me that those women didn't matter, and if they did, they would be where I'm at. She said I had to be confident and know that Jabril loved me, and I knew that. Plus she told me to stay off the Internet, and I tried my best.

"Zakiya, you packed yet?" Claudette yelled down the hall.

I texted Bril and told him I couldn't wait to see him. He texted me back that he missed me, too. He was flying straight from Phoenix where they had played the Suns.

"No."

"The car will be here in a few minutes. Hurry up."

The black Lincoln Town Car drove us to the airport. The driver took our luggage and handed it to the skycap and checked us in at the curb. We had plenty of time before our flight so we went to eat at Chili's.

"So, you excited to go to LA?" Claudette asked.

"I used to live there."

"Yeah, I did think Bril mentioned that to me." I liked Claudette. She treated me like a daughter.

It was nice coming back to Los Angeles. It was a different experience this time. Our limo met us at the airport and whisked us right away to the hotel. Jabril had already arrived and had flowers waiting for me and Claudette.

I called Elena immediately.

"Elena, I'm in town."

"You should come up to the store," she said, and we headed out.

When we walked in the store, I said, "See, I told you I'd be back," as I gave Elena a hug.

Claudette said hi. She was mad because the mall didn't have any high-end stores. "How long before she gets off, because they don't have a Saks in this mall."

"She is almost off."

We all went shopping on Rodeo Drive. It was one of the best times—I was happy and I had money. And there was bebe.

* * *

After our shopping trip, Jabril took me to a party. It was good to relax and I was meeting all these celebrities. They were excited to meet Jabril, and then he would introduce them to me. Everyone touched my stomach and wished us luck and said that we made a beautiful couple.

Jabril was back on the road. Claudette was going back to New Jersey and I was going back to Okalahoma to be all alone again. I came in and Wendell brought my bags up. I called Adrienne and she said she would call me back. So then I checked in on Lisa, Miles, and Kyle.

"How are things going?"

"Good."

"Where are the boys?"

"Asleep. You know it's late and they have school tomorrow. They kept me on as permanent at my job, so I'm no longer a temp. I have benefits and I got a raise."

"That is so good."

"Yup, I'm so happy. So I can't talk long. I have to get ready for work."

"Well, tell my nephews I love them."

"I will, and Aunt Tina said call her."

"Just give her my number."

After talking to Lisa I was tired. I turned on the television to see what was on. Not much. I turned my computer on. I knew I wasn't supposed to be looking at pictures but I couldn't help it. I went to Skirts on the Scene. I went on a few pages but I didn't see pictures of us. And then on the fourth page, I clicked on the picture to make it bigger and couldn't believe what I was viewing on my screen.

The pictures they had of us online looked awful. I looked huge. My eyes looked like they had dark rings under them. My eyes didn't look crazy like these pictures, and my nose wasn't that big. They took the pictures from the worst possible angles. I looked so ugly. Pictures lie, I thought. All weekend everyone said how cute I looked. I logged on to the Web site. I scrolled down. The first comment was in large caps and read,

Ballerchick202
HATED IT HATED IT HATED IT. *She need to go* . . . .
Stevebaby288
What does he see in her . . . she is going to have a monster baby.

There were all these comments dogging us. They had a zoom-in of my feet and said I had a corn. What the hell? Every comment was about how I didn't deserve to be with him because I was so ugly. I had to go look at myself in the mirror. Did I really look that bad? I held a second mirror up. I didn't look like that picture. Then I turned my face to the side. My nose was bigger. But I was still cute. Fuck it, I had to go online and defend myself. It was like cyber mean girls. They kept picking on me and I didn't even know them. First comment I wrote: *They are a real cute couple. All y'all must be haters.* Then the second comment: *I think she is the bomb. Her hair and makeup are the bomb. Look at her bag—it costs at least $2,500. Where's yours?*

Chapter 62

Cherise

There had to be a fire in the building. That was the only explanation for why someone would be knocking on my door at three in the morning. I put on my slippers and robe and ran to the door. I looked through the peephole and saw DeCarious. What the hell? I opened the door. "Yes?"

"Can I come in?"

"No, it is four in the morning. What are you doing, knocking on my door this time of the night? You can't just come around here. It's been two months—you don't know if I have company." I stepped outside the door.

"Do you have company?" I detected a little bit of jealousy.

"No, I don't, but you can't just show up at my house whenever you feel like it."

"I just came to tell you you were right, Cherise. I was wrong. I was so wrong. I love you. I handled us wrong. I should have come to you like a man and told you how I was feeling. You are my soul mate, my best friend, the only woman I should have married. I never met anyone like you. You handle your own business. You are just perfect. I used to tell you that all the time. You are so beautiful and smart. I love you. I need you, Cherise. I want to be with you." I smelled alcohol and I was not impressed with DeCarious's drunken rant.

"DeCarious, are you drunk?" I asked, looking at him intently.

"No . . . well, all I had was two drinks. That's all. But that doesn't matter. Did you hear me, Cherise? I love you. I want you. I need you. I'm sorry about all of this. I want to make it up to you." DeCarious then pulled me to him.

"Tell me you love me. Look at me, Cherise. Tell me you love me, too, Cherise." I wanted to tell him that I loved him. I wanted to, but I just couldn't. I was too hurt and facing too many emotions at once. I knew he would be back and I loved him. I prayed for this. I hoped and wished for him to come back. I wanted him to come back unmarried and ready to commit to me, but I didn't like the way he left. He left me hurt, alone, confused, ashamed. He lied to me and left without thinking about how I would feel.

"DeCarious. I can't do this right now. Maybe we can get together and talk at another time." I went back inside and closed the door. He knocked on the door and I told him to go away. Why was he doing this? Why now?

"Please open up this door, Cherise. I need you. I'm sorry," he said, whimpering. I walked away from the door. I was not going to let him in. I couldn't believe what was going on. And then he began to knock hard on my door. Each knock made my heart hurt. First it was a pat that turned into a *boom boom boom*. I couldn't ignore the knocks.

I walked back to the door and screamed, "DeCarious, I need you to leave! I'm not opening the door for you."

The knocking stopped and then I heard footsteps trailing down the hall and then the fire escape door open.

I sighed. As much as I wanted to pick up the telephone and

call him and tell him to come back, I wouldn't and I couldn't. Instead I dialed Toni.

"What's wrong?"

"DeCarious just came to my house drunk."

"Are you serious?"

"I wouldn't let him in." As soon as I completed my sentence, I heard another call coming in. "That's him calling. What should I do?"

"Just hear what he has to say and tell me what he said in the morning."

I answered the call. "Yes."

"Please hear me out, Cherise." I wanted to hang up, but I listened.

"I know you think I've been drinking, but I know what I'm talking about right now. Cherise, I am so in love with you. I know I messed up with you. But I will do whatever it takes to be with you. There hasn't been one day that went by that I haven't thought about you. Cherise, there is no other woman for me. I know I messed up. I know I fucked up. I love you."

"You love me? If you loved me you wouldn't have married another woman. If you loved me you would have been there for me. You left me, DeCarious. You left me. You made that decision and now we have to live with what you did."

"Can I come to you, Cherise? Please? I need you, Cherise."

"No, you don't need me. Stop lying. Go wherever you've been all these months. You left me. *You left me.* I had to go all this time wondering what I did wrong."

"I know you are hurting. I hurt you when you loved me. I wasn't used to someone loving me without wanting something in return. I don't want to be with her. I just thought she was pregnant."

"DeCarious, it's too late. I don't want to ever hear from you in life. Your daughter's mom ruined you. You don't know what love is," I said as I hung up the phone and began crying uncontrollably the rest of the night.

I had a hard time concentrating at work the next day. De-Carious had been calling nonstop. It wasn't flattering. Instead of having a forgiving heart I was angry. I was so very mad. Now that I was strong and I could look the other way, he wanted to come back.

Chapter 63

Adrienne

If me, Asia, and DeCarious weren't going to be a family, then he wasn't going to see his daughter. And I was going to take all his money and destroy him. He was going to regret the day he ever met me. Angelique gave me this real good attorney's number. Her name was Holly Byrne.

I took the elevator up to the ninth floor. Ms. Byrne greeted me herself. She had a decent size office, but said she was short-staffed today. She invited me back to her junky office. It was a mess—boxes and stacks of paper in every direction.

"So, what's going on?" she said as she sat down and began to look in a small compact and layer her outer eye with black eyeliner. Something about her was very masculine and hard, and I couldn't believe she was applying makeup, but I began speaking anyway.

"Well, my husband is trying to get our marriage annulled as well as take custody of our daughter, and doesn't want to pay me any alimony or spousal support."

"How long have you been married? Where did you get married?"

"Three months, and in Vegas."

"Ugh," she said as she stopped applying the eyeliner.

"Okay, three months is not a lot of time. What does he do?" she said as she went back to tracing her outer lid.

"He is a player in the NFL."

She stopped as if she became interested again and said, "Really. Well, maybe we can handle this. Do you know who is representing him?"

"His attorney is out of Atlanta. I think a Joseph Martin. Before we married they only gave me a little child support and I don't want it to happen again. He is hiding money. I know he has millions. He has a recording studio and property. But he is trying to put everything in his mother's and cousin's names so he won't have to give me anything."

She stood up and said, "My retainer to handle this case will be at the very least twenty thousand dollars. But I assure you that when I finish with him, twenty thousand will not be anything. I will take his house and make sure you get half of everything. We will go to the media if necessary. Has he hit or shoved you before?"

"Well, no. He walks away. But he put me out of his car before."

"He shoved you out of the car—perfect. That is domestic abuse. Trust me, he doesn't want that type of label. None of them do. I had a case like this before. I set up a press conference and before my client reached the microphone, his attorney wanted to make a deal."

"But he is not a big star."

"It doesn't matter. The NFL affiliation alone is enough to garner media attention and embarrass him."

I was excited. She was saying everything I wanted to hear. She was like a vicious attack dog. It was like all I had to do was say *get 'em, sic 'em, girl,* and she would go and bite De-Carious right in the ass.

Chapter 64

Cherise

DeCarious sent flowers to my job. He called, e-mailed, and texted me tens of times, saying how sorry he was. I didn't want to hear his sorry. I didn't know what would make him think he could just walk out of my life and then come back and everything would resume as normal. I was not having it. I refused to answer his calls and return any of his messages.

He couldn't get me on the phone or by text, so he decided to show up at my job. As I was walking out of the building, he grabbed my arm and said, "Can we please go somewhere and talk?"

"No, I just want you to leave me alone. I want you to stop sending me flowers and stop calling me."

"Please, Cherise. Please, Cherise, will you talk to me?"

"I'm tired. It has been a long day."

"Please, I just have a few things I need to talk to you about." Seeing his face made me angry. I felt like taking my fists and pounding his chest and asking him why he'd hurt me.

"I am so sorry how everything played out, Cherise. I thought I was doing the right thing for my daughter, and with Adrienne being pregnant again, I just wanted to give it one last chance."

"I don't care, DeCarious. I don't want you, and I don't date married men."

"Cherise, I'm trying to get the marriage annulled, but she is not having it."

"DeCarious, we can't have this conversation here. Let's talk in my car." I figured if he said everything he needed to say, then he would finally leave me alone. He followed me to my car. Once we were in, he just began pouring everything out and I just sat and listened.

"She has a lawyer already and she said she is going to the press and will tell them that I hit her, and is making all this stuff up. I talked to my attorney and he said I don't have anything to worry about. She married me under the false pretense that she was pregnant. That is reason enough for annulment. Whatever it takes, I'm getting out of the marriage. I might have to give her temporary alimony, possibly a small lump sum, and definitely child support, but I don't have an issue with taking care of my daughter."

"I just can't take you back into my life, just like that. I'm too hurt."

"I understand and I want to do everything in my power to make it up to you. So what's next, Cherise?"

"I don't know. Day by day."

"Can I come home with you? I don't want to go home. I'll just sleep on your sofa."

I let DeCarious sleep on my sofa. I wanted to be around him. I didn't want him to leave. I handed him a blanket. We said good night and I went into my bedroom and closed the door. I wanted DeCarious to get in the bed with me. I wanted to join him on the sofa, but his presence alone gave me peace.

Chapter 65

Zakiya

I had decided to forget about the stupid blogs and the girls on them. Jabril loved me. Even though we weren't even sure what we were having yet, he got a tattoo with *JS II* in cursive letters on his bicep.

He said that once the baby was born he was going to put the baby's face and birth date underneath. On his forearm he got my name tattooed in big Greek-style letters and he begged me to get his name tattooed on my back.

"You are crazy, boy. Please, stop marking your body up." I laughed.

"I only have eight tattoos. I know people who have like twenty. This dude when I was getting my last tattoo had a few tats on his face."

"That's next for you." I laughed. "You are going to be looking like Lil Wayne."

"Never."

"Hurry and get dressed, Kiya, so I can see JS2."

"I'll be ready in a few."

We were on our way to the doctor's office. Jabril couldn't go to all my doctor appointments with me, but he tried to go to most. I was getting my ultrasound done today to see what I was having. Last time we tried to see, the baby's hands were blocking the view and they couldn't make out if the baby was a boy or a girl.

The ultrasound tech came in the room. Happy and cheerful.

"Y'all ready to see what you're having?" she asked as she applied this cold brown gel to my stomach.

"I think she is having twins. Look how big her stomach is," Jabril joked.

I tried to punch him playfully. I saw the image of the baby coming on the screen.

The woman laughed herself, and said, "This is a big baby." She adjusted the band around my stomach and went over to the screen and then told me to turn to the side. I turned to my side and then she kept swiping the instrument back and forth across my stomach. Then she said, "I'll be right back." Jabril and I kept laughing and playing until the woman came back in the room with my doctor.

"Doctor Fisher," I said.

He said, "Hi, Zakiya." His sternness let me know something was wrong. He looked at the screen and said, "I don't want to alarm you, but your baby is not moving and does not have a heartbeat right now."

"Huh?" we both said together. We both looked over at the screen.

Then Dr. Fisher said, "I'm sorry, your baby is dead." The words hit me like a bag of bricks. *Your baby is dead*. I started screaming at the thought of not meeting my baby in the next ninety days. I had a dead baby inside of me.

"You didn't do anything wrong. Sometimes things like this happen. We will not know anything until we check for congenital birth defects, such as heart malformations, in the baby."

I don't remember anything after that. They offered me

counseling and all sorts of things and the next day they induced my labor I had to push the baby out, but I knew there was not going to be a crying baby. When I finally pushed out Baby Smith, the room was somber. No cameras, taking pictures, or celebration. Jabril was crying, I was crying, and so was Claudette. How could this happen? What did I do wrong? They asked me if I wanted to see him. I said no. I wanted to get up and just leave. I didn't want to name him or give him a service, but Jabril insisted that we bury our son. He made all the arrangements.

They wrapped our son up in a blue blanket. The funeral home came to pick up our child and we buried him a few days later.

Chapter 66

Adrienne

I tried to give DeCarious one more chance to see if he would come to his senses and wake the fuck up. See if he would realize he had more to gain with me than without me. Somebody needed to inform him that it is cheaper to keep her. My attorney is so good. If he still wanted to go through with the divorce, then fine, because my attorney said that he didn't have a case against me. He couldn't prove that I didn't know I was pregnant. He couldn't prove that I didn't have a spontaneous abortion. But if DeCarious wanted to play hardball he could. And if he did, I was going to go right ahead with the domestic abuse allegations and release all the threats he left me to the news media. I would ruin him, and I tried to explain that to him, but he was stubborn and dumb. If he knew what's best for his finances, he would heed my advice.

"DeCarious?" I yelled into the phone.

"What?" he yelled back.

"I just wanted to say—"

"I don't want to hear anything you have to say. Get it through your damn head. We are never going to be together. Stop calling my damn phone. I have the woman I love back. She loves me. She has her own money, career, and she would love me tomorrow if I was broke. Listen, don't call me if it is not about Asia."

He hung up on me again, and I called him right back.

"DeCarious?"

"What, Adrienne? I thought I just told you not to call my phone if it was not pertaining to my daughter."

"I'll call you whenever I feel like it. Okay? You like your house, right?"

"What the hell is that supposed to mean, Adrienne?"

"It means exactly what you think it means." I tried to take the bass out of my voice and sweeten up my tone. "DeCarious, I didn't call to argue, but I do want to explain something to you."

"You don't have to explain anything to me. I don't want to hear it, Adrienne. Something is really wrong with you."

"I'm going to tell you anyway. By law, I'm entitled to half. I'm your wife! I know you have an attorney, but he is giving you wrong information. My attorney is a beast, and she is not playing. So you might want to think twice about trying to move forward with this annulment." I paused. "I am willing to make it work with you. But if we don't make a deal, I will make sure that you *never see Asia again!*" I screamed, and then I hung up on him.

He called my phone and left a message. I listened to the scathing words he left for me. "Adrienne, if you keep my daughter away from me, I will hurt you. I will kill you, bitch. They will find your dumb ass in a ditch."

I called him back and said, "DeCarious, thank you for leaving me more threats. Don't say I didn't warn your dumb ass. And did you just say you were going to kill me and they are going to find my body in a ditch? A judge will love to hear this. Maybe I need to call your girlfriend's job or FOX 5 and let them know that DeCarious Simmons is a deadbeat dad and abuser, and he is threatening to kill me. I think I'm going to get a restraining order on you now, because I'm scared." I laughed and then hung up on him again.

"Adrienne, you are really crazy."

"Yeah, well, my crazy ass is going to hang up so I can call the police now. I think I have some photos from when you choked me, too. You know I bruise easily."

"Adrienne, you are the fuck crazy. No one is going to believe you."

"I bet they will."

"No one likes a man who beats on his women and doesn't take care of his child. You are going down. I'm taking everything, DeCarious. Everything. You hear me? Your house, your money, and your life."

"You can't take my house or my money."

"Watch me. Start packing your shit because you are getting evicted," I said as I hung up on him again. I was done playing nice. I called my attorney and told her to go ahead. She could do whatever was necessary. I'd do a news conference with my big, black, round sunglasses on, and sniffle for the cameras as I wiped away imaginary tears. I laughed at the thought. I didn't want to do it to him like this, but he did it to himself.

Chapter 67

Cherise

DeCarious ran in the door, huffing and puffing. I was scared to ask what was wrong.

"What's wrong?"

He then went to the door, opened it and slammed it, and began punching his fist into his palm. "How can this bitch think she can just take my money? How can she say she deserves half? She never worked hard a day in her life. I want to kill her."

"Calm down, baby. What is going on? I don't understand."

"My attorney called Adrienne and asked her if she was served with the annulment papers. I called her and she told me to call her attorney. So now her attorney is threatening to have a news conference saying that I'm an abuser."

"She doesn't have any proof," I said.

"She does. She was making me so mad, I did leave on her voice mail that she was going to make me kill her."

"DeCarious, you didn't."

"I did. It was dumb, but she kept calling me and saying how I won't be able to see my daughter, and I just got so angry. So my attorney called back and said that they want spousal support and child support. She wants my house. I was willing to give her five hundred thousand. So then Adrienne calls me and says that if I don't give her what she wants she will take half of my income. Then she said she was going to the media and say that I have been physically abusing her. She is trying to ruin me. I hate her. I swear, I hate her. I'm ready to have someone kill her."

"Stop talking crazy. We will work this out."

"I worked hard for all this. I'm not super rich, but I'm doing okay. I did this work. I ran them miles. I get up at 5 a.m. I went to college, worked out in the snow and rain in high school. This was my sacrifice. I will kill her before she gets half of everything I've worked for. I swear on my daughter. I will kill that bitch."

I had to calm DeCarious down. I could never understand how someone could want to kill someone, but this woman—someone needed someone to do something to her. She was insane. I wanted to kill this bitch myself.

"Babe, just calm down. We are going to figure this out." I couldn't help but think if he had never gone back to her none of this would have happened.

DeCarious had a meeting with his attorney and wanted me to accompany him, so I did. We came into the office and had a seat. He introduced me as his girlfriend. I knew they were probably thinking, *Aren't you still married?*

"DeCarious, listen. This is going to hurt, buddy. But she has this attorney, and she is threatening all types of allegations. She asked for two point five million dollars to walk away."

"Two point five million dollars? Is she crazy?" I said.

"Are you joking? I was married to her for two months. Does she really think I would give her a million dollars for every month that we were married?"

"No, it is a game, but they have to start high and we are going to have to meet them in the middle. Around one million."

"What? That's too much money. You said I would only have to give her half of that."

"I know. That's what we thought initially. But you have a contract extension on the table and you don't want her to find out about that. And she is saying you hit her and she has proof. She said something about voice mail messages that they will release to the media. And we just don't walk that path at all. It would be a public relations nightmare. The league just doesn't need this. Think about your franchise, team, and fans."

"But it is not true."

"It doesn't matter, DeCarious. I've been trying to keep this negotiation a secret, but as soon as you sign this new deal and you are still legally married to her . . . then she can ask for half. You have to get out of this marriage as soon as possible."

Chapter 68

Tanisha

Thanks to God I had all my children, and my Kevin back. We were taking things slow, but I was going to move back in with him. I think everything I've been through has made me more compassionate, understanding, and less judgmental.

I wanted to meet with Adrienne. I had been so evil to her, and she didn't deserve it. She is lost and confused and she needs someone to help her. I had to let her know that I didn't blame her about everything that happened to me in my life. At first I was going to call her, but I decided I was going to visit her in person. I called her and asked if she was available for lunch.

"What's up, Adrienne? What are you doing?"

"Just leaving my lawyer's office. Why? What's up?"

"I wanted to meet up with you."

"Is everything okay?" she asked.

"Yeah. I think we have a lot that we need to discuss and just need to meet up face-to-face."

"I'll let you know," she said.

That didn't sound very promising. I really wanted to talk to her. I wasn't sure where she lived. "Adrienne, I just wanted to let you know I forgive you. I am sorry I blamed you for everything. You were only being a friend. You thought that was the best thing to do at that time. I don't know why all this happened, but I know it has made me stronger. I don't blame you. You gave me advice and I took it. It is not your fault.

"But since I've been through all this, I feel like I have to tell you. You have your life—don't waste it. I feel like I wasted so much time. You have your health and you are beautiful. You have a healthy, beautiful child, so you need to stop playing with your life. I'm so serious. Stop playing with your life."

"Tanisha, thanks, but no thanks. I get it, but please don't tell me how and what I should think. I love DeCarious and I want to be with him. If he doesn't want to be with me, then I am entitled to whatever he has."

"One day you will wake up. You can't do dirt and stay clean."

Chapter 69

Zakiya

It's been a few weeks since the baby died. Everyone keeps telling me I will get over it, but I haven't yet. I keep thinking about the plans I made that included the baby. Jabril is doing fine. He just said he was going to get me pregnant again, but I don't want to ever get pregnant again. I never want to go through all this heartache and pain ever again.

Since I came home from the hospital I haven't been able to do anything. Jabril has been there for me and is trying. But I'm a wreck. Every time he is about to leave to go anywhere I start crying and I don't know why I feel like a baby, but I just do. I just feel so sad, like I don't want to move on. My phone was ringing, but I didn't want to talk to anyone, but since it was Elena, I answered.

"What are you doing? I haven't heard from you," she said.

"I lost the baby. I'm not pregnant anymore."

"Oh no, chica. You okay?" Elena asked, her voice getting elevated.

"No, I feel like shit. I just want to die. I swear I just want to die."

"No, don't say that. You don't mean that."

"Yes, I do mean it. Every night I just get up and think my

life would be so much better if I wasn't here. I actually think of how I'm going to do it."

"Do what, Zakiya? Stop talking crazy."

I started sniffling. "Elena, I'm so not playing. I don't have anything to live for. I can't even have a baby, right? All women can have children. I'm worthless."

"You're not worthless, Zakiya."

"Yes, I am and Jabril hates me. Do you know how much Jabril hates me?"

"He doesn't hate you. Where are his uncle and mom?"

"They're not here. I don't like his dumb-ass uncle anyway. I think he is happy my baby died. You should have seen the smirk on his face when I first came home. I'm just tired. I'll call you later."

After I hung up, I walked into the bedroom. I was really done with life. I just wanted to die and be with my baby and my mom. I couldn't wait to see them.

Chapter 70

Adrienne

When DeCarious tried to call me, I had three words for him: Call my attorney. Then I turned my phone off. I didn't have time for him. He had his chance to make a deal with me. He wanted to do it his way, so now he would pay. So he wouldn't talk to me. I guess he figured that he would have his mama do his dirty work for him because Miss Anne was ringing my phone. I answered the phone like, *I don't want to talk to you, either, bitch.*

"Yes, Miss Anne."

"Hi, Adrienne. How's Asia?" This bitch ain't called me in forever. Now she wants to ask about her granddaughter? *Get to the point,* I thought.

"She's good. What's up, Miss Anne?"

"Adrienne, I was just calling to talk to you. I have to be honest with you. I don't like what's going on with you and DeCarious. Either y'all going to be together or not. But either way, y'all gonna have to find a way to come to some type of agreement without anyone getting hurt."

"Miss Anne, you need to tell your son that. I have been trying to work things out with him. And he is the one who doesn't want to compromise. I didn't want a divorce—he does."

"Okay, then maybe you can come down here and you two can sit and talk."

"No, it's too late, Miss Anne. I'm done."

"You sure?"

"Yes, I am. No one is thinking about me or really concerned about Malaysia. So I'm done talking. I will see him in court."

"Okay, Adrienne, if that's the way you want it. I just don't understand why it has to end angry. You both have to do what's best for Asia. One more thing—if you continue to work out of greed, Adrienne, everything around you will collapse. I guarantee you."

"Miss Anne, I have to go." She could give that same tired speech to her son. I wanted at least a million dollars, which wasn't a lot if he wanted me to sign the annulment papers.

I drove down to my attorney's office. She said she had some good news for me. I walked into her office. Her receptionist offered me something to drink. I was too nervous to drink anything. He was on the computer checking e-mails. He said that Ms. Byrne would be out shortly. She came right out and said, "Come in, Mrs. Simmons." I had a seat and Ms. Byrne stood up and then walked to her window and opened the blinds, letting more sunlight inside her office. She walked back over to her desk and leaned on the edge and said, "I just had a conversation with your husband's attorney. Apparently they just want this to be over with, and want to settle."

"Really? For how much?"

"Five hundred thousand, and I think their offer is more than reasonable, Mrs. Simmons."

"You do?" I asked, confused. "Ms. Byrne, what about all you said about wanting to get the media involved and asking for two million but getting at least a million out of the deal?"

"Well, he has hired the best attorney in the state of Georgia, and he is licensed in Pennsylvania, and they are going to draw this thing out so long that by the time you receive any money, your legal bills will eat a large percentage of the money. If we have to go before a judge, the first thing they are going to ask you is why aren't you working? What is wrong with you? You have a college degree and are perfectly able."

"But we already knew all this."

"We did, but as I reviewed everything, I think this is your best option."

"But you said that I could get the house and would walk away with at least half of what he is worth. He is worth way more than a million dollars."

"I did say that, but let me ask you this, Mrs. Simmons. Are you employed right now? You'll say no, and then the next question will be, What's wrong with you? You have a college degree and are perfectly able. Then his attorney may say that you are able bodied and you just don't want to work. They are going to dig up dirt and try their best to make you appear like a gold digger."

"But I'm not a gold digger."

"I know you are not, and I know you just want what's best for your daughter. However, the court may not see it that way. Ultimately, it is your decision. However, I say take the money. It will be a good nest egg for your daughter and yourself."

"I don't want to settle. I want to make sure me and his daughter are secure. What are they offering in child support?"

"Let me look," she said as she walked back over to her desk and looked on her computer screen.

"Sixty-five hundred per month, and that includes day care and nanny expenses."

"That's it. No. He is worth way more than that. No, absolutely not." DeCarious and his lawyer were really crazy if they thought that they could get over on me like this. I looked at her, tears almost coming out of my eyes. "This is crazy. No, I don't agree. I won't accept."

"Think it over and I will give his attorney a call on Monday and see if they want to come up with something better." I said okay as I exited her office. I was really upset with her. I expected so much out of her. What happened to all that gangster talk she was talking in the beginning? I was frustrated as hell. I walked down Walnut Street to the parking garage and gave the attendant my ticket. As I waited, the only thing that came to mind was maybe I should fire Ms. Byrne. I didn't want to, but how could she think that bowing down to DeCarious and his attorney was acceptable? What happened to everything she promised me—the media, the house, etc.

I didn't have any change so the attendant brought me my car and all I could say was thank you. I drove angrily down Twentieth and headed toward the Parkway. I saw a strange number appear on my phone with an area code I didn't recognize. I didn't have time for any surprises, so I did not answer. And then the number called again. I Googled the area code 323 at the next light on my phone. It was Los Angeles, California. *Who do I know there?* I thought, *If they call back I will answer.* When the phone rang again, I didn't give the person a chance to say hello before I shouted out, "Who is this?" I was not in the mood for games.

"Hi, this is Elena, Adrienne."

"Who?"

"Elena—Zakiya's friend from Los Angeles."

"Oh, she is not with me. She is in Oklahoma. If she calls I will tell her that you called."

"That's not what I called for. I just spoke with her and she doesn't sound so good."

"Well, Zakiya is very sensitive and you know pregnant women go through it. She'll be all right. When I talk to her, I'll tell her you called."

"You know about her losing the baby, right?"

"No, when?" I asked.

"She had a miscarriage a few weeks ago and is really upset."

"Oh no, I didn't know that. Let me call her now."

"Now, that's why I was calling, because when I talked to her she didn't sound too good. And now her phone is off, but I'm trying to reach her. I haven't talked to her in a few hours and I'm getting scared."

"Why? What do you mean, she didn't sound good?"

"She just seemed real depressed and kept saying she didn't want to leave the hospital without the baby, but they made her leave and she was crying and crying. Then she said she was going to call me back."

"Okay, I'm going to try to get in touch with her. I'll call her and Jabril."

"When you get in touch with her, can you call me back?" she asked. I told her I would and began trying to reach Zakiya. I felt bad. She had called me a couple of times and all she wanted to talk about was the stupid comments on the Web sites and blogs. I should have answered, but I didn't know she was going through all of this. I called her, the phone rang and rang, and then she picked up the telephone. She sounded awful.

"What's going on with you, Zakiya? Why do you sound like that?"

"Adrienne, I just can't take it anymore."

"Huh? Where are you at? Where is Jabril?"

314 **Daaimah S. Poole**

"I'm sitting in the nursery and Jabril is not here because he left—because he hates me."

"He doesn't hate you."

"Yes, he does, and I'm just done. I can't take it anymore."

"What are you saying, Zakiya? What do you mean?"

"I mean . . . Why me, Adrienne? Why me?" she sobbed.

"Stop crying, Zakiya. It is going to be okay."

"I can't. I try to stop crying, but I can't. I keep thinking about my baby son. He was going to be here soon. I had so many plans for us. His name was going to be Jabril Smith the second, and we were going to be a family. And now he is not here and I miss him, and I never got to hold him, Adrienne. I want my baby. They wouldn't let me bring him home. They said he couldn't come home with me. I want my baby. I don't want to live without my baby."

I was at a loss for words. I should have called her back sooner, but I had so much going on in my life. Instantly I felt bad. I didn't know what to say. She sounded crazy.

"Zakiya, I'm so sorry about the baby, but it wasn't the right time. You have to calm down and think about what you're saying. You don't mean any of this."

"I do mean it. I mean it all. You even said it, Adrienne. That I was having a boy. His first son—that was special. And I went back on that Web site and they said my baby had died, and I was ugly and fat and couldn't carry a baby."

"Forget that Web site. You'll get pregnant again."

"No, I won't. I never want to have a baby again. I never want to leave this house again. I don't care anymore. I hate my life. I have to go. I'll talk to you later, Adrienne."

"Zakiya!" I screamed into the phone. But she had clicked the phone off. I kept calling her back and calling her back and she didn't answer. I was so scared. I couldn't get to Oklahoma. Why did she have to be so far away? I didn't know what to do. When I got home I called her back on my house phone and she answered. I knew I had to calm her down and talk some sense into her.

"Zakiya, listen. I want you to talk to me. I don't want you to do anything stupid." I had her on the speakerphone and texted Elena for her to call the Oklahoma City police and tell them to send a cop over, that I had her on the phone and I was going to try to keep her on the line. She texted me back "Okay."

"I just want all this pain to end. I'm in a lot of pain. I don't feel good. I don't want this pain anymore, Adrienne. I want to see my mom. I miss my mom."

"No, Zakiya, listen to me. Please don't do anything to yourself. You hear me?" She didn't say anything. "Are you listening to me? God has a plan for all of us. And I don't know, maybe he knew you weren't ready and he wanted to give you a little more time."

"Adrienne, I can't go on no more. He is not paying any attention to me. I was just the person that was having the baby, and now the baby is gone. I feel empty," she cried. "I'm going to leave, and as a matter of fact, I'm going to leave this world. Who cares? I'm not going to stay here anymore." She wasn't making me mad but she wasn't listening. I was so upset.

"Zakiya, stop talking crazy. You have to stay around— your sister needs you. I need you. Okay, it's a bad time right now, but you will get through this, okay? I will come out there and visit, me and Asia." She still wasn't responding . . . so I called out her name again. "Zakiya?"

"Huh?"

"What are you doing? Promise me you won't hurt yourself."

"I can't promise you that. I'm just tired, Adrienne. I'm going to go to sleep forever. I never want to wake up."

"Please don't do anything silly, Zakiya. Please, you got

your whole life to live for." I didn't know what else I could say or do to keep her from doing something to herself. "Zakiya, pray, okay?" As I told her to pray, I began praying to God. "Oh God, please don't let her hurt herself. Please, oh Lord, I beg you, please." I got on my knees. I cradled the phone and tears streamed down my face. I was becoming sick with fear. I was feeling like she was about to kill herself and there was nothing I could do about it. I already envisioned myself at her funeral. I didn't want to be at her funeral—she was a good girl who didn't deserve it. She didn't deserve it. I called out her name several times. She wouldn't respond.

Elena texted back that the police were on their way. I just began praying again. I asked God to please not let her hurt herself, and asked Him to help her get over this setback. I tried to think of everything Miss Anne had told me and I just kept praying and praying that the police got there before Zakiya got to herself.

Chapter 71

Tanisha

I've dreamed of being next to Kevin. Him forgiving me, him loving me again. But never in a hundred million years did I ever dream it possible. I hoped and dreamed, but when you have been through so much you kind of give up on hope. But that's the problem—you can't ever give up on hope. Hope and faith are what protected me through all the nights and crazy, cold days in Detroit. Hope made Kevin's heart not be cold toward me. I love Kevin. I will always Kevin. I know one day I will be Kevin's wife, but right now I'm so happy he has forgiven me and that we are in each other's lives.

Chapter 72

Zakiya

I broke down. I mean it literally. I don't remember what happened, but there was a loud knock on the window and the police were surrounding the car. I didn't know where I was going, but when the police arrived I was crying hysterically in the car.

I broke up with Jabril. It hurt like hell. He was and is my first love, and I don't know what's next. He calls me and tells me he loves me all the time. He wants me to come live in Oklahoma and said he would pay for me to go to school, and if I didn't want to stay at his house he would get me a place. I want to go back, but I am so scared of being trapped or stuck in a relationship I no longer want to be in. I'm not sure about what I'm going to do. I love Jabril, but I wish I could have him without all the extras. People want to be in the "lights, camera, action," but they have no idea how hard it is. Sometimes I think I'd rather be a regular person with a regular job, where nobody judges you.

I've matured so much in the last year. I just want to be by myself, no one in the house, and just do Zakiya for a moment.

Chapter 73

Cherise

DeCarious got a text and I was too scared to even ask him what it said because his mouth was wide open. Then he passed the phone to me and it was from Adrienne.

DECARIOUS, I WILL SIGN THE PAPERWORK. MY ATTORNEY IS SENDING OVER THE INFORMATION TODAY. I DON'T WANT TO FIGHT AND ARGUE WITH YOU. LIFE IS TOO SHORT. WE HAVE TO DO WHAT IS BEST FOR ASIA.

He picked me up and spun me around We were so excited—it was over! Adrienne had conceded. He could sleep and stop being so stressed. DeCarious had started stashing all his assets in other people's names. He even asked me to put my name on his studio to keep it away from Adrienne. Now he didn't even have to do all that.

There is a freedom to loving without a deadline or restrictions. Toni and Dave are separated and Toni is so happy to have her freedom. It is odd our reversal of fortune. I'm the one in a relationship and Toni is on the verge of being single. Toni still has her opinion on my relationship with DeCarious. She thinks I shouldn't have taken him back and that he is not the right one for me. I love my sister, but she couldn't be more wrong. DeCarious is more than the right one for me—he is my soul mate, and he is everything I ever wanted. And I know DeCarious feels the same way. Not only does he verbalize his feelings for me, he shows me. He was always sweet and considerate, but now he is the best man any woman could ask for.

When I awake next to him, I touch him because I don't know if I'm dreaming or awake. I don't know what's next for us. We have been through so much. Some might say any relationship that can survive all this is either bound to fail or meant to be. I am still thinking positive, so I'm going to say meant to be. I love DeCarious. I really don't know what I would do without him in my life. But during all that we went through, my love never waned, even when I thought he was never coming back. When Toni was telling me to give up, there was something inside me that never let go. I couldn't let that flame die out. I wouldn't give up on him. I always knew that DeCarious was my soul mate.

With all that said, I know his daughter's mom will always be around. I also know it will be difficult to keep our relationship out of the gossip columns, but it is the chance I am willing to take. The worst that can possibly happen has already happened. Some couples are perfect from day one, they spend every day together and never have an argument, and still end up in divorce court. Then what about the couples who meet and in two months are married?

Cherise Long will be hyphenated with Simmons, definitely . . . Stay tuned.

Chapter 74

Adrienne

Sometimes you really have to know how to take an "L," and I think in anyone's eyes five hundred thousand tax-free dollars for a few months' worth of work is not really a loss. That's why I signed the annulment. I really care about DeCarious, but if he doesn't care about me, then fuck him. Who cares. I'm a half mil richer and DeCarious is a stupid moron who doesn't know what he wants. I could have played the game with him a little longer and got more, or even made him love me, but I'm tired of playing games with an old toy. I'm throwing away the old and starting over, and the best thing about starting over is the clean slate. There is another rich man out there who doesn't know anything about me. I can start all over and write our story the way I want it to go. And my next man doesn't have to be an athlete, either. I'm so over them. I think next time around, I want an intellectual—some type of a businessman. I want him to be so busy with work he has to compensate me with money and gifts.

Right now I'm just glad Tanisha's life is fixed and Zakiya has got herself together. Both were unnecessary weights weighing down on me. I didn't necessarily put either one of them in the position they were in, but I guess somehow I

Discussion Questions

1. Do you agree with Adrienne's philosophy on men and money?

2. Do you think Adrienne ever really loved DeCarious?

3. Was Cherise wrong for hiding her relationship with DeCarious from her coworkers? Did she care too much about what people thought?

4. Should Zakiya have just ignored the blogs and Web sites?

5. If you were Cherise, would you have taken DeCarious back?

6. Should Zakiya go back to Jabril?

7. Did Adrienne get what she deserved?

8. Do you think Tanisha and Kevin's relationship will last?